THE STONE GIRL'S STORY

BY SARAH BETH DURST

CLARION BOOKS
Houghton Mifflin Harcourt
BOSTON   NEW YORK

Clarion Books

3 Park Avenue

New York, New York 10016

Clarion Books is an imprint of Houghton Mifflin Harcourt Publishing Company.

hmhco.com

The text was set in Adobe Jensen Pro.

Library of Congress Cataloging-in-Publication Data
Names: Durst, Sarah Beth, author.
Title: The stone girl's story / Sarah Beth Durst.
Description: Boston ; New York : Clarion Books/Houghton Mifflin Harcourt,
[2018] | Summary: A girl made of stone, forever twelve years old, has outlasted the
father who carved her and gave her life, but now the magical marks that animate
her are fading and she must leave her mountain home and find help in the valley
below if she wants her story—and those of her family—to continue.
Identifiers: LCCN 2017012702 | ISBN 9781328729453 (hardcover)
Subjects: | CYAC: Stone carvers—Fiction. | Authorship—Fiction. |
Storytelling—Fiction. | Adventure and adventurers—Fiction. | Fantasy.
Classification: LCC PZ7.D93436 St 2018 | DDC [Fic]—dc23
LC record available at https://lccn.loc.gov/2017012702

Printed in the United States of America
DOC 10 9 8 7 6 5 4 3 2 1
4500701107

For Anne Hoppe,
a great sculptor of stories

Chapter
One

Turtle had stopped moving last week.

He'd warned Mayka and the others a year ago, when he first began to slow — but he moved so slowly anyway that she hadn't believed him. Not really. She'd always thought they'd have one more afternoon. On the mountain, there was always another afternoon. Another sunset. Another sunrise. Until there wasn't.

She still visited him every day and talked to him as if he could hear her. He had moss growing on him over the faded markings on his shell, the way he liked it, but this morning, Mayka had had the idea he'd also like flowers. Yellow ones, like tiny suns. She decided to plant them in a circle around him, even though she knew he couldn't see them.

Kneeling next to him, she plunged her hands into the dirt, fingers first, using them like spades to dig a hole. She then picked up a flower, cupped its roots in her palms, and gently placed it in the hole. As she scooped dirt around the plant, she wondered what it would feel like to cry, like Father used to. When he was sad, tears would drip down his soft cheeks, curving through his wrinkles. She remembered she used to reach out and catch a tear on her finger. He'd tell her they tasted like the sea, which seemed miraculous to her.

Mayka would never cry. Like Turtle, she was made of stone, carved by Father long ago, and she couldn't cry, even when she very much wanted to.

"You picked a pretty spot to stop," she told Turtle, as she planted a second flower. He had chosen to stop on her favorite overlook, the one with the pine trees. *I could stay here for hours,* she thought. *Even days.* From here, she could see the sun spread across the valley, brightening the low-hanging morning mist until the mist shredded itself into strips of clouds. Far below, a river cut through the forests and fields. Reflecting the sky, it looked like a curling line of blue paint, with the forests as blots of dark green and the fields like smears of yellow and the quarries as patches of gray. It was so peaceful that she —

The pine trees rustled.

Immediately, Mayka held one hand up over her head.

Thwack.

A stone ball hit her palm. She closed her fingers around it.

"Throw me hard, Mayka!" the ball squeaked.

Well, it was *peaceful,* she thought. *Sorry, Turtle.* Standing, she wound her arm back and threw the stone as hard as she could. It sailed over the edge of the cliff.

"Woo-hoo!" the ball cried as it unfurled its wings. Feathers extended, the ball-that-was-really-a-bird swooped up and then looped in a figure eight before flying back to the cliff. He landed on a branch near Mayka and cocked his head so he was looking at her sideways. "Did that make you feel better? Because it made *me* feel better." When he wasn't curled into a ball, Jacklo looked like a gray songbird, with three tail feathers that stretched a few inches beyond his feet, carved out of smoky quartz. He had a crest of stone feathers on his head. "Are you okay, Mayka? Everyone's worried about you."

"I wanted to be alone, Jacklo," Mayka reminded him. She'd been clear this morning: she'd wanted a few hours with Turtle, to say goodbye. She'd informed all her friends at once, in hopes they'd listen. "I told you that."

"But now we can be alone together!" He nestled into the crook of the branch.

Mayka looked at him for a moment as she considered how to explain that wasn't what she meant. *He won't understand,* she thought. But she couldn't be angry with him. It was just the way he showed he cared. "Yes, Jacklo, we can."

Kneeling again next to Turtle, she planted another flower. Around her, the wind rustled the pine needles, making a shushing sound. She wondered what these flowers smelled like and if the wind would carry their scent down the mountain.

"Risa says I'm not good at being alone," Jacklo chattered. "She thinks I can't do it. She says I can't ever sit in silence and just—"

"Jacklo?"

"Yes, Mayka?"

"Silence means no talking."

"Oh. Right." He ruffled his feathers, which sounded like pebbles tumbling down a slope, then fell quiet again.

She wiped a bit of dirt from the ridges around Turtle's eyes. He'd begun the trek here months ago, though it wasn't far from home. He'd pondered each step before laboriously shuffling forward. She should have realized—

"You know, sometimes when I listen to quiet, I hear all the noises in it, and it's not quiet at all," Jacklo said. "There's the wind and the birds and the bugs and—"

"Jacklo?"

"Sorry."

She dug the last hole. Turtle had realized on his own that the marks Father had carved on his stone shell to awaken him were fading—rubbed away by wind, water, and time—and he'd calculated how far he had to walk in the weeks he had left. He'd made it to the exact place he wanted before he stopped. She only wished she'd understood sooner. Without a stonemason to recarve his marks, Turtle would sleep forever.

"You know what, Mayka?"

Lowering the last plant into the hole, she said, "Yes, Jacklo? What is it now?"

In a tiny voice, he said, "I think I'm scared."

Mayka looked up at the bird. He was hunched over, with his shoulders up and his head ducked low. His wings were tight against his body. "You are? Why?"

"I don't want to become silent, like Turtle."

"Oh." And like that, her annoyance melted away. *This* she understood. She'd been trying hard not to think about exactly this for the past week. *Me too*, she thought, but she didn't say it out loud. Instead, she held up her hand. "Want me to throw you again?"

His head shot up, and his wings unfurled. "Only if it will cheer you up too."

"It will," she promised her friend. "We'll cheer each other up."

Pushing himself off the branch, he rolled into a ball as he flew toward her. She caught him, pivoted, and threw him as hard as she could.

He arched up toward the sun and then — with another "Woo-hoo!" — flew higher. Circling around, he flew back to her hand. She caught him and threw him again, over and over, until the sun was high overhead and it was midday.

"I think . . . it worked, a little. Thank you, Jacklo." She smiled at him and realized she hadn't smiled in several days.

Her cheeks felt stiff, as if they'd forgotten how to move without cracking. "Let's go home."

He flew in a circle above her and then up toward the trees. Several flesh-and-feathers birds were startled from their branches and also took to the sky, and for a second, Mayka lost track of which one was her friend as he swarmed with them over the pines.

Kneeling next to Turtle once more, she patted his head. "I'll come visit you again soon."

He didn't answer her. Deep in his long hibernation, he *couldn't* answer. But she still stayed beside him a few seconds more, out of habit or hope, before she trudged back through the pines toward home.

Needles crunched under her bare stone feet. She skipped over rocks in a stream that trickled between the trees, and then she walked out of the woods and into the sun. It warmed her as she climbed the slope, until she was as warm as the rocks on the mountainside.

Ahead, on a bluff below the peak, was home.

Still beautiful, she thought, *despite all its years.*

The house walls were marble that gleamed different colors in the sun, depending on the time of day: yellow in the morning, white in the afternoon, and dusky rose-blue in the evening. Its roof was slate, each tile carved like a petal, and the chimney was a spiral of basalt. Rocks were artistically positioned around the house and covered in wildflowers, and the garden was in front.

Their garden was full of plump heads of lettuce, rows of carrots, and overflowing vines of squash and pumpkins. Mayka and her stone friends didn't need the vegetables, since they didn't eat, but the chickens, goats, and rabbits liked them. After Father died, the owl, Nianna, and the cat, Kalgrey, had advised freeing the flesh-and-blood creatures and letting them fend for themselves with the wild animals on the mountain, but Mayka and the others had insisted on keeping them — Dersy because they reminded him of Father, Jacklo because he thought they were fun, and Mayka because they made her feel as if she was part of life on the mountain, rather than watching it all pass by. Also, the chickens made her laugh.

Currently, they had four goats, sixteen chickens, and twelve rabbits. As she approached, Mayka saw the others were already feeding the goats their midday meal. Dersy, one of the two stone rabbits, was snipping lettuce leaves in the garden, using his ears as if they were shears, and then hopping with the greens over to the goat trough, while the stone cat, Kalgrey, carried delicately, with her sharp obsidian incisors, various scraps that had been rejected by the chickens — hard-to-chew broccoli stems and melon rinds — and added them to the meal.

Outside the goats' pen, the stone fish swam through a channel carved into the rocky ground and pressed their heads against a lever — this changed the direction of the stream so that it sloshed into a second channel and poured into the goats' bucket. When the bucket was full, the fish pushed the lever in the opposite direction and cut off the flow.

Leaving the lettuce, Dersy hopped to the garden gate as Mayka reached it. Rising up on his hind legs, he pushed the gate open with his nose. "Welcome home, Mayka. You're late. I was beginning to worry."

She smiled for the second time in the same day. *Dersy should have been carved like a mother hen, not a rabbit,* she thought. He was always worrying about something or other: a chicken that had molted early, a carrot that had grown crooked —

He clucked his tongue against his buckteeth. "You were careful by Turtle's cliff, weren't you? If you fall and break, we can't fix you."

"Yes, Dersy, I was careful."

"Good. Now, come on, there are chores to do." He hopped across the garden. "First, could you please check Harlisona? I know you think I'm overreacting, but I think her marks are getting worse, and she refuses to let me look at her in decent light. You might have better luck."

Mayka froze for an instant, her smile etched on her face — when Turtle had stopped moving, she'd told herself they didn't need to worry. He'd been the oldest of all of them, carved by Father before he even came to the mountain. The rest of them wouldn't slow for years and years. But it was getting harder and harder to believe that. *Stay calm,* she told herself. *Don't let him know you're worried.* It wouldn't do any good for Dersy to think she was beginning to agree with all his doom-and-gloom talk. Coming through the gate, Mayka followed him. "I'll take a look."

Lately it seemed like little things were always breaking. Their marble house was still beautiful, yes, but it had pockmarks from wind and hail, visible only if you looked closely at it, and a few of the roof tiles were broken. One of the troughs had cracked last month, and they'd patched it with mud that hardened in the sun. But worse were the marks of age on her friends. The lizard, Etho, had thin fissures between his scales. Nianna had chipped a feather, though luckily not a wing feather. And now Harlisona . . .

Mayka crossed the garden to the rabbits' warren. The two stone rabbits had dug themselves a hole beneath the hutch where the flesh-and-fur rabbits lived.

Over the years, they'd just kept digging. The ordinary-looking hole led to a maze of rabbit tunnels that stretched for miles and miles within the mountain — up to the peak, around the summit, and all beneath the pine forest. It didn't serve any particular purpose that Mayka could see, but it made the rabbits happy. Harlisona spent most of her time digging. Mayka had lost track of how many years she'd devoted to burrowing.

Flesh rabbits didn't need an elaborate warren. They were happy enough in their hutch. Mayka plucked a bit of clover from the ground and pushed it through the mesh wire of the rabbit cage, and then she knelt down to talk to her friends. Content, the rabbits in the hutch nibbled and munched.

"Harli, it's Mayka! Can you come out?"

She listened, wondering if Harlisona was nearby or deep within the tunnels. If the latter, she might not come out for days. But a few seconds later, Mayka had her answer: she heard the scrabbling of stone against stone, and a second stone rabbit — Harlisona — poked her head out of the hole. She wrinkled her nose as if sniffing the air, even though she couldn't smell any more than Mayka could, then hopped out.

"Do you mind if I take a look at you?" Mayka asked. "Just to check your marks." *Maybe I'm overreacting. Surely we have decades and decades left. Dersy is a worrier, and Jacklo's so trusting he'll believe anything he's told.* She'd examine Harli, then reassure Dersy and Jacklo that there was nothing to be scared of.

The rabbit nodded. She didn't talk much. Or really, at all. Not in years. She'd lost the mark for speech soon after Father died — it had chipped off in an accident, and they hadn't known how to fix it. Scooching closer, Harlisona let Mayka examine her back. Dirt clung to the grooves of the rabbit's markings, and Mayka gently cleaned it out with her fingers. She felt along the marks. The ridges were less sharp, and a few of the symbols were harder to read than she remembered.

Oh no. It is *worse.*

Mayka looked again at Dersy, more closely this time — his marks weren't crisp anymore either. In fact, the one on his leg that said he could jump high looked chipped. *Is it all of us?* Ever since Turtle stopped, she'd been hoping it wasn't true. *I've been lying to myself.*

"Mayka, I know you don't want to hear it, but . . ." Dersy began.

"You're right," Mayka said. "I don't."

Stay calm, she told herself. *Stone should be calm.* She needed to steady herself and think. Crossing to the fishpond, she sat on a rock shaped like a tree stump and peered into the water. Streams fed into the pond, and they'd planted lilies all around it — she didn't know how many years ago, but since then, the plants had spread and multiplied into a bank of curved green leaves. In the height of summer, they bloomed with orange flowers.

Back from giving water to the goats, the stone fish swam in lazy circles. Only three of Father's miraculous fish were left. He'd been so very proud of them, but the water eroded their markings quickly, and the ones that remained could no longer speak. *We're all fading,* she admitted. *First the fish, then Turtle. Next, all of us.*

We don't have decades.

Maybe not even years.

Maybe it was only months until the next one of them felt themselves slowing, or weakened and chipped. *You need to face the truth,* she told herself.

She held out her arm and twisted it in the sunlight to look at her marks. Father had carved her last, using every scrap of skill that he, the finest stonemason in the world, possessed to create a living stone girl. But even on her, the edges of her marks had begun to dull and the lines were less distinct, with curves in the symbols instead of sharp corners.

Jacklo landed on the rocks by one of the streams that fed the pond. He had a smear of dirt on his cheek and a sprig of leaves wedged between his stone feathers. He must have been playing in the woods again, instead of flying directly home. "Mayka, why were you planting flowers by Turtle?"

His sister, a stone bird named Risa, fluttered down beside him and smacked him with her wing. It clinked, the sound of stone hitting stone. "You bothered her this morning, didn't you?"

"Ow! And no. Well, yes, but no. She didn't want to be alone."

"She specifically said she wanted to be alone!"

Jacklo preened his feathers with his beak until they lay flat again, like slate tiles on a roof, perfectly ordered. "She was alone with me."

"That's not what that word means," Risa said, then her voice softened. "Mayka, you said you wanted to say goodbye, but you didn't, did you? Did you give Turtle flowers? Oh, Mayka, you know he can't see them anymore." Hopping closer, she laid the tip of her wing gently, comfortingly on Mayka's hand.

Looking away, Mayka didn't know how to answer her. It had just . . . felt right to do. Just like visiting him every day felt right. He was still part of the family, even if he slept.

"She's been telling him stories too," Jacklo added. "I heard her yesterday. She tried to read his story but couldn't, so she read him hers. Mayka, will you read us your story? Please, pretty please, with pinecones on top?"

Mayka studied her arm. Each mark on it was a piece of a story. Combined, they made her. If they rubbed away, like Turtle's . . . She didn't want to think about it. "How about I tell you one of Father's favorite stories instead?" she asked Jacklo. A story would make everyone feel better. *Including me,* she thought. "Once upon a time . . ."

Jacklo danced on the rock. "She's telling one! Everybody, come!"

"There was a little boy who was lonely. His mother and father worked hard in the city, and he was alone all day, every day. His house was too far from other houses for him to have any friends to play with, and he had no brothers or sisters. His only friend was a rock that sat in the middle of his family's garden."

The stone rabbits, Dersy and Harlisona, hopped over to the pond to listen.

"He talked to that rock every day. Told it about his dreams, his wishes, his thoughts, and when he ran out of all that, he started making up stories about the birds in the sky, the fish in the streams, and the adventures that he would go on if only he were old enough."

Out of the corner of her eye, Mayka saw her other stone friends emerge from around the house: the cat Kalgrey, the owl

Nianna, the lizard Etho, and the badger who, like Turtle, was just called Badger. They formed a circle around her.

"One day, his father slept late and had to rush down the mountain to the city to work, and he forgot his tools. The boy tried to follow him to bring him his tools, but the boy's little legs were too slow, and so he returned home to the rock with the tools in his hands. His father worked as a builder in the city, constructing the bridges and roads that people used every day, and so his tools were hammers and chisels."

Jacklo sighed happily. "I love this part."

"Shhh," Risa hushed him.

"You love this part too."

Risa opened her beak, then shut it. "You're right. I do. Please, keep going, Mayka. 'The boy took the tools in his little hands...'"

Mayka smiled at the two birds and at the others who had come to listen. Even the fish were swimming closer to the surface of the pond. How many times had they gathered exactly like this to listen to her tell stories? She'd lost count — the days blurred into one another, like afternoon dissolving into dusk. She'd thought they'd do this forever. "The boy took the tools in his little hands, and with a *tap-tap-tap*, he began to carve his stories into the rock, all the while talking to the rock and telling it tales. He worked through the day, through his lunch without stopping, through his naptime without stopping, until dinner, when his mother and father came home. And then at night, he snuck out again to the rock and kept carving."

Father had told her this story so many times, she could almost hear his voice. Telling it made her feel as if he were there, with his hammer and chisel, ready to fix their marks so they'd last forever and none of them would have to worry or be afraid.

"When dawn came the next morning, the boy's father and mother went to the boy's bed to wake him — and he wasn't there. Frightened, they searched all over the house, and then they ran outside . . . and found him curled up against his rock. As they hurried over, the rock spoke to them. 'Hush,' it said. 'He's sleeping.' And that is the tale of the first stonemason."

Mayka looked at her friends: the birds, the animals, the fish, all her father's creations. She felt a lurch inside of her that she couldn't name. *Sooner rather than later, we'll all stop,* she thought. *Just like Turtle.*

I can't let that happen.

"I think . . ." she said slowly, the idea taking shape, "we need a new stonemason." As she said the words, she felt them roll around in her mouth and in her head, and they felt right. The birds began to squawk, and the animals muttered and chittered to one another. *Yes, that's what we need,* she decided. *A stonemason, like Father!* A stonemason could recarve their marks, maybe even awaken Turtle and the sleeping fish! And then everything would go back to the way it was supposed to be.

Fluttering his feathers, Jacklo chirped, "But, Mayka, we don't know any! We don't know anyone. How can we —"

Mayka stood up on the rock, beside the pond, and looked beyond the garden, toward the pine forest and the valley below. She balled her hands into fists and tried to sound brave. "I'm going to find one."

Chapter
Two

Very brave words. Mayka congratulated herself. *But Jacklo's right. I don't know any stonemasons.* There weren't any on the mountain. She'd been all over it, and only Mayka's family and the woodland animals lived on the forested slopes. *If I want to find one, I'll have to leave.*

"Ooh, ooh, an adventure!" Jacklo chirped.

Risa shushed him.

With a whimpering moan, Harli curled into a ball, tucking her head under her front paws. The other rabbit, Dersy, hopped in a tight circle at Mayka's feet. "Yes! This is what I've been saying! We must act, before it's too late! One of us must go down into the valley, find a stonemason, and ask him to come visit us."

Go down into the valley. He said it so simply, but it was a thing none of them had ever done. A real adventure, out in the world beyond the mountain! Mayka felt as if the stone within her was churning. She had never planned to journey beyond.

Everything she ever wanted was right here—*but it won't be if I don't fix this*, she thought. "I will do it. I'll leave today."

The stone owl, Nianna, swiveled her head to fix her polished black stone eyes on Mayka. "No one is going anywhere. Least of all on an adventure. Father wanted us to stay here and be safe, and that is what we will do."

Yes, he had wanted that. Mayka remembered how he used to like to stroll around the house at dusk—he had a routine: check on the chickens, the goats, the rabbits; view the garden; lock the gates—before he'd come inside and light the candles on the table in the cottage. He knew every inch of their home. *It's our sanctuary*, he liked to say. *Nothing here will ever harm you.* It used to make him so happy, to know they were all safe here.

But we aren't safe here, she thought. *Time has found us.*

"There will be stonemasons in the valley," Mayka said. "All I have to do is find other stone creatures and ask them to guide me to whoever carved them."

"Guide *us*," Jacklo said.

"Guide *me*," Mayka corrected. "There's no need for more than one of us to go."

Spreading her wings, Nianna glided from her perch onto a rock beside the pond. "My darling girl, *our* darling girl, you are so very young and so very brave. Father carved you well, and we are all proud of you. But this plan—it's madness. We don't belong in the valley. We are made to stay here, safe, together."

Father had come from the valley. He hadn't talked about

it often, but Mayka knew that much. He'd been born in the city of Skye, a cluster of lights that she saw far below and far away at night. They looked like clumps of stars, and she remembered she'd once asked him why so many stars had fallen in the same place. He'd laughed and told her she was seeing lanterns clustered together, like bees in a hive. But when she asked him to tell her more, he told her a story instead.

"Do you remember the story of the two brothers?" Mayka asked.

Nianna clicked her beak open and shut. "Whoooo? The fools?"

"They were acrobats," Jacklo said stoutly, "not fools!" *Gallant Jacklo,* Mayka thought. He'd defend anyone who was attacked, including two mythical brothers.

"*Foooools,*" the owl said.

Mayka thought back to the story. She hadn't told it in a while, but she never forgot a tale. "Once there were two brothers who lived in the sky —"

The cat, Kalgrey, snorted.

"That *is* how it begins," Risa said. "Let her tell it."

Kalgrey lifted one paw and licked between her toes. "Of course. If she wants to tell *that* version. If she wants to tell the truth, she'll begin with the baby. It was her crying that led the brothers out of the sky."

"Yes, yes, but that comes later, Kalgrey," Dersy said. He thumped his hind paw on the ground, a nervous twitch that made the flesh-and-fur rabbits freeze in their hutch. When no hawk dove from the sky, they relaxed and returned to chomping their lunch. "Go ahead, Mayka."

Mayka settled back down on the rock. "The two brothers argued all the time, and every time they fought, the valley would shake with thunder and lightning. It was so bad that the people would send men and women up into the mountains to talk to the sky brothers and beg them to stop and leave the valley in peace . . . but the sky brothers were so busy yelling at each other that they never heard the humans pleading. Now, it came to pass one day that they had both yelled so much that they had to take a breath at the same time . . . and in that breath of silence, they heard a sound."

"The baby's cry," Kalgrey said, with a thwack of her tail on the rock. Mayka wondered what the cat thought of her idea to find a stonemason. She always disapproved of everything — it was her nature. *But does she dislike my idea or Nianna's rejection of it?*

"Be nice," Risa said to the cat. "Mayka's telling a story, and the rest of us want to listen."

"I'm never nice," Kalgrey said. "I'm a cat. Read my story if you doubt me." Stretching herself, she arched her back, displaying a series of marks: *This is Kalgrey the cat. Sharp of tongue and claws, nimble of paws and mind. She climbed to the top of the chimney and scolded the sun and then slept when it hid, frightened, behind a cloud.*

"Look here," Mayka said, pointing to another mark on the cat's back. "You curl up every night by the door to watch over us, and you keep the rats out of the chicken feed," she read.

The cat sniffed. "That's duty, not niceness."

Jacklo fluttered his wings. "Can't Mayka finish her story?"

"Not if it ends with her leaving," Kalgrey said, but then she curled around Mayka, which was as close as Kalgrey ever got to an apology.

Mayka rubbed Kalgrey behind the ears and continued her story. "The sky brothers heard the baby cry, and they came down into the valley, somersaulting and flipping from cloud to cloud, and when each brother saw the *other* brother hurrying to the baby, it only made him flip higher and somersault faster until by the time the two of them reached the earth, they'd generated so much wind that they'd blown everything around the baby away: the houses, the people, the trees, even the river. The baby lay on a blanket alone in the center of an empty open field."

"How come the baby didn't blow away?" Jacklo asked. "That never made sense to me. If the wind was strong enough to redirect a river, shouldn't the baby be airborne too?"

"Stories don't have to make sense," Risa told him.

"It's nice when they do."

"But they don't have to. So listen."

"One brother, who had sunset-red hair, reached the baby first and said, 'Why are you crying? You don't have a brother who vexes you every day. You are all alone. You should be happy.' And he scooped up the baby and began to dance with her all around the empty field." Mayka liked to picture him dancing like wind, his feet barely touching the grass. She smiled as she told this part of the story. "When he stopped dancing, the baby cried again. And the second brother, who had twilight-blue hair, said to the baby, 'Why are you crying? You aren't all alone. You have earth beneath you, the sky above you, and me to make you laugh.' And he began to perform tricks, transforming himself into different shapes: a tree, an elephant, a rabbit, a dragon, for his body was like a cloud and easy to change. The baby cooed and clapped. 'See, she likes me better,' the blue-haired brother said.

"'I made her laugh first,' the red-haired brother said.

"'But I made her laugh harder.'

"And they argued and argued, and as they fought, they rose higher into the air, and the sky stormed around them. Left behind on the ground, the baby began to cry once more. So the brothers hurried back, and each began endless tricks, flips, and somersaults until the babe was laughing again. This continued until the sun set in the sky, and soon the baby, hungry and cold, began to cry in earnest, and neither brother could console her."

Nianna snapped her beak open and shut. "Fools I called them, and fools they were. This was a child made of flesh and blood, not clouds and sunlight."

"What happened to the baby?" Dersy asked.

"For the sake of the baby, the brothers stopped arguing," Mayka said. "The storms ceased, and the people came back to the valley. They fed the baby, clothed her, and built homes for themselves and her. Eventually, those homes became a town, then a city, which was named Skye after the brothers. And the two sky brothers stayed earthbound, performing tricks and flips for the children of the city, making them laugh instead of cry."

As she finished the story, Mayka felt even more certain she was making the right decision. She could tell the tale had worked on the others too. Everyone had calmed down. The fish were swimming in slower circles, and Kalgrey had closed her eyes as if asleep. Badger had waddled back into the bushes, and Etho lay still on a sunlit rock. Even Nianna seemed less ruffled.

"The people in the valley will help us," Mayka said quietly. "Like they helped the baby."

Nianna sighed. "Very well. But we must not all go. Our father wouldn't have wanted that. One is sufficient for this task. Therefore, only one will go. Only Mayka, if she's willing."

"I will go, ask for a stonemason, and return with him," Mayka promised. "He'll recarve us, and then everything will go on as it has before. You'll see."

It should have been simple to pack.

No food. (She didn't eat.) No blankets. (She didn't sleep.) Her clothes were stone, carved as part of her, and her bare stone feet had never worn shoes. Mayka circled through the cottage and wondered what she *did* need to bring.

Sunlight filtered through the windows in long shafts, illuminating specks of dust. It made the kitchen sparkle as if coated in gold flecks. *Nothing in here,* she thought — she hadn't touched the forks and knives since Father died. His plates and bowls had become birdbaths out in the garden, and his pots served as extra water bowls for the goats.

The bathroom had been converted into an extra chicken coop years ago, the stone tub filled with grain for the winter months. And as for the two tiny bedrooms . . . she had filled hers with rocks she'd collected over the years. A nice piece of quartz with streaks that looked like clouds. A chunk of basalt. Flakes of mica. One rock with an imprint of an ancient fern and another a piece of amber with a fly suspended in it.

She'd left Father's bed untouched.

Her most precious possessions were in the heart of the cottage. Above the mantel was a row of clay figures, the models that Father had made before he carved her friends from stone. There was one for each of them, except for her — he'd said she was his masterpiece, born from his heart, and he'd needed no model for her. She loved looking at the figurines. Even in clay, he'd captured Dersy's worry in the way his ears perked, Harli's shyness in the curve of her shoulders, and Jacklo's endless energy in the shape of his outstretched wings. Mayka touched each one, skimming her fingers over the clay. Hairline cracks ran through all of them, so she didn't dare move them. *They'll have to stay here,* she thought. As much as she wanted to take a token of her friends with her, she couldn't risk breaking them.

Equally precious, her father's tools hung on the wall by the hearth, in a place of honor. She fetched a cloth from beside the sink and cleaned the tools, polishing them until they shone again: his hammers, his chisels, his rasps. One by one, she returned them to the wall, exactly the way Father had left them when he'd told her he'd carved his last.

In the end, she packed nothing, because everything she touched seemed to belong exactly as it was.

I belong here too, she thought. *Exactly as I am.*

But she knew she wouldn't stay exactly as she was, not without help.

"I'll miss you," she told the house.

It didn't answer, though Mayka still felt as if it heard her. The house was stone too, built from marble blocks that Father had carved out of the mountainside and hauled here, long before he'd made her. He'd told her once how it had taken so many days that it was months before he had even one wall and years before he had all four. He'd lived under a canvas tarp, like a traveler, and worked on his home every day. On the inside of the house, onto each stone block, he'd carved pictures: flowers, trees, birds, and animals, and she had painted them with colors he'd made from crushed berries and plants. The paint was faded now. *I should repaint them.*

Looking around the cottage, she saw many things that should be done: the quilt on Father's bed should be washed, the jar of honey that drew bees to the garden had to be refilled, the flowers she'd picked to brighten the table had shed a circle of petals around the vase . . .

She puttered around the house, neatening and washing and fixing, until the shafts of sunlight faded and shadows began to spread.

Jacklo landed on the windowsill. "Mayka? Are we going on our adventure now?"

"*We* aren't going," she corrected him. "*I* am." She didn't know what to expect in the valley. It was best if she went alone and didn't put anyone else at risk. "You heard Nianna. Only one is needed for this."

Gathering up her courage, Mayka walked out the door — and saw sunset. Rosy clouds filled the sky above the mountains, and the valley was already deep in shadows.

Kalgrey curled around her ankles. "You missed the light," the cat said.

"Darkness won't hurt me," Mayka said. But she hadn't meant to leave at night. In every story, adventures always began on a crisp, clear day. *I shouldn't have delayed.*

"You could trip and fall and break in the darkness," Kalgrey said. "Don't be foolish." In cat speak, that was almost *I love you.*

Risa flew to them and landed on Mayka's shoulder. "She's

right. It isn't practical to leave at night. Begin at dawn. Like a bird."

"Or. Don't. Leave. At. All," Etho the lizard said. He always talked slowly, each word punctuated by a flick of his tongue.

"I'll be back soon," Mayka promised. She estimated that it would take her a day to reach the valley, a day or two to find a stonemason, and another day to return — less than a week. *I can be away for less than a week, can't I?* It was a snap of the fingers, compared to how long they'd lived here. Badger had once spent an entire week studying a single mushroom, and Jacklo had once devoted two weeks to thinking up every rhyming word he could. "Come on, let's feed the animals."

While the stone rabbits readied the greens for the flesh rabbits, Etho slunk off his rock to gather mushrooms in the forest for the goats. Badger tossed seeds to the chickens, and the stone fish refilled the water buckets.

Mayka let herself into the coop, and the chickens clustered around her, pecking at her feet. She shooed them back as Badger threw them another pawful of seeds. She checked the roosts for fresh eggs — they could be given to any foxes or predators from the forest who were tempted to snack on either the chickens or the rabbits. Nianna, with her night vision, would watch for them while Kalgrey patrolled the fences.

"Will you all be okay while I'm gone?" Mayka asked.

Sitting on a fencepost, Kalgrey spread her claws and made

a show of examining them. Father had worked hard to make her claws retractable — each claw was made of diamond. "I will take care of the chickens."

"Very funny," Mayka said.

"If I wasn't meant to hunt, Father wouldn't have given me instincts. But I will *try* to leave the chickens intact. Can't understand why you like them. Messy creatures. You do realize you will be among *lots* of messy creatures in the valley, don't you? Not only chickens, but humans and their flesh creatures. Horses, donkeys, pigs, dogs." At the word *dogs*, Kalgrey shuddered all the way to the tip of her tail.

Jacklo fluttered down on the fence beside the cat. "Oh! What if you meet others like us? What if you like them better than us? What if you don't want to come back?" Agitated, he flapped his wings to demonstrate his bravery — and promptly fell off.

He righted himself. "Meant to do that."

Squatting, Mayka dusted him off. "Of course I'll come back. This is home! And you're my family." All of them drew closer, clustering around her.

Badger, the oldest of them now that Turtle slept, pushed forward and took her hand in his large paws. His voice creaked, for he seldom used it, and his words were stilted, as if he were reciting poetry. "We *are* family. No blood binds us, for we have no blood, but we are bound by time and love. You will carry our love and hope with you to the valley, and it will strengthen you."

Mayka looked at all her friends, and she felt warm, as if the sun shone on her brightly. *I'll go in the morning,* she told herself. "Will you all watch the stars with me tonight?"

They climbed, flew, or were helped onto the roof of the cottage as the last of the sun dropped out of sight and deeper blueness spread across the arc of the sky. Lying side by side, they watched the stars pop out one by one, until the sky was filled with so many that they could see stars between the stars.

Sometime late in the night, she told an old story about the stars. And then a tale of the pine forest. And then another about birds learning to fly.

Together, they watched the stars until dawn.

And at dawn, Mayka climbed down from the roof and began to walk — away from the cottage, away from home, taking nothing and leaving everyone.

Chapter
Three

Mayka looked back only once — to see her friends gathered by the gate, waving, while the chickens pecked and clucked in their coop and the goats munched on pinecones that they'd found in their pen and the rabbits nibbled on clover. She waved back and wished she could etch the moment in stone. It all looked so perfect in the morning light, with the pine trees framing their home and the peak of the mountain above them.

I'll be back, she promised silently. *Very soon.*

She followed a deer trail between the trees. The dirt was padded with a mat of old pine needles that tickled the soles of her feet. Rocks and roots jutted into the trail, so she had to watch where she stepped and skip between them. After a while, she heard the trickle of a stream up ahead, and then the trail twisted to run alongside it. When the trail narrowed so that blueberry and dingleberry bushes were scraping her ankles, she splashed through the stream, holding her arms out for balance as she hopped over the slick rocks.

As she walked, she felt her mood begin to shift. She wasn't looking back anymore; she was looking forward. *This is my first adventure,* Mayka thought. *I never thought I'd have one.* She found herself wondering what the valley would be like close up, and she imagined what she'd say when she encountered her first stranger. She'd never met a stranger before.

Maybe she would meet another stone person. Maybe a girl. She'd never met anyone like her. *That would be amazing,* she thought, *to share stories with someone just like me.*

Overhead, birds tweeted and squirrels scurried up and down the trees and into the bushes. She saw a deer once, through the trunks, frozen as it stared at her before it bounded away, leaping over logs as if it had springs in its knees.

After a little while, she noticed that the tweeting birds sounded very much as if they were arguing.

"Hey, this is *my* branch."

"You can't own a branch. They're for everyone! Besides, I saw it first."

"You landed second."

Ordinary birds did *not* talk. Scanning the trees, she looked for her friends. "Risa? Jacklo? Did you follow me?"

"Um . . ." Jacklo said. "No?"

Mayka put her hands on her hips and glared at the trees. "Tell the truth."

"Yes?" Jacklo said.

She heard leaves rustle. Turning in a circle, she spotted them: high up in an oak, two gray birds side by side on the same branch. Risa smacked Jacklo with her wing. "You shouldn't have said that."

"She said tell the truth."

"You could have evaded."

"She figured out we're here," Jacklo said. "She's very smart."

Risa made a birdlike snort, which was more of a whistle. "If she were so smart, she would have brought us in the first place, instead of making us have to sneak behind her."

Mayka glared at them both. "I didn't *make* you sneak behind me! You were supposed to stay home! Didn't you hear Nianna yesterday? Father wanted us to stay home; it's bad enough that I'm leaving." The birds looked at each other, and Mayka put her hands on her hips, hoping it made her appear fiercer. "Besides, you have tasks to do! What will the chickens do without you?"

"Peck at things," Risa said, with a shrug of her wings.

"The others will take care of them," Jacklo said. "We were elected to come with you."

"Oh? Who elected you?" Mayka asked.

"It was a small election," Jacklo said. "Very small. Only two votes. But we won in a landslide! There was a lot of cheering."

Risa sprang off the branch and glided down to Mayka's left shoulder. Jacklo followed her, landing on Mayka's right shoulder. "Don't be stubborn," Risa said. "With us helping you, we'll find that stonemason and be back before Nianna even notices."

"She's not the boss of us anyway," Jacklo said.

The water from the stream rushed over Mayka's feet, tickling her toes and burbling as if it wanted to talk. She felt the cold and wetness, but it didn't distract her — it would take a long time for water to erode her feet. "I don't need help."

"You will," Jacklo said confidently.

"How do you know that?"

Jacklo dropped his voice. "Because you might meet . . . the giant monsters!"

Risa sighed. "Jacklo!"

"What giant monsters?" Mayka didn't know what she'd find in the valley. Aside from a few stories that weren't true anyway — there was no such thing as sky people — she didn't know anything about life there. "Do you know stories I don't know?"

"Er, um . . . Well, there *could* be giant monsters. Maybe?" Flapping his wings, he flew into the air and circled above her head.

Mayka rolled her eyes at him. *No monsters.* He was inventing excuses. "Jacklo —"

"If we're with you," Risa said, "we can scout ahead and warn you about any danger. Even if it's not monsters." She leveled a look at her brother.

"You say you don't want us, but we know you do," Jacklo said, still circling Mayka.

"Father left the valley for a reason," Mayka said. "It could be dangerous." *But that's a reason to let them come,* part of her whispered. *You don't have to face this alone.* Just because she'd claimed this as her quest didn't mean it was only hers, no matter what Nianna said. It would be nice to have Jacklo and Risa with her.

"At least let us come with you to the bottom of the mountain," Jacklo bargained, "so we can tell the others that you made it down safely. Please, Mayka!"

That sounded reasonable. And truthfully, Jacklo was right: she was glad to have their company. *We can be alone together.* "Fine. Come with me." As Jacklo began to cheer, she added, "But only until I'm down the mountain. No promises after that."

"Very well," Risa said. "For now."

With Jacklo flying above and Risa still on her shoulder, Mayka continued downstream. She liked the sound her stone feet made when they clicked on the rocks in the water, and she liked the feel of the water-worn pebbles. A few tiny fish darted in the deeper pools, and she thought of the stone fish at home. They'd never left the pond by the cottage. She wondered if they ever thought about swimming in a stream down the mountain or about what it would be like in a lake, or even the sea.

"How far from home have you flown?" she asked Risa.

Jacklo answered from above, flapping his wings to stay close to them. "All over the mountain," he said proudly. "Even up to the top! Ooh, you should see the view! You can see forever from up there! I think you can even see so far you can see tomorrow!"

"But the valley? Have you flown there?"

"Father never wanted us to," Risa said, from Mayka's shoulder. "And we didn't want to make him unhappy."

"Now that you're going, though, we can fly far and wide!" Jacklo performed a loop-de-loop in front of them.

"You said you'd go back when I reached the bottom," Mayka reminded him.

Finishing his loop, he dipped down as his wings drooped. "Oh. Right. Unless you change your mind and want us with you. It's not that we don't want to be home. It's only that we want to see the world! And then we can go home."

Mayka understood that: now that she was on her way, she was eager to see the valley too. It was a strange, unexpected feeling. *I think I'm actually excited.* She resolved not to tell Nianna that, after this was over. "What have you seen of the valley from the sky?"

"Houses," Jacklo said promptly.

"And fields, with rivers between them," Risa added.

"And tiny people who look like ants swarming a garden."

Mayka halted midstep. "*What?*"

"Jacklo, you are hopeless," Risa said. "They only look tiny because we're far away. Up close, I am sure they're ordinary size. And I don't know if they're stone or flesh."

"Oh." No giant monsters and no ant-size people. She felt foolish for thinking he meant it, even for a second. *It's only that I don't know what to expect.* For all Mayka knew, the people in the valley could breathe fire. She wished she knew more recent stories in addition to the long-ago myths. "I guess we'll see."

They traveled on in silence.

The forest was still thick on either side of the stream, with branches that wove together into knotted clumps that looked to have no beginning and no ending. Ivy vines grew over all of the underbrush, masking the individual plants, so that the forest blurred into a solid mass of green. Now that they were farther down the mountain, Mayka noticed that there were different kinds of trees. Plenty of pine still, but she also saw a lot more oak trees with gnarled, maze-like bark, and birches with white papery bark. She loved the birches. They stood out like white candles against the dark forest. In fall, their leaves were a yellow so bright it looked like flames, but now they were deep summer green. A woodpecker hammered somewhere nearby, its *rat-a-tat-tat* echoing through the forest.

"This is it," Mayka said, "the farthest down the mountain I've ever been."

"Congratulations!" Jacklo said, and she grinned at him. She didn't want to say it out loud, but she was glad the birds were with her. Something this momentous should be shared.

After a little while, she began to hear a steady sound in the distance, like a *whoosh* or a *whir*. "Jacklo, can you go see what that is?"

He flew forward, while Risa stayed on her shoulder.

It sounds, Mayka thought, *like a windstorm.* She'd been through plenty of storms, huddled in the cottage while the wind and rain pelted the face of the mountain, with all her stone friends and all the flesh-and-blood animals safe around her. She'd retell Father's best stories to keep them calm. But today the sky was blue, and she didn't feel more than a breeze. The trees weren't even swaying.

It was getting louder as Mayka walked on.

"Jacklo? Where are you? What is it?"

If Jacklo answered, she didn't hear him — any answer was drowned in the *whoosh-crash*. The stream she'd been following had deepened and widened, and it ran so fast that it frothed as it jumped from stone to stone. Other streams ran beside hers too, also burbling as they raced over rocks. Ahead, the streams merged together, which was fine, she thought, as long as they didn't knock her off her feet.

Perhaps I should —

And as she began the thought, the water slapped harder

at her leg, and she stumbled. Stepping on slippery rocks, she couldn't get her balance. Her arms windmilled on either side. Risa took flight with a cry.

Above her, Jacklo screeched, "Waterfall!"

He dove toward her, waving his wings, but she was already falling, crashing into the stream. The bubbling water flew into her face. Splashing, she grabbed for a root that jutted over the stream. Climbing onto it, she wiped the water from her eyes.

"Very, very long way down," Jacklo said, landing on the root. "Don't go that way!"

Risa flew forward and then back. "He's right."

More carefully this time, Mayka crawled off the branch. Her feet squished into mud, and it sucked at her toes as she inched forward through the stream.

Several streams ran into one another and then spilled over the edge of a rock. *So this is a waterfall,* she thought. She knew what one was, of course, and she'd seen plenty of little ones all over the mountain. The forest was full of streams that cascaded off of rocks, but she hadn't known it could sound like this, as if there were thunder just ahead.

She waded farther into the water, toward the falls.

"Don't!" Jacklo cried.

"I just have to see . . ." Grabbing behind her, she held on to a branch, wrapping both hands hard around it, and leaned forward. Only a few inches, and she'd be able to see where all the water was going.

But she couldn't. It was tumbling into air, into a cloud of droplets.

"Wow! That's amazing!" she cried.

"Come back!" Jacklo called.

She retreated. Maybe if she went *beside* the waterfall, she could climb down. Picking her way carefully across the streams, she finally reached solid land. She inched to the edge and looked down — straight down.

It was a cliff.

Beside her, the water plummeted into empty air, churning with bubbles and foam, until it crashed down on the rocks far, far below. Directly below her, also far below, were more rocks.

She looked left, then right. Left again.

In both directions, as far as she could see, roots and vines dangled over the drop-off. *I could climb*, she thought dubiously. She usually avoided cliffs. It was only sensible.

If she fell hard enough, she could break. Her fingers were fragile. The braids in her hair could snap off. Her nose. Her ankles.

"We'll go around," Mayka said. "Can you scout to see which way will be faster?"

"Jacklo, fly north," Risa said. "I'll fly south. Return after fifty wingbeats."

"Aye-aye, Captain!" Obeying, Jacklo flew along the cliff, and Risa flew in the opposite direction. Mayka settled against a rock to wait.

Telling herself not to worry, she looked out beyond the cliff at the valley. What had looked like a patchwork quilt from high on the mountain now looked like rolling fields, with rivers splicing them. Farmhouses dotted the valley, nestled in groves of trees or framed by golden and green stretches of land. And was that the city of Skye in the distance? Maybe. She couldn't tell. Anyway, she didn't plan on traveling as far as Skye. All she needed was to reach the valley itself—the nearest stonemason would do. She would locate a road, then a house, and then ask directions, either from a stone creature or from a flesh person. It was a simple plan, but that was fine. It didn't need to be complicated to be good.

It will work, she told herself. *Risa and Jacklo just need to find me a way down.*

She thought again of what it was going to be like to meet her first stranger, and wanted to be on her way. *A new person! It's going to be as incredible as seeing a waterfall.*

Risa flew back first. "It's worse that way. Sheer rock for miles. It will take at least two days to reach someplace where you could climb down safely."

Mayka felt heavy, as if all the stone of her body wanted to sink into the earth. She'd been hoping to reach the valley by morning at least. She stared out at the valley — so close and so far, still so very far.

"Where's Jacklo?" Risa asked.

Mayka pointed in the direction he'd flown.

"He knows how far he's supposed to fly before he returns. We've done this before," Risa said, landing on a root near Mayka. They waited for a few more minutes. "Sometimes he gets distracted."

They waited some more.

Still no Jacklo.

Risa settled her wings around her. "I'm *not* going to look for him. I'm not his mother. He's not my pet. If he can't be responsible —"

Seeing a shadow slip through the sky, Mayka pointed. "There he is!"

He danced with the clouds, flipping and somersaulting in the air, clearly performing for them as he swooped in front of the cliff.

"Jacklo, that's enough!" Risa called.

"Oh, but the wind is so wonderful! Can't you feel it, Risa? Northerly wind! I could fly for hours in it!" He swooped past them again, and Mayka felt a breeze on her face as his wings were inches from her nose.

"The cliff, Jacklo!" Mayka called. "How far does it go?"

He did a figure eight. "Not sure. But I found something.

Come see!" They followed him along the edge of the cliff for several minutes. Mayka climbed around brambles and ducked under branches. And then, without warning, Jacklo soared out over the cliff and plummeted down. Sighing, Risa flapped after him, while Mayka crawled to the edge and peered over.

As in the area close to the waterfall, vines were everywhere, woven like a rug over the rock. Lying on her stomach, she watched as the birds, working together, grabbed at vines with their beaks and pulled them backwards. Was that . . .

Jacklo crowed, "Stairs!"

Stairs?

But who would have carved . . .

Father.

It had to be Father. "Once upon a time," she whispered, "there was a man who wanted to live in the mountains . . ." She didn't know all of her father's story, but she could imagine at least a piece of it.

If it was a story, she could begin to understand it.

He had to want to come here badly enough to climb this cliff. She looked out again at the valley — the distant city, if that's what it was, was beginning to sparkle as shadows spread across the fields and rivers. The sun was sinking. The sky was still lemon yellow, but the low light made the rocks glow amber. "He encountered a cliff, and so he carved himself stairs . . ."

Reaching down, she began to yank at the vines near the top.

Jacklo and Risa pulled others away, snipping leaves with their beaks, until they had exposed a step. It wasn't a very broad step, and dirt had settled into its grooves. But Mayka knew stone, and she knew the chips in it weren't natural. A tooth chisel had touched this rock. She stretched out her arm and touched the scratches filled in with dirt.

Working patiently, the two birds pulled and yanked and snipped at the greenery on the cliff as the sun set and shadows settled over the forest. As the moon came out, they kept working, clearing away greenery, while she waited at the top — able to hear them but not able to see much more than movement as they made their way down.

They worked through the night.

At dawn, as the moon faded from view and the sky lightened, she saw that the two birds were done: crude steps were revealed on the cliff face. The rising sun painted the rocks with yellow and rosy pink.

The two birds landed on her shoulders as Mayka began to climb down. They issued instructions: step here, watch that one — it's loose — hold there, move a little left, now right . . . As she climbed, her fingers touched the grooves that her father had carved so many years ago. He'd climbed up these steps and never climbed back down.

Or had he?

Why did he make stairs if he never returned to the valley? He could have used ropes to climb up, or found a way around, but instead he'd carved permanent steps into the cliff. She wondered if he *did* return to the valley.

But no, he couldn't have. One of her friends would have known if he'd ever left, and they would have told her. They wouldn't have kept that story from her.

Maybe he didn't return. But maybe he meant to.

She wondered what he'd think if he knew she was on his steps now. Would he be angry, or proud? She didn't know. But she did know she was more determined than ever to see Father's valley.

At last, she was at the bottom.

"See?" Jacklo said smugly. "We were useful."

Risa fluttered her wings. "Now will you stop being all noble and silly, and agree to let us come with you the rest of the journey? You know we're going to do it anyway."

"Please, Mayka!" Jacklo begged. "Please, please, please say you want us with you!"

Of course she wanted them with her. They were her friends! She'd never been apart from any of them for more than a few hours. If Jacklo and Risa came with her, it would feel like bringing a piece of home. But was that a good enough reason to agree? She'd meant only to risk herself.

Dusting the dirt off her hands, Mayka looked back up at the cliff with its crude stairs. She couldn't have done that without the birds, right? Maybe she'd been foolish to think she could do this alone. Maybe it wasn't going to be as simple as she'd thought. She might need help, if she was going to return as quickly as she wanted.

Now, that's *a good reason!* Even Nianna would have to agree with her logic, now that the birds had proved this wasn't a task for only one. She grinned at her two friends. "Yes, I'd like you to come."

The two birds cheered, and together, they continued on through the forest that covered the mountainside — down toward the valley.

Chapter
Four

Mayka walked out of the woods with two birds on her shoulders — and she stopped and stared. Ahead was a golden field, flat, so very flat, with soft stalks of pale yellow grasses that swayed in the wind. Beyond it was a river that cut through the land, and she saw trees on either side of the river's edge. A wooden fence ran through the field, and sheep grazed on one side of the fence. She'd never seen a sheep, but Father had described them: fluffy white clouds with feet.

Squaring her shoulders, she stepped forward, off the mountain. The dirt in the field was soft, and she sank into it. She drew her foot back — she'd left a print, but not a deep one. The grasses had bent and broken under her foot. It felt strangely significant.

I never meant to leave my mark on the valley.

She stared at her footprint and then began to feel silly for staring. It was just a dent in the dirt, but it felt like the most phenomenal step she'd ever taken. *Come on, Mayka, move. You can't just stand here.*

"Ready?" she asked the birds.

"Of course!" Jacklo cried. "On to adventure!"

Adventures used to be only in stories told on a summer night, or in stories whispered to comfort your friends in the middle of a storm. She wasn't supposed to have adventures. *Maybe this was a mistake. Maybe I shouldn't have left home. Maybe I should turn around right now.*

No, she told herself firmly. *This will be a grand adventure, and I'll love every minute of it. And then in a few days, it will be over, and we'll be home safe and sound and with a stonemason.*

Risa fluttered on her shoulder. "Jacklo, we should talk about what your definition of *adventure* is. I don't like the lack of trees."

"Aw, you sound like Dersy," Jacklo said to Risa. "What are you worried about? There's plenty of sky for us to escape to!"

"But there aren't enough trees for Mayka to hide in if she gets scared," Risa pointed out. "And we're here to look out for her, remember?"

"It's okay," Mayka said, before they could launch into another argument. "I'm not scared." And she found that she was smiling. *I'm really doing this!*

She set off across the field, while Jacklo and Risa rode on her shoulders.

The wind blew gently across the valley, and the wheat bent

as if it were brushed by the palm of an invisible hand. With a coaxing whisper, the wind curled around Mayka, unable to move her stone hair, but she felt it on her stone face and body. Unblocked by trees, the sun warmed her.

"Lots of sheep," Jacklo said. "It's a shame they can't talk."

Hearing him, one of the sheep raised its head and bleated, "*Maaaaaaaah!*" It sounded a lot like Father's goats. Somehow she'd expected sheep to be . . . more elegant than goats. She'd heard plenty of stories with picturesque meadows full of sheep. Never goats.

Closer, the sheep looked more solid than clouds. Also dirtier, as if the cloud had been plunged into a mud puddle. But still, her first sheep! And there, beyond the flock, was a road, a dirt path that up close looked like an inverted riverbed, minus the river, winding through the field. She aimed for it.

Far wider than the deer path from the mountain forest, this road looked as if it had been trampled by many feet and wagons —tracks were worn into the dirt. Reaching the road, she knelt and touched one of the grooves. She wondered how many people had passed this way, where they were going, whether they were on an adventure too. From the top of the mountain, she'd never been able to see the travelers, only imagine them. But she hadn't ever imagined she'd be one of them. She felt giddy, as if her stone head were filled with bubbles.

"Should we follow it?" Jacklo asked.

"There aren't a lot of options," Risa said. "I don't think the sheep can help us."

"This *is* the plan," Mayka said. If there was a road, it had to lead somewhere. That's how roads worked in every story she knew. Roads had purposes, and, with luck, this one would serve their purpose. "Find the road, find a guide, and find a stonemason."

"We'll scout ahead," Risa said, and took flight.

"Ooh, wait for me!" Jacklo followed her. "Don't worry, Mayka, we won't fly far!"

On the left side of the road, Mayka saw a few person-shaped footprints, deep in the mud, and she stepped in them. The prints were large, and the walker had worn shoes. She placed her foot in the steps, hopping to match the long-gone traveler's stride. *Amazing,* she thought. She continued along the road, enjoying the sensation of placing her feet where human feet had been. Usually in the forest, when she found well-worn trails, they were made by deer, sometimes bears. Not feet shaped like hers. She wondered if any of the prints belonged to stone girls. Maybe someone like her had passed this way.

The birds circled back above her. "Found someone!" Jacklo called.

"But I don't think he can help," Risa added.

They led her off the road, across the field, to where a sandstone boulder lay against a lone apple tree. As she came closer, she saw that the boulder was shaped like a horse. The carving was rough, but she could make out the intended shape. It lay on its side, with its head resting against the trunk of the tree. Its stone eyes were open, gray, and sightless. Just stone.

Moss grew on its back, and weeds wound around its folded legs. Its hide was coarse, as if the carver hadn't known how to polish rock. More the idea of a horse than a horse itself.

"Hello!" Jacklo shouted at it. He landed on the horse's head and turned his neck sideways and upside down to look in the horse's eye.

"Oh, hush," said Risa, landing on a branch in the apple tree above the horse. "He can't hear you. Not anymore." To Mayka, she asked, "Can you read who he was and why he's here?"

The markings were on his back — or at least they had been. Mayka touched the grooves in the stone. Most had eroded so badly she couldn't read them. She ran her fingers over them, trying to make sense out of what they could have been. "Strength," she said. "I think this is the mark for strength. He was strong. And . . . tireless? Patient? He never tired."

"Except that he did," Jacklo said. He pecked at the horse's ears.

"Don't do that," Mayka told him.

"Why not? He doesn't mind."

"It's not . . . I don't know. Just don't." She ran her hands over the horse's back, feeling the chisel marks. The rock was raw. He'd been shaped quickly, more like one of Father's early models than a finished creature, but he had marks etched into him. He'd been alive, as rough as he was. "I wonder why a stonemason didn't recarve his marks."

"It looks like the stonemason didn't do such a good job on him the first time," Risa said as Jacklo scurried forward and pecked at a bug that was crawling along one of the grooves.

"Be nice," Mayka chided her.

"I'm only being honest," Risa said. "It's clear he wasn't made by a master."

She's right. Still, no matter how rough-hewn he was, it was troubling that he'd just been left here in a field. Like Turtle. If there were stonemasons in the valley, he could have been fixed, his marks recarved, his edges smoothed, his shape fine-tuned. Maybe the stonemasons were too far away to find him. *Maybe they don't know he's here,* she thought.

Straightening, Mayka looked across the field. From up on the mountain, she'd been able to see the valley stretching out like a blanket, as far as the distant city of Skye on a clear day. But now she could see only field after field, rolling gently into the distance. "We should keep going."

Leaving the horse, they headed back to the road and continued on. Mayka wondered how many more stone creatures there were in the valley. At least they'd found one, even if he was still and had been that way for some time. So that meant there must be more, didn't it?

The sun trekked across the sky, journeying with them, and

she felt it warm her shoulders and hair. The birds sometimes flew ahead and sometimes rode on her shoulders — they were never out of sight. The fields continued: golden grasses in some and brilliant green in others. The green grew in neat rows, with rich brown dirt between them. The river sometimes flowed through the fields and sometimes along the road.

She looked around her as she walked, memorizing it all so she could tell the others when she and the birds were home again. They'd want to hear about everything, and she wanted to remember everything.

Returning from one of her scouting trips, Risa reported, "There's a bridge ahead."

More evidence of people! Mayka supposed the neat rows of green and the fences were also proof of people, but a bridge was a sign of someone who could work with stone. *We're getting closer!* She picked up her pace, hurrying in a loping kind of run across the rolling hills. Soon, at the top of a hill, she saw the bridge. "That's it?"

It was made of wood.

Flat planks had been laid one after another to arch up in a rainbow-like curve over the not-very-wide river. She walked down the hill toward it. Wood posts supported the bridge from beneath. "Well, someone had to make it, even if it's not stone." At least that meant . . . something? *Not much*, she admitted. She didn't need a woodworker or a bridge builder; she needed a stonemason.

She'd expected to find one by now. Or at least find someone.

Crossing the bridge, Mayka tried to tell herself that the wooden bridge was a good sign, since its existence meant there were people somewhere in this valley. The boards creaked under her feet, as if whimpering from the weight. Stone would have been a better choice for a bridge, but maybe the stonemasons were too busy to build a bridge out to where only sheep lived. *Or maybe there aren't any stonemasons*, a thought whispered. *No stonemasons to build a bridge, no stonemasons to fix the horse, no stonemasons to save your friends.*

She refused to believe that.

They traveled another hour before they saw the farmhouse. It too was built of wood, and it was nestled in a grove of trees. Around it were more gold and green fields. Mayka sped up — running didn't tire her stone legs, and now that she had a clear goal, it was easy to race down the road toward the house.

Closer, she saw that it was actually a collection of houses, rather than a single home. Several of them reminded her of their chicken coop, but much larger: these were barns, with wood plank walls painted with spirals and geometric patterns. One building, in the center, was bright blue with a sunny yellow porch and lots of windows. *Someone must live there!*

As she drew even closer, she saw a man in front of the farmhouse. He was wielding an ax and chopping wood into smaller chunks. She couldn't tell at first if he was stone or flesh and blood — he wore a red shirt and his hair was black, but he could have been painted stone.

Flesh, she decided as she approached the yard. His skin had a sheen of sweat on it, and he was panting in great heavy breaths. His chest was so broad that she thought he could bend a tree with every exhalation.

"Excuse me?" Mayka called from the road. "Hello!" Her voice sounded higher than normal. *I'm meeting someone new!* What would he say? What would she say? Would he like her?

The man looked up, wiped his brow, and squinted at her. The sun was behind her, aimed directly at his eyes. "Hello, my dear, who are you?"

"My name's Mayka, and these are my friends, Jacklo and Risa." As the last living sculpture Father had carved, she'd never had to introduce herself before. She reveled in the new sensation.

Jacklo chirped. "Hello!"

Eyes widening, the man dropped the ax. It landed on the hardened ground headfirst and then the handle thumped down.

"You should watch your tools," Risa advised. "You don't want to accidentally cut yourself. That looks sharp."

The man pointed. "Your . . . birds! They talk!"

"Yes, they're my friends," Mayka said. He seemed overly surprised, as if he'd never met a talking bird. Surely he'd seen carvings like Jacklo and Risa before. Or maybe not?

"Jacklo talks too much," Risa offered.

Jacklo sniffed. "You're the only one who has ever complained about my talking."

"I'm the only one who gets a word in edgewise," Risa said.

"Incredible," the man breathed. "I'd heard about such creatures — so lifelike they look real. Out here, we have workhorses, farm cats to catch rats, that kind of thing, but none of the toys. Only the wealthiest families... Who are you, girl? Are you lost?" He bowed awkwardly. "I'm just a humble farmer, but if I can be of service, say the word."

What a strange reaction, she thought. Jacklo and Risa weren't toys; they were birds. And she'd already said her name. As to the other question... "We're not lost. At least, we're not really lost — we know where we are — but we don't know where we're going." Leaving the road, she crossed the yard toward him. A dog with matted fur yapped at her, and she noticed it was chained to a stake. The fur near its collar had been rubbed down to the skin, and she wanted to tell the man to untie the dog, please. But maybe it was chained for a reason. She was acutely aware of how new she was to all of this, and how far from home they were. "We're looking for a stonemason. Could you tell us where to find one?"

"Well, now, there aren't any hereabouts, of course. You'll want to be asking in —" He stopped abruptly and stared at her, hard, shielding his eyes from the sunlight. She halted, halfway to him. He waved his index finger at her. "You... Are you... *You* can't be stone! Why, you're so..." He stalked up to her and poked a meaty finger at her shoulder. "Stone! Extraordinary!" He clamped his hand down on her shoulder as he twisted to shout at the house. "Berin! Berin, come out! You have to see this!"

With a twisting pull, Mayka squirmed out of his grip and backed up. "You were about to say where we can find a stonemason?" She didn't like the way he'd called her "this," or the way he'd grabbed her. But she didn't retreat all the way — he'd been on the verge of telling her what she needed to know. The stonemasons were in the valley, but where? "Please, all I need to know is where to find a stonemason."

Risa whispered in her ear, "We should leave."

On her other side, Jacklo said, "He could be just curious. Sounds like he never saw anyone as fine as us. We were made by a master carver."

Maybe he was right. The horse had been crude, and if that was an example of the type of stone creature this man knew, then it was logical he'd be curious.

"If he hasn't seen anything like us, then he's unlikely to be able to help us, right?" Risa said. "Let's go. You run, Mayka. We'll fly. He won't be able to catch us."

This farmer was the first person they'd seen in the valley. She didn't want to just flee. He hadn't done anything threatening, though she hadn't liked how he'd touched her shoulder. Before Mayka could decide what to do, a woman came barreling out of the door to the house. She was taller than her husband and equally broad, with thick leather gloves over her arms and a leather apron tied around her waist. "What are you yelling about, Afre? Just got the ax blade hot. Won't set right if I have to reheat it."

"Look at this!" Afre said, gesturing to Mayka.

The woman, Berin, noticed Mayka for the first time. Her expression softened slightly, making her cheeks look spongy. "Hello, child, what are you doing out in the middle of nowhere?"

"Come closer, Berin. Look at her! She's *stone!*"

Berin gasped. "No! Truly?"

Mayka took another step backwards as Berin bustled toward her. She could still run, she told herself, if she needed to. Their flesh legs wouldn't carry them as tirelessly as her stone ones. "Yes," she said, "and we're looking for a stonemason. Do you know where one is?"

Berin shoved her face close to Mayka's. Her breath was warm, and her mouth was wet. Mayka stared at Berin as Berin stared at Mayka.

"Never seen anything like it," Berin marveled. "A real live stone girl! So realistic. From a distance, you can't even tell — except she's so gray. Even the 'fabric' of her dress. Can't imagine how much this must have cost. And impractical — she's no plow-horse. How could she ever work enough to repay her cost? Who owns you, stone girl? Do they know you're here? They must be worried sick, a treasure like you. You didn't run away, did you?"

"Of course I didn't! I'm here to find a stonemason, for my family."

"Ah, an errand girl," Berin said.

"Out here?" Afre asked.

"You are far afield from any place a stonemason would live," Berin said. "They go where the wealth is, which means Skye. Plenty of stonemasons in the city. But that's a fair piece away, and the roads wind a bit. Didn't your keepers give you directions? Which stonemason do they want you to find?"

"Someone skilled who doesn't mind travel," Mayka said. *Skye.* Father's birthplace, the city that lay far across the valley. She'd never planned to go anywhere near it, but if she had to . . .

"How do I get there?"

"I think she's a runaway," Afre said. "Only thing that makes sense."

Berin was nodding as she appraised Mayka. "You're right. No one would let something as exquisite as this out of their sight. She must be worth a fortune."

"There's bound to be a reward if we return her."

Risa squawked. "And now you *really* should run!"

Mayka didn't wait another instant. She pivoted as Afre shouted, "Grab her!" She felt meaty fingers seize her arm, and she yanked away, hard. The fingers slipped, and she ran. She heard them shouting behind her, running after her, but she pounded her feet faster, running toward the road.

She didn't look back. She didn't slow. She just ran.

Chapter
Five

She ran until the sun sank behind the mountains and the stars came out, and then Mayka kept running, because her stone body didn't tire and because the moon cast enough light on the road that she could see the path stretching like a gray river between the dark grasses . . . until a cloud covered the moon, and the shadows on the road merged together. Her toes found a rut that she hadn't seen — and she sprawled forward.

Lying there, she felt the cool earth against her cheek. She had mud on her, she knew, but at the moment she didn't care.

The two birds landed beside her.

"Are you all right, Mayka?" Risa asked.

"Yes."

"Those were *not* nice people," Jacklo said. "I'd envisioned . . . Well, I thought we'd make new friends. Guess not with them. He called us toys."

Mayka rolled onto her back and looked up at the stars and

wished with all her heart that she were still on the roof of their cottage, with all her friends beside her. *Even the sky looks different here*, she thought. She was used to the mountain cutting off a part of her view, but here in the valley, the whole arc of the sky was open. It felt so big. And beautiful. But right now, she missed *her* sky.

"He'd never seen anything like us," Jacklo continued. "Or like you, Mayka. It must be because they live so far away from anyone else. Ooh, maybe that's *why* they live away from everyone else! No one wanted them near since they're so rude."

"At least now we know where to go," Risa said, practical as always.

"Do you think they'll be nice in Skye?" Mayka asked.

"Of course they will," Jacklo said. "There are lots and lots of people in the city. That's what makes it a city. And all the people will be different, like we're all different."

The word *city* felt so foreign. She couldn't conceive of that many strangers living together side by side. You couldn't know everyone's name or story. You'd walk past people and never know their history — where they'd come from, where they were going, what they dreamed of.

Jacklo's right, she thought.

Everyone had a different story. Her friends were all very different: wise Badger, ponderous Etho, opinionated Nianna, superior Kalgrey . . . Father had carved them all with unique stories. Like her friends, the people who lived in the valley would be different from one another too, with their own personalities and past experiences to shape them. *We'll meet friendlier people*, she consoled herself. *And we'll see Skye!*

But still, she lay in the road looking up at the stars for a long time, with the birds nestled against her, until dawn began to creep across the sky and the road began to vibrate.

It started slight at first, a little tremble. She turned her head and saw a puddle was shaking. And then the birds took flight.

"Get off the road, Mayka!" Risa shouted.

Mayka rolled to the side into the grasses. She ducked down, hiding among the golden stalks, as a wagon trundled across. She peered out and saw a stone horse as crude as the one in the field. Its hooves were pounding the dirt as it pulled a wagon behind it. The wagon was piled high, with a tarp strapped over a dozen crates. A few leaves poked out beneath the tarp.

Mayka scrambled out of the grass. "Hey! Hello! Can you wait, please?"

But the horse didn't stop. It didn't even turn its head to look at her.

Jacklo and Risa flew after it and in front of its face. But the horse kept plodding forward, pulling its load, until it was out of sight. The birds flew back to her.

"He couldn't hear us," Risa reported.

"Or didn't want to," Jacklo said. "Maybe he's shy."

"He also couldn't speak, or didn't want to," Risa said. "Either way, he won't be helping us. Are you all right, Mayka?"

Mayka looked down at herself, grasses stuck to the mud that covered her dress. She looked like she'd rolled around in the goats' pen. She couldn't meet new people like this. "Is there a river nearby?"

"Yes," Risa said. "It waters the fields. Follow me."

Trailing Risa, Mayka tromped across a field full of corn. She picked her way between the stalks, crushing the old dead leaves. Jacklo flew behind her, low to the ground, and used his stone wings to wipe away her footprints as best he could. He'd done it before, when playing hide-and-seek with Kalgrey and Badger. It made Kalgrey so angry when Badger's tracks disappeared. "Kalgrey's funny when she's angry," Jacklo had said.

Risa glanced back at him. "I don't think the farmers are following us. Mayka ran fast. Flesh creatures couldn't match her pace."

"They could if they used wagons," Mayka pointed out. There hadn't been any passengers on the wagon that had passed by earlier — the horse was pulling a load of what looked like vegetables — but there was no reason why he couldn't also pull a load of people, if he wanted. "I'd rather be safe. Thank you, Jacklo."

"It's so strange that they wouldn't believe you," Jacklo said.

Mayka didn't have a reply to that. She wasn't used to not being believed. All of her friends trusted her, and she trusted them.

Ahead, Risa flew low through the tops of the corn, guiding

them toward the river. Mayka heard the babbling of the water before she saw it, so she wasn't surprised when the corn ended and the field sloped down into a riverbed full of cattails. She walked along the edge until she found an open area on the bank, then she knelt and splashed water on herself, rinsing the mud off her stone dress, arms, and legs.

"We need to be more careful who we talk to," Risa said. "Or not talk to anyone."

"We have to talk to someone," Mayka said. "We don't know which road leads to Skye. We need a guide, or at least directions." She didn't want to start fearing everyone just because of one bad experience. She didn't want to think that the valley, which looked so peaceful from high above, was full of unkindness.

It could be, though, she thought. Father had left the valley, and he'd never said why. Had he encountered unkindness? She wondered what had happened to him here.

Jacklo poked at the riverbed with his beak, overturning stones as if he were a flesh-and-feathers bird looking for worms. "Risa and I could search ahead . . ."

"No," Risa said. "We don't leave Mayka alone."

"Maybe the next time, you two shouldn't talk. Just fly onto the roof and pretend to be ordinary birds. Can you do that?"

"That sounds sensible," Risa said. "Then we can warn you if anything seems amiss."

"Ooh, like this!" Jacklo tilted his head back and let out a

warbling cry that sounded like a rooster was dying. *"Errrr-cooo-currrrr!"*

"Maybe more subtle than that," Risa said. "Three short chirps and one long." She demonstrated, sounding like a songbird. "If you hear that, you run."

"And what's your warning for us?" Jacklo asked Mayka. "I know! You could bark like a dog! Or howl like a wolf! *Hoooooooowwwwwl!*"

"How about I just shout 'fly'?" Mayka suggested.

"Boring," Jacklo said.

Clean, Mayka sat on a rock and held out her arms, letting the sun dry her. She didn't mind being wet, but she didn't want the dust and dirt from the road to stick to her and turn into mud again. "Okay, so the plan is unchanged: we need to find a guide." All she knew from seeing the lights in the valley at night was that Skye was "far away." She'd never paid attention to how the roads and the rivers and the hills and the fields connected.

"The next stone creature—we'll *make* him answer us," Jacklo said.

Risa snorted at him. "What if he's like the horse and doesn't want to? How are you going to make him?"

"I'll annoy him until he answers. I'm very good at being annoying."

"That is true," Risa conceded.

With that decided, they returned to the road, looking for

someone who could give them directions. *A guide would be ideal,* Mayka thought, *but really just simple directions would do for now.* Once they'd traveled far enough in the right direction, Jacklo and Risa would be able to spot the city from the air without losing sight of Mayka.

Mayka jogged down the road while Jacklo and Risa flew on either side of her, just above the corn. As the sun continued to trek across the sky, her stone body dried. Only her feet were mud-covered now.

She'd never crossed so many miles before. In the mountains, it took time to scramble up the slopes. Here, where it was flat, it was possible to feel the distance pass beneath you. There was something rather wonderful about that. The rhythm of her feet was hypnotic, and as she ran, she let the unpleasantness of the farmhouse fade behind her. She tried to pretend it was part of a tale that belonged to someone else from long ago and far away.

"Ahead! Out in the fields!" Jacklo called.

"Look to the east!" Risa said, swooping down to fly level with Mayka. "Three stone creatures, on the move. Follow us!"

Veering off the road again, Mayka ran across the fields. These were unplanted, fresh-plowed fields, with the soft earth piled in parallel lines. Her feet sank into the soil, every step a reminder that she wasn't on her rocky mountain slope anymore. Eastward, she saw three shapes: bumps in the landscape. "Did you try to talk to them?" she called.

"Didn't get that close," Jacklo said. "We thought you'd want to be there, to hear what they had to say."

She did. She ran faster.

The bumps were moving across the field, pulling a curved blade behind them. It dug into the earth, churning it. Closer, the stone creatures looked like wide horses. Cows? Oxen? *Oxen*, she decided. Father had described them to her in a story about a farmer with three children, whose clever wife harnessed the very first ox.

Like the horse, they were crudely shaped sandstone, with no polish to their skins. Their features were rough, with little shape to their mouths, noses, and eyes. They plodded ahead without acknowledging Jacklo and Risa dancing on the breeze around their heads. "Hello, stone kindred!" Jacklo shouted. "Up here!"

The oxen didn't look up.

They continued to plod.

Mayka caught up to them. "Excuse me? I'm sorry to interrupt your work, but we need to ask directions. We're trying to find a stonemason and were told to look in the city of Skye, but we don't know which way to go. Does the road go there? How far is it?"

"And where do we look when we get there?" Jacklo asked. "Where do we start? Who do we look for? Do you know the name of a stonemason? Where can we find him? Why are you ignoring us?" He flew in front of the oxen. "Hello? Can you hear us?"

"I don't think they can," Risa said.

Jacklo shouted, "Hello! I'm Jacklo! We need help!"

The oxen just kept tromping forward, like the horse with the wagon on the road. Running in front of them, Mayka spread her arms and legs wide and shouted, "Stop!"

They halted.

"That's better," Jacklo said, and he landed on one of their horns. He leaned forward so he was upside down, his eyes even with the ox's eyes, like he'd done with the motionless horse. "Hello."

Arms still open wide, Mayka said, "Can you please tell us how to get to Skye?"

No answer. They stood there, silent.

"Maybe they can't talk," Risa suggested, "like Harlisona."

"Or the fish," Jacklo said. "Always wondered what they felt when their marks for speaking were washed away, whether they were sad, whether they like the quiet, whether they're happy just swimming around and around and around —"

"Can you see their markings?" Mayka asked as she circled the beasts — they were so huge that the markings could be any-where. The birds darted over, under, and around them. At last, she spotted marks tucked behind one of the ox's front legs.

There were only a few, barely a full story. Just the symbol for strength and a few others. She reached out and touched the marks, trying to decipher them. "Pull? Shape? 'This is ox. He's strong and steady. He plows the fields day and night.' That's all it says. Or something like that." She ran her fingers over the marks. She'd never seen such a simplistic story before on a living creature. "That's it. No individual name. Nothing about his history or experiences. Just . . . he plows."

"That's horrible," Risa said.

"No wonder he can't talk," Mayka said. "His carver didn't give him a voice." The ox was trapped in this rough body, limited by his story. She wondered how aware he was of his fate. Most likely, he didn't even know what he was missing — he couldn't know what he didn't know. Still, she knew, and she felt sorry for what he'd never hear, say, think, feel, or experience.

A tiny, high voice piped up from the grasses: "You could try talking to *me* instead."

"Hello?" Mayka called. She scanned the grasses, but saw no one. Bending, she looked for frogs, lizards, even bugs. "Who said that?"

Risa fluffed her feathers to make herself appear larger. "Show yourself!"

Out of the field waddled the strangest creature that Mayka had ever seen. She was knee-high, and she had a lizardlike head, scales over her squat body, and wings. She was carved of orange stone streaked with red. "Hi!"

"What are you?" Mayka breathed. Father had carved Mayka and all her friends out of stone he'd harvested from the mountain, either granite, marble, or quartz — they were all various shades of gray, sometimes with black spots and sometimes with flecks of mica. Mayka herself was as gray as a shadow at dusk. None of them were this translucent incandescent orange. Plus, all of Mayka's friends were based on real flesh-and-blood creatures. This new creature looked as if she came straight out of a story.

As she stared at the creature, Mayka realized how rude her question was. It was just . . . she'd never seen stone look like fire before. "I'm sorry. I meant *who* are you?"

Regally, the creature rose onto her hind legs and nodded at each of them, as if she were a (small and somewhat reptilian) queen greeting her adoring subjects. "I am Siannasi Yondolada Quilasa."

All of them stared at her.

"That's a lot of name," Jacklo said finally.

The creature giggled. When she laughed, her wings clinked together, sounding like little bells. "I know. Everyone just calls me Si-Si."

"Nice to meet you, Si-Si. I'm Mayka, and these are my friends, Risa and Jacklo." She wasn't sure exactly what to say next. So far, the only new people she'd met were the farmers, and that hadn't gone well.

"And to answer your other question," Si-Si said, "I am a dragon."

Chapter
Six

Mayka gasped out loud. "Truly?" She supposed she shouldn't have been surprised — stone could be carved into any shape — but Father had never talked about anyone carving anything legendary.

Jacklo stared at Si-Si. "Whoa! Like in the story?"

The little dragon nodded proudly. "I was inspired by the great dragons of legend, whose bones formed the mountains, whose breath birthed the wind, and whose flame gave life to the land." She spread her wings to their full width and drew herself up to her full height — which would have been impressive if she'd been more than two feet tall.

Under Si-Si's wings, near the joints, Mayka saw carvings: an intricate pattern of lines and swirls. These weren't simple marks like on the oxen. This was a new story, exquisitely drawn! "May I read you?" she asked politely. *Please say yes!* She hadn't gotten to read a new story since Father died. If she could go home with a stonemason *and* a new story —

Si-Si dropped her wings. "You can read? Really?"

"My father taught me." Mayka knelt next to the little dragon, who raised her wings again to display the marks. She had gorgeous wings with streaks of red that glistened when the sun hit them. Mayka had never seen stone so beautiful, though she'd heard Father mention it: firestone, because it looked like the heart of a fire.

"No one's ever read my story to me before." Si-Si was trembling, causing the light to shimmer on her scales. "I've heard retellings, of course — everyone knows the story of the Mountain Dragons — but no one has ever read *me* before. Ooh, I'm so excited!"

Sitting cross-legged in the field, Mayka began to puzzle out the marks. She recognized several, but there were swirls within swirls . . . "Risa, can you find me a stick?"

Risa fluttered off a few feet away and then returned with a twig. Mayka began to draw in the earth, meshing symbols together. Often marks were combinations of other marks — if she could find the right mix of symbols that matched the one on Si-Si's wing, then she'd have the key . . .

"Got it," Mayka said, pleased with herself. Now that she knew how the carver had combined the marks, the rest should be easy to decipher. "Once, a very long time ago, when the earth was so new that she changed her clothes with the seasons . . ."

Si-Si craned her neck to look at the underside of her wing. "Wow, does it really say all that?"

"Well, you could also read it as 'there were lots of earthquakes and volcanoes,' but the swirls — see here?" Mayka pointed to the way one flourish curled up like a fern. "This means the story is supposed to be poetic and old. So I'm telling it that way."

"You're making it up?" The dragon recoiled as if she'd touched something sticky.

Mayka wondered if she should be offended — stories were an art, not a science, and Father often said not everyone understood that. Kalgrey, for instance, had little patience for extra embellishments. But then again, the cat didn't have much patience for anything, except for stalking field mice she didn't intend to eat. "The marks aren't words exactly; they're more like a guide. Father and I used to practice all the time. He'd draw marks in the dirt, and I'd read them into stories. He even added a new mark to *my* story to commemorate my new skill, when I felt I was ready." She held up her palm so that the little dragon could see. In the center of her hand was a symbol that looked like an eye with other tiny marks held within the pupil. "It tells of how I read stories to Father while he worked on his carvings, how I made him laugh and cry, and how all my friends would come and listen as the moon rose over the mountains. But you could also just say it means 'Mayka reads,' and that would be correct too."

"Wow!" Si-Si leaned so close that her nose nearly touched Mayka's hand, then she drew back. "You say your father carved you? Who's your father?"

"He carved all of us." She closed her hand and cradled it against her chest, as if she could hold the memory tight in her fist. "His name was Kyn, and he was a master stonemason."

Si-Si fixed her flamelike orange eyes on the two birds. "I didn't know that it was possible for anyone to carve birds that can fly. I'd heard stories, and I've dreamed—" She cut herself off. "How *is* it possible? You're stone, aren't you?"

"One hundred percent and proud of it!" Jacklo demonstrated by thumping his wings together so they made a *thwack* sound. "Just like you."

"Not just like me." Si-Si lifted her wings, flapped them once, and then dropped them by her sides. "See? I can't fly. Do you think . . . Would your father recarve me so I could?" The longing in her voice was so clear that it almost hurt to hear.

"He can't." Mayka looked at the oxen who still stood motionless in the field. "He . . . stopped moving a long time ago. We buried him under a tree that he loved and put stones above him." It was strangely hard to say the words, even though it had happened so long ago. She'd never had to tell anyone else before. Everyone she knew had been there. Telling the story of his death made it feel like it had just happened, and she suddenly missed him so badly that she ached, as if winter cold had spread into her body. She wondered what he'd think of their quest and of Si-Si. *He didn't want any of us to leave the mountain,* she thought. *But I think he would have liked to meet Si-Si.*

"That's terrible to hear," Si-Si said. "I'm so sorry."

"It's terrible to say," Mayka admitted. The words made it more real. Words always did, even when you didn't want them to. "I don't want to tell that story right now. May I finish reading yours?" She gestured to the dragon's wing.

"Oh! Yes, please." Si-Si lifted her wing again so Mayka could see the marks.

Leaning closer, she read the elegant symbols, "Back when the earth was new, dragons ruled the skies. They scorched the earth, and they boiled the seas. When they walked, they shook the ground, and the land split beneath their massive feet. No other creature could survive in such a dangerous world."

"Wow, that's dramatic!" Jacklo said. "I wish I wore a story like this. Do you think I'd be braver if I had a legend carved on me?"

"Hush," Risa scolded.

Mayka continued. "After a time, the dragons became lonely. They thought it would be nice to have other creatures around them. Creatures that flew through the air, swam through the sea, and crawled on the earth. And so they landed and began to craft them out of the clay and out of the sea. They used their fire to breathe them to life. But these new creatures were too fragile —when the dragons took to the air again, their creations began to weaken and die, for while the dragons flew, the air was filled with fire and the sea boiled. And so the dragons came down from the sky and lay still on the earth. Over time, their breath cooled, and their bodies hardened to rock, and they became the mountains."

"All of that is written on me?" Si-Si asked, craning her neck to see.

Mayka pointed to the mark that represented the story of the dragons. "Just beneath it, it says, 'This is Siannasi Yondolada Quilasa, carved to honor the dragons who created all those made of flesh and blood. She will . . .'" Mayka faltered. What did that next mark mean? She thought back to her lessons with Father. She'd seen it before, on the blocks in the walls of the cottage. *Decorate.* "She will decorate her home and remind all who see her of our beginnings." Mayka looked up at the dragon, feeling suddenly awkward. It ended so abruptly. "That's what it says." It was strange that the marks didn't mention any of Si-Si's own strengths. Father always included marks that told personal stories. But Si-Si's story was all about the heroics of other creatures, going so far as to end on a clear reminder that it wasn't about Si-Si herself.

Si-Si lowered her wings. "It says . . ." A shudder ran from

her nose all the way down to her tail, and her voice shrank to a wavering whisper. "Then it's true. I *am* just a decoration. No more than a bauble . . ."

Maybe I shouldn't have read her story out loud. Mayka had never had that thought before — stories were meant to be told — but this one had clearly upset their new friend. "It says you're a tribute to the great dragons who created all flesh-and-blood life. That's good!"

Si-Si sank to the ground, her dragon head resting on her paws, her wings collapsed by her side. "This is why I can't fly. I'm only an ornament. Nothing special about me. Good for nothing. Useless."

"You aren't useless," Mayka said. "You can help us! The oxen won't" — *or can't,* she thought — "and the people we've met, when we asked them . . ." She trailed off, not sure how to describe what had happened.

"It didn't go well," Risa said dryly.

"We're looking for a stonemason to recarve our marks," Mayka said. "But we need directions. From up on the mountain, it's easy to see the city, but here in the valley . . ."

Si-Si lifted her head. "You're going to a stonemason? Yourselves?"

"Yes. We need to ask a stonemason to come home with us and recarve the marks on us and our friends — they're beginning to fade. If a stonemason would fix the marks —"

"You plan to just *ask*?" Si-Si's eyes were wide. The sun reflected in the stone, making it look as if flames were trapped within her pupils. "But . . . you can do that?"

"Mayka can do anything," Jacklo said confidently.

"Not anything," Mayka corrected. "But yes, I plan to just ask. Why shouldn't I? All we have to do is find a stonemason and convince him or her to come up the mountain."

Si-Si got to her feet and shook out her wings. "Do you think . . . Could I . . . Maybe I could ask him to recarve me?"

"Of course," Mayka said. "What do you have to lose by asking?"

The dragon looked again at Jacklo and Risa. "If a stonemason could fix me so I could fly . . . I could be more than a decoration. Maybe if I had new marks and wings shaped like yours. They said . . ." Her wings drooped again, hitting the ground.

"Who said what?" Risa asked.

"The other stone creatures at the estate. They said I was useless, that I was an 'extravagant luxury' that no one needed. But if I could change, if I had new marks that made me useful, if I could *fly* . . . I'd prove them wrong."

"They *are* wrong," Mayka said firmly. They should have appreciated how unique and beautiful Si-Si was, carved from a stone that Mayka had never seen. Whoever had carved her must have valued her — there was such care in the detail of her scales and the shape of her face, with all the wispy lines that looked like feathers on her cheeks. "Come with us to the stonemason. Show us the way to Skye, and you can ask him yourself. I'll help you ask, if you'd like. Together, we'll convince him to aid all of us."

Si-Si smiled, revealing teeth carved from black obsidian. She pawed at the ground and flapped her wings, prancing in place. "Yes! I'll help you, and you'll help me."

"Ooh, do you know the way to Skye?" Jacklo asked.

Risa flew in a spiral above the little dragon. "We know it's in the valley, far away from our mountain. But we don't know what road to follow. Not without flying away from Mayka, and we won't do that, not after the farmers."

Si-Si pranced higher, her wings making a tinkling sound like crystal — the music of her wings seemed to reflect her mood, and it sounded like hope. "I know how to find it! I'll take you there!"

Si-Si hopped like a bunny.

Mayka hadn't expected that. She'd imagined that a dragon would skulk more. Or stride across the landscape, belching fire everywhere. But no, the little stone dragon sprang in hops, leaping forward and then catching her back legs up. Her wings flapped, and her tail wagged with each hop. She looked, in a word, adorable. But Mayka wasn't about to say that without knowing how the little dragon would take it.

"Why were you out here in the field?" Mayka asked, following her.

"Um . . . I like the fresh air," Si-Si said.

Jacklo whistled. "You can smell fresh air?"

Soaring above, Risa let out a half snort, half tweet. "She can't. She's stone. All air is the same to our kind, you know that. Question is: why is she lying?"

Si-Si ruffled her wings. "It's a common expression! And you will see that city air is different. Dirtier. Everyone says so. But if you must know, I was only in the field because *you* were in the field. I was curious. It's not often you see masterpieces like you out in the countryside."

"How did *you* get here, out in the countryside?" Risa asked.

The bird sounded so suspicious. "Risa!" Mayka said. "Be friendly."

Si-Si drooped. "No, it's all right. You don't know me. And I'm . . . I am no one."

Jacklo circled around her head. "You're Siannasi Yondolada Quilasa. You aren't no one!"

"You heard what my marks say about me. I'm not good enough to have my own story. I exist in the shadows of others . . . Others who could fly."

"If you did have your own story, what would it say?" Mayka asked. "Where were you before you were here?"

"Tell us," Jacklo said. "We'll listen."

The little dragon looked at them, as if to see if they meant it. Mayka gave her an encouraging smile. Si-Si hopped quietly for a moment before she began. "My keepers had a summer villa, until they had to sell it. I only know what I could hear listening at windows — there was a lot of arguing. They'd spent money they didn't have, and lost money they used to have, and could no longer afford to keep the house." Her voice quivered, and she wasn't looking at anyone as she spoke. "Most of the others . . . they took them along, back to town, to keep or resell, but I was forgotten. Left behind, alone at the villa. I waited for them to come back for me, but they didn't, because who needs a decorative dragon? I'm so unimportant that they didn't even remember me for long enough to resell me."

"I'm sorry," Mayka said, then asked, "What do you mean 'keepers'?" The farmers had used the same word.

Si-Si didn't answer. She seemed caught in her own sorrow. "If I were bigger, I'd make an excellent guard. If I were smaller, I could be a spy. If my teeth were sharper and less fragile . . . If my claws could grip better . . . If I could fly . . . Oh, if I could fly! Feel the wind on my face! Soar above everyone and everything! If I could fly, it wouldn't even matter what anyone said or thought of me!" She craned her neck to watch Jacklo and Risa, who were soaring overhead in the midst of a flock of flesh-and-feathers birds. They swooped down again, flying alongside Mayka and Si-Si. "My keepers used to have a stone heron. He waded in the ornamental pond and would wax on about philosophy to anyone who would listen. He couldn't fly either, but the family called him wise. They would always bring visitors out to meet him and ask him questions, as if he were some kind of oracle. I didn't like him very much. He always thought he was so much smarter than everyone else. He's the one who told me the family wouldn't be taking me with them, because they thought I was worthless. I told him he was wrong, but he was right."

"So you left then, after they were gone?" Mayka asked. "And you've been alone ever since?" Poor Si-Si. At least Mayka had left home voluntarily, and Jacklo and Risa had come with her of their own free will too.

"She's not alone now," Jacklo said stoutly.

Si-Si shot him a grateful look. "And once a stonemason fixes my wings and my marks, I'll never be alone again. I'll be one with the sky! And I won't be worthless anymore."

"You're not worthless," Mayka said.

"My story — the story *you* read — says I am," Si-Si said.

None of them knew what to say to that.

As they walked on, the sun continued to cross the valley. Eventually, it set, and the mountains glowed amber and rose. Mayka looked back at their mountain — the tallest peak, covered in forests and waterfalls — and wondered how her friends were. She wondered if they were worried, if they had guessed where the two birds had gone, if they'd know the right thing to say to

Si-Si to make her feel better . . . Nianna would have scolded her, told her how fortunate she was to be alive. Badger would have said something profound. Kalgrey would have mocked. Dersy would have tried to comfort her by sharing his own worries . . . *All right, maybe they wouldn't have known what to say either.*

As Mayka walked and thought, the stars began to appear, and the moon shone down, clouds drifting over its smooth face.

Si-Si caught the moonlight on her scaled back every time she hopped, which made her easy to follow. But the uneven ground was harder to see, and several times Mayka stumbled. Once she fell all the way to her knees, but she stood back up and kept going.

"Shouldn't we wait out the dark?" Jacklo asked.

"What for?" asked Si-Si.

"So we can see our way, of course," Risa said. "I've already flown into three cornstalks, and Jacklo has leaves stuck in his feathers."

"I can see by the light of the moon. Can't you?"

"Not as well, obviously," Risa said. "We should wait for dawn."

Si-Si said in a tiny, sad voice, "But . . . but . . . I finally have hope."

The sadness in her words made Mayka feel as if she'd stepped on a baby chick. "All right. We'll keep going." Aside from their having to be more careful, it didn't make that much difference that it was night. A few cornstalks wouldn't hurt the birds, and even if she fell in a ditch, anything short of a tumble from a cliff was unlikely to damage her.

Besides, the faster we get there, the sooner we'll be home. After meeting Si-Si, though, Mayka couldn't help being curious what other wonders the valley held and what they'd find in Skye. She wanted to see what the cluster of lanterns looked like up close. She imagined telling her friends about Si-Si — they'd want to hear everything about her.

Jacklo circled above them. "But, Mayka, night is for stories!"

"At home, we liked to watch the stars, and I'd tell stories," Mayka explained to Si-Si. To Jacklo, she said, "You can still have your stories while we walk. Si-Si's already being kind enough to show us the way. The least we can do is get us all there faster."

"Then I want a story about travelers," Jacklo said.

Mayka ran through the list of stories she knew that fit that description. "How about 'The Tale of the Wandering Tree'?" Both Jacklo and Risa landed on her shoulders, one on each side. She took that for a yes. "Once upon a time, a master stonemason wanted a garden, but in the land where he lived, nothing grew. The rain didn't fall. The soil was empty of life. Even the worms wouldn't crawl through it . . ."

"How did he eat?" Si-Si asked.

"The story doesn't say," Mayka said.

"All flesh creatures need to eat," Si-Si said. "And they need water too, which I don't understand, since they just put it in one end and send it out the other."

Mayka giggled. She'd noticed that too.

"You're interrupting the story," Risa said.

"I'm curious!" Si-Si said. "He couldn't live in a place with no food and no water. And where is this place anyway? Not the valley, certainly."

"Mayka, just tell the story," Risa said from Mayka's shoulder.

The crickets were chirping throughout the field, and the sound made a nice background to the storytelling. Night in the valley was just as peaceful as it was in the mountains, Mayka was happy to see. *It's the sky,* she decided. *No matter what the story is, it's all under the same sky.* Even if they saw it from a different angle. "What he did have a lot of were rocks. So the stonemason carved himself a garden filled with stone flowers and stone bushes and one great, big, beautiful stone tree in the center with flower buds just open, as if caught in a perpetual spring. He carved marks all over it, trying to make it into a tree that could grow and produce fruit . . . but instead he created a tree who could speak."

"I've never heard this story before," Si-Si said. "What would a tree have to say?"

Mayka grinned. She'd asked Father the very same question. "At first, he talked about the wind, then birds, then the clouds, and then, quite quickly, he ran out of things to observe. So he picked up his roots and walked to the edge of the forest to see what he could see."

"But trees can't —" Si-Si began.

"A stone tree could. It doesn't need the soil or water or anything to live, any more than we do. It only needs its marks, its stories. Every day, the stone tree would wander a little farther, then return and tell the man what he saw. He walked in every direction until he had seen all there was to see. By then, the stonemason was no longer alive to hear what the tree had to tell. So the tree simply kept walking."

"Like us," Jacklo said with a sigh.

"You're riding," Risa pointed out. "And you haven't done any walking at all."

"But we're far from home, farther with each mile," Jacklo said. "Like the tree."

Si-Si squawked. "We are *not* lost! I know precisely where we are, or I will, as soon as I see a landmark. I can do this! I think I can. Unless I'm useless, which I am . . ."

Mayka stopped walking. "Are you saying we're currently lost?" She looked around, but in the darkness, everything blended into the same black-gray. She listened to the crickets. Somewhere there was the gurgle of a stream, with the croak of a bullfrog, mournful.

"No! Maybe. I don't know!" Si-Si wailed. "Go on with your story. Please. I'll check ahead just a little bit. Just to see."

The little dragon bounded forward, crashing through the field. Mayka listened to the sound of her crunching across the grasses.

"Mayka?" Risa said. "I think we're lost."

Mayka was beginning to think that too. She also was thinking that the tale she'd picked was not the best choice. Because the tree never did return home. He kept wandering, and for all anyone knew, he was wandering still.

Chapter
Seven

As soon as the sun peeked over the mountains, Jacklo and Risa took to the air to scout north and south for any sign of the city. Shoulders slumped, Si-Si paced in a circle around Mayka. "I failed."

"You tried," Mayka said as comfortingly as she could.

"I tried to defy my story. I should've known I couldn't. I'm useless."

In the south, Jacklo was a spot against the clouds. Risa had already disappeared from view, flying high northward. The birds hadn't wanted to leave her alone, but Mayka had pointed out that she wasn't alone. She had a dragon to protect her, albeit a small, insecure one. "You brought us closer to the city," Mayka pointed out. "That was helpful."

Si-Si dragged her wings in the dirt and sighed heavily.

Mayka squatted next to her. She thought of all the times she'd comforted an anxious Dersy, and all the times Badger and

Nianna and others had comforted her, especially after Father died. *Si-Si doesn't have anyone to comfort her.* "Maybe ... maybe you can be more than your story." She winced as soon as she said it — as Father had often told her, even flesh-and-blood people were the sum of their stories. Si-Si couldn't be other than what she was, any more than Father could have changed the fact that he was a stonemason who'd left the valley and climbed a mountain.

Si-Si let out a whimpering *pffft* sound.

Searching for something to say, Mayka tried changing the subject. "Tell me about the city. I've never even been to a town. Or, well, anywhere."

"It's big," Si-Si said. "Lots of people and lots of creatures, living close together, and ..." She wilted again, her shoulders drooping even lower until her chin rested on her paws. "I've never been there either, at least not in a way I remember. Soon after I was carved, I was brought from Skye to the estate in a cart under a cloth so I wouldn't be damaged. My home was the first place I saw outside my carver's workroom."

"Do you know how to find the workroom where you were made?" Maybe they could ask the stonemason who had made Si-Si to help them. He'd done a beautiful job carving the dragon. She was far more detailed than the oxen and horses they'd seen. Exquisite, really.

"No, but he's not who we need. He wasn't skilled enough

to make me fly when he created me; he won't be skilled enough now. I need a better stonemason. Like your father."

If Father were still alive, he could have changed Si-Si the way she wanted. Hollowed out some of the stone in her torso to make her lighter. Reshaped her wings to be more aerodynamic. Added marks that would let her fly.

Risa was the first to return. She glided down and landed beside them. Preening her feathers, she settled onto a rock. "It's north. Not far."

Si-Si perked up. "We're close? I brought us close?" The little dragon climbed onto one of the rocks in the field near Risa and craned her neck, but her head was still much lower than the tops of the cornstalks.

"Where's Jacklo?" Risa asked.

"He's not back yet," Mayka said.

Risa sighed. "Probably got distracted by something shiny."

Mayka wanted to head north right now — Skye was close enough for Risa to see! But if they continued on without Jacklo, he wouldn't know where they were. No, they had to wait.

Sitting on the ground between the cornstalks, she waited.

Up on the mountain, she'd never minded when time went by. Waiting was easy. She'd spent days waiting for a flower to bloom. She'd waited for the moon to be full. She'd waited for the wind to shift. She'd waited for winter. She'd waited for spring. And it hadn't felt like waiting. It was just . . . living. Time flowed on, and you watched the world, inhabited the world, loved the world.

Somehow, though, it felt different here. She felt as if her stone skin were itching. Her feet wanted to *move*. She felt a powerful pull northward. *Is this what it feels like to be impatient?*

She was used to being in one place, her home, and not wishing she were somewhere else. She'd always been exactly where she wanted to be. Standing up, she paced, like Si-Si, simply to keep her feet from feeling that odd itch.

Soon I'll see the city!

She occupied herself with imagining what it would be like: stuffed with both flesh and stone people and creatures, living side by side, in houses as close to one another as trees in a forest. She wondered if being so close together caused them all to like one another or hate one another. She wondered if she'd make new friends. *It's going to be amazing!*

"He'll be back," Risa said. "He always comes back, usually with ridiculous tales of his adventures." She settled her wings around her and tucked her head beneath one of them.

But Mayka couldn't quit pacing.

She spotted Jacklo first: a black dot against a star-filled sky, like a tiny cloud, and then she saw him flapping toward them. He circled once before he landed.

"You would not believe what I saw!" Jacklo cried. He didn't wait for them to respond. "Giant monsters! Three of them! Large as . . . as . . . that farmhouse. Legs like tree trunks." He hopped from foot to foot, ruffling his wing feathers around him. "They are incredible!"

"Dangerous?" Risa chirped. She spread her wings, ready to flee.

"Oh no, they'd stopped. Long ago, from the looks of it. Grass is growing over their bodies, and their faces are crumbling into sand. But oh, they must have been so incredible when they were awake! Imagine giants striding across the valley! Mayka, Risa, you have to come see!"

"But the city is north!" Si-Si said.

"And the giants are south!" Jacklo cried. "Mayka, don't you want to see them? To read them? Such stories they must have had!"

Standing, Mayka looked to the south, but she couldn't see through the field. All she saw was more corn. Could it be true? Were there fallen giants in the valley? Father had never told any stories about them. If it was true . . . Their bodies would hold untold tales. Secrets and mysteries she could unlock. Dreams she hadn't yet imagined!

But north was the future.

North was the city that could be the answer to their hopes and dreams. North was where stonemasons *created* stories, where people like Mayka were born, where they'd see wonders beyond anything she'd imagined: a place full of more people and creatures, both flesh and stone, than she'd ever known.

She stood for a moment, torn between past and future. But

then she looked at Si-Si, whose blazing eyes were fixed so hopefully northward, and she thought of their friends waiting for them back home.

"We go north," Mayka decided.

"Good," Risa said. "Let's go." She took to the air and, without waiting, flew north. At a jog, Mayka followed Risa. Si-Si hopped beside her, and Jacklo flew to catch up.

But Mayka glanced back to the south and wished she knew what stories lay there, buried in the past.

They ran, flew, and hopped through the day and the night. Farther north, the fields of corn and wheat became sheep and cow pastures, which were easier to run across, but also dotted with piles of manure. Mayka stepped in several, washed off in streams, and then ran on.

They saw farmhouses, lit from within by lanterns and candles. And near dawn of the third day, they encountered their first stone wall. Up until now, all the fences had been wood, but this one was made of chunks of mountain granite that sliced across a pasture. Hefty and gray, it lurked as a linear shadow in the weak predawn light.

"Look!" Mayka said. "It's proof that stonemasons must be near!" She hurried toward the wall, and the little dragon bounded across the field behind her.

"Wait!" Si-Si called. "It might not want you to cross!"

Putting her hands on the wall, Mayka swung her leg up —
and then, suddenly, the rocks shifted beneath her. With a cry,
she was tossed backwards, landing on her rear in the dirt.

The stones formed a face. Its features were cobbled together
from multiple rocks. In the gray predawn light, she was able to
see that the wall had mimicked this pattern elsewhere too —
every few yards, there was another face.

"This is private property," the wall said, stones crunching
together. "Do not enter!"

"You're alive!" Jumping to her feet, Mayka dusted herself
off. Chirping angrily at the wall, Risa and Jacklo circled above
her. "No, no, stop," she said to the birds. "It's incredible!" To the
wall, she said, "I'm very sorry. We didn't know you were alive.
Could you please tell us where we are? Are we close to the city?
How many miles do we need to go?"

Si-Si tittered as if Mayka had just said something ridiculous. "It isn't going to answer you! It's just a wall."

"But it talked!" Mayka said. "It's awake."

"Don't be silly. It's only interested if you try to cross it.
Watch this." Hopping up to it, she swatted the wall with her tail.
She then hopped backwards.

The rocks shifted again before it spoke. "This is private
property. Do not enter!"

"Huh," Risa said. "Weird."

"Don't insult it. Just because it doesn't share its feel-
ings doesn't mean it doesn't have them." Leaning over, Mayka

examined the nearest face. A mark had been carved into the stones that made its forehead. It was still too dark for her to read, but she ran her fingertips over it.

The face repeated its warning, "This is private property. Do not enter!"

"Hush. I heard you."

The mark was so short and simple that she could read it with her fingers. Gouged deep into the stone was a single symbol, the word for "wall" or "guard." She knew from Father's reading lessons that it was usually combined with other symbols, to create a creature who excelled a guarding a house. But this . . . there were no other symbols, no story about this wall, no history. It simply *was*.

How sad, Mayka thought. "Can you say anything else? You must have seen things, must think things, being here. You watch the sky. You see the seasons turn. You must have stories of your days."

"It's just a wall," Si-Si said. "Come on. We can go around it."

Mayka touched the mark again, firmer, waking the face. "Please, we don't mean any harm. All we want to do is pass through."

The rock face shifted to speak again. Pebbles spilled from its lips, forming a beard of rocks. "This is private—"

"I know. But can't you make an exception? We don't mean any harm to whoever lives here. We won't bother them. They won't even know we're there. We'll run straight across."

"Do not enter."

"Just climb it," Jacklo said, landing on the wall. "It can't —" He squawked as rocks rolled around his feet. "Ack! Help! Help, I'm stuck!" Flapping his wings, he tried to pull away.

"Jacklo!" Risa flew down to her brother. Hovering in the air above him, she tried to yank on his wing with her talons. Mayka joined them, pulling on his body. When that failed, Mayka dug into the rocks — they'd rolled together to pin him to the wall. As she dug, the rocks rolled against her too, trying to trap her fingers with the bird. Knocking them back, she pulled the stones apart, and Jacklo shot up into the air.

Si-Si giggled. "Are you okay? I know I shouldn't laugh. But . . . the wall . . . you." Swallowing, she tried to stop giggling and hiccupped instead. "You can't — *hiccup* — cross a wall. You have to go around. That's how walls work — they keep you out."

Rubbing her hands, Mayka backed away from the wall. She'd never seen anything like this — unthinking stone that reacted. "I think maybe you're right." As she walked along the wall without touching it, she kept studying it. It seemed so wrong that a stonemason would bring a wall to life but make it unable to communicate anything more than a warning. It must have other thoughts trapped within its mortar.

Or maybe it didn't. Maybe it was alive but not aware. Worms were alive but not capable of advanced conversation. You couldn't reason with a flower.

"Why bring it to life at all if you don't make it able to be more?" Mayka asked.

"Because the land needed protecting," Si-Si said. "My keepers had a wall like this around their entire estate. I was just lucky that it had been ordered to keep people out, not in, or it would have been a lot harder to leave after they abandoned me."

The sadness was back in her voice. Mayka wished there was something she could say or a story she could tell that would make the little dragon feel better. It had to have hurt so much to be forgotten. She patted Si-Si's back, between her wings. "I'm sorry. Do you want to talk about it?"

"No," Si-Si said, shifting away from Mayka. "It's upsetting, and I don't want to be upset on my way to change my destiny." She arched her back and lifted one foot, posing as if she wanted someone to admire her bravery.

Mayka thought about repeating her apology but decided the best choice was to change the subject again. "Risa, how far out of our way will this take us?"

"A few miles. But, Mayka, there are walls as far as I can see. We'll have to take the roads into the city. And there are people on the roads."

"Maybe they'll be friendly." Mayka didn't know if everyone here was like the farmers, and they were going to have to risk it at some point — they still had to venture into the city, with all its people, to find their stonemason. "I'm not going to be afraid of the unknown."

"That's okay, Mayka," Jacklo said. "I'll be afraid for you."

"I've met lots of people," Si-Si volunteered. "Or at least a few people. Sometimes we'd have visitors at the estate. All of them were very different from one another. One of them liked to eat seeds and spit the shells on the floor, and another incessantly washed his hands . . ." Mayka listened as Si-Si rattled off person after person, more than Mayka had ever imagined meeting. She tried not to feel overwhelmed.

Si-Si continued to talk, and the faces in the wall continued to watch them as they walked alongside it, careful not to touch it, until they came to a road. By now, it was properly dawn, with pale yellow light flooding the valley.

The road was packed dirt, with deep grooves from wagon wheels and indents from hoofprints — Mayka couldn't tell just from the prints if they'd been made by flesh or stone. She stepped out from behind the wall and into the middle of the road and started to walk.

By midday, she saw it: ahead, in the distance, was the city of Skye.

From here, it looked like a streak of white and gray, gleaming near the horizon. Leading to it, the road rose and fell over hills that were dotted with farms and houses, some clustered together and others tucked in between trees or beside rivers. People and creatures were walking and riding to and from the city — from here, they did look like ants, just as Jacklo had described. It was . . . Mayka tried to think of an adjective large enough to encompass it: *magnificent, stupendous, extraordinary.*

"Wow!" Si-Si said.

Mayka agreed. That word worked too.

"I never thought I'd have to come here," Risa said.

"I never thought I'd *want* to come here," Mayka said. "But I do!" She began to jog toward it. *So close, and so incredible!* She was really going to see it, the city from the stories, the birthplace of their father, the legendary Skye!

"Come on!" Si-Si called, breaking into a deerlike lope. "Faster! Our future awaits!"

Chapter
Eight

*A*s Mayka jogged down the road with Si-Si, she tried to sort through her emotions — tried to imagine how she'd feel if this were one of Father's stories. *Am I nervous? Or excited?* She felt as exposed as a rabbit in a field, but also thrilled to be out on the road, in sight of all the other travelers. She wanted to race forward *and* bolt in the opposite direction at the same time.

At first the other travelers were far away, but as Mayka and her friends drew closer, she found herself wondering what they'd see when they looked at her: a stone girl, composed of gray mountain granite, with bare feet and a dress carved to look as if the fabric were ruffled by wind. Mica freckled her cheeks and arms, and a streak of white quartz striped her hair. Hints of black stone clustered on the skirt of her dress, like black stars in a gray sky. She'd been polished smooth, except for her hair, which curled into braids with the natural ripple of the rock. Thinking of the farmers, she wondered how nervous she should be.

Everyone's different, she reminded herself. It was true for her and her friends; it would be true for the people in the valley. *They'll see me for me.*

She wondered if Father had ever felt this way coming into the city, this mix of wow-can't-wait and no-don't-want-to. She wondered if any of the other travelers felt this way.

The first person they passed was flesh and blood, steering a wagon pulled by flesh horses. He had a hat pulled over his ears, and Mayka felt his eyes on her as they jogged by. She made herself smile and wave. "Hi! Are you going to the city?"

His eyebrows shot up. "Yes."

"Keep going," Si-Si advised Mayka. "He's not a stonemason."

"How can you tell?"

"It's obvious," Si-Si said with a roll of her fiery eyes. "All stonemasons have to wear badges to prove they're registered with the guild. No one's allowed to carve stone without one. It's the law." She picked up her pace, and Mayka matched it. Soon they were past the man and his wagon.

Next were three stone horses, like the one they'd seen two days ago, pulling a load without a driver. One was gray, one was black, and one was pink granite, and all wore leather harnesses hooked to their carts. The horses didn't acknowledge Mayka or Si-Si in any way. They just kept plodding forward.

Mayka wondered if Father had had a stonemason badge. She'd never seen him wear one, and she'd never found one in the house.

After they passed several more travelers, Mayka decided she felt more excited than nervous. *What a tale this would have made!* Their journey to Skye. She imagined herself and her friends gathering around Father, maybe on the roof at night with the moon overhead, fat and low in the sky as if it wanted to listen too. He'd tell of their journey, and Jacklo and Risa would jump in — Jacklo with embellishments, and Risa with commentary. Dersy would faint at the part with the farmers, and Nianna would want to hear more about the fallen stone giants that Jacklo saw.

Ahead were the city walls.

White stone, they gleamed in the morning light. Quartz and mica sparkled — it looked as if someone had collected stars from the night sky and then wrapped them around the city. Beyond the walls, she saw spires and domes, sheathed in white and blue, gold and bronze. *I didn't know it would be so beautiful,* she thought. The story of the sky brothers had never mentioned that. But the city was a jewel, shimmering and glittering and shining so brightly that Mayka couldn't look away.

All roads led toward a stone arch, and all the travelers streamed together. Mayka and Si-Si were within the crowd flowing toward the city, while the two birds flew above. At first, Mayka watched all the faces — waiting for someone to yell at her or try to grab her, like the farmer—but no one seemed to pay any attention to her or Si-Si, or to notice Jacklo and Risa flying above. She began to relax, and even to enjoy herself.

Over the road, at the peak of the arch, was the face of a friendly turtle with a broad smile and sagging eyes. The rocks around him were patterned to look like a shell, and the arch itself was made of his legs, spread wide for people to walk through. He spoke in a booming voice. "Welcome to Skye! Home of a hundred dreams and a thousand opportunities!"

If Turtle could see this... She thought of her old friend, high on an overlook. Clear nights on the mountain, you could see Skye twinkling in the distance, but she knew he'd never imagined a turtle on the entrance to the great city. She grinned and waved up at the arch, and was rewarded with a smile back from the great turtle. *When a stonemason wakes Turtle, I'll tell him all about it.*

As she passed through, she felt as if the city were wrapping her in sounds: voices, bells, whistles, footsteps, wagon wheels across cobblestones. She turned in a circle as she walked, trying to see everything at once, but within the press of people, it was impossible.

In the city, Mayka had expected to see other dragons like Si-Si, but even here, the little dragon seemed unique. Mayka didn't see any legendary creatures. The stone creatures were like Mayka's friends, forest and farm animals: horses, pigs, dogs, rabbits, all carved out of a variety of stones. White quartz. Rose quartz. Obsidian. Marble. Limestone. Even stone she didn't recognize. And the people were just as colorful, with skin that ranged from pale pink to deep black and with hair that was colored every shade of the earth, sea, and sky from cornsilk yellow to sunset rose and river blue.

She felt as if she were being drowned in shapes, voices, and colors.

Calm, she told herself. *Stone should be calm.*

But there was nothing calm about the stone-filled city around her.

"Festival vendors, this way!" a voice trumpeted. "This way to the Festival Square! Straight ahead to the Inn District! Lodging for weary travelers available! Left to the farmers' market, bakers' row, and the Garment Quarter!"

Trying to see the speaker, to orient herself, she stopped and craned her neck, and people jostled her. Mayka wished she were taller, less childlike. Someone bumped hard into her shoulder.

"Sorry," a man grunted, then he looked at her and his eyes widened. "Well, look at that: a stone girl! Remarkable!" She noticed a few other people gawking at her. Most, though, seemed not to care.

She made herself smile in what she hoped looked like a friendly way. "Yes, mountain granite," she said, and then she herded Si-Si deeper into the crowd. People closed around her, and when she looked back, the man had been swallowed by the masses.

She was glad that Jacklo and Risa were flying high above, and she wished she could join them. Now that she was within the city, it seemed . . . too full, too much. This deep in the forest of people, she couldn't see anything but more people.

She wormed through the crowd. Both flesh people and stone creatures were pushing their way forward, and many were pulling carts and wagonloads full of food and wares. They chattered to one another in such a din that it all blended into one sound, words blurring into one another so that she couldn't distinguish them. She felt as if she were beneath an avalanche, battered by sounds and shapes and bright colors falling down on her, and she forded ahead, aiming for a spot of openness in front of her.

Away, she thought. *Run.* As much as she'd wanted to come here when they were out on the road, she now wished she could flee and run out of the city, across the valley, and back up her mountain, back where there weren't all these people or creatures or buildings, back where there was quiet.

She was shaking, her stone fingers clacking against her palms. She breathed in and out, and tried to think calm thoughts: a lake, a mountain, the sky. She could barely see the sky from here. The buildings leaned against one another, as if they were trying to block it from view. Everything was stone or wood, all of it carved into intricate shapes and patterns. Even the street beneath her feet, which was chunks of smoothed stone, had been crafted by expert hands. Carver hands, like her father's. She tried to let that fact calm her.

"Are you all right?" Si-Si asked. "You don't look all right."

"Just . . . it's a lot."

"Come on," Si-Si said. "I'm good at finding quiet places." She hopped over the cobblestones, weaving between people. Following the little dragon, Mayka ducked into a canyonlike space between two buildings.

Above, the sky was only a thin streak of blue. But the roar of the city felt muffled, smothered by the walls. She took a deep breath, the way Father used to do every sunrise, to shed the nightmares. She'd never had a nightmare or any kind of dream, since she didn't sleep, but she imagined one felt a bit like this: as if the world were squeezing you. "Where are we?"

"It's an alley, a space between buildings too narrow to be a road," Si-Si said. "It doesn't lead anywhere. We had a bunch of narrow spaces like this at the estate, between the barns. I used to seek them out when the other stone creatures were picking on me."

"I didn't know there would be so many people." *I didn't know so many people existed!* She'd never felt this way before, like she didn't belong. She should be where she could see the wide, open sky, where the valley was laid out at her feet, safely far away.

"It helps if you don't try to look at all of them at the same time."

Peering out of the alley, Mayka gazed at the people, trying to make herself focus on them one at a time, rather than seeing them as "Eek, lots!"

It helped, a little.

They came in all shapes and sizes, wearing more colors than she knew existed: a boy in a more-orange-than-a-pumpkin hat, a woman wearing a dress of feathers, a man with a bare chest but a many-layered skirt with tassels dangling all around. Between them were stone creatures, plenty of them. Stone rats scurried through the street with rolls of paper strapped to their backs, carrying messages. A stone squirrel with a bucket around its neck was scrambling across the face of a building as it cleaned the windows. Other stone creatures — bears, wolves, and bulls, some crudely carved and others exquisitely detailed — blocked the entrances to the fancier houses, acting as guards.

Jacklo and Risa flew into the alley.

"This is amazing!" Jacklo cried. "There are so many of us!"

"It's a good sign," Risa agreed, as she landed on a stack of crates. Jacklo perched beside her and folded his wings. "There must be many stonemasons in this city."

She's right. Someone had to make all these creatures. It was *good* the city was so crowded with so many stone creatures. *You wanted to come here,* Mayka reminded herself.

"This should be easy," Jacklo said. "All we have to do is ask anyone."

Mayka didn't want to move from the alley. It felt comfortable there, like being in a cave, safely cocooned in shadows. She took a step backwards, knowing she should be taking a step forward, and her foot squished. Looking down, she saw she'd stepped on a pile of rotted fruit. It oozed between her toes. Shaking her foot, she tried to scrape it off on the cobblestones. *I can't stay hidden. We're so close!* "Come on. Let's find a stonemason and go home."

Before she could reconsider, she forced herself to walk out of the alleyway, back into the crowd. It swallowed her almost instantly. But this time she rode the wave instead of letting it crash over her. She went up to a woman who wore a headdress of bone antlers and a dress painted to look like a sunset. "Excuse me, but do you know where I could find a stonemason?"

The woman frowned. "Ask your keepers. You should go to their stonemason."

"But I don't —"

"It's their business, not yours. Go home, stone girl." The woman walked on, and Mayka saw she was holding a leash, with a stone dog trotting behind her. Sculpted out of sandstone, the dog was painted pink and wore a collar of diamonds and rubies. Glancing at Mayka and Si-Si, it sniffed as if it had smelled garbage.

"I know who to ask," Si-Si said, hopping into the crowd. "Excuse me? Excuse me! Oh, hello, could you please direct us to a stonemason?"

Pushing forward, Mayka saw the dragon had stopped in front of a pillar with a stone owl carved at the top. His legs and tail feathers were part of the pillar itself, barely chiseled, holding him immobile, but his head and body were free to move. His head swiveled to watch in all directions, and his wings were directing traffic, pointing down streets. "Ahead for the Inn District, right for the Festival Square and festival preparations, left for all other business!"

"Hello? We're looking for a stonemason." Si-Si hopped higher so that the owl could see her. "Hi? We need directions. Please help us."

When he didn't answer, Jacklo landed on the owl's head and twisted his neck to look him in the eye. "Hello! It's not polite to ignore the little dragon lady. Could you please answer her question? Which way to a stonemason?"

"Interrupting my work is not polite," the owl said. "And lingering by the city entrance is not permitted. You must keep moving." He waved his wings in a circle. "Keep moving. Moving, moving, moving." He swung his wings until Mayka and Si-Si scooted out of the way. Jacklo launched into the air.

"You'd think the one giving out directions would have been the best choice," Si-Si grumbled. "Do you want to try?

Pick one to ask." She stuck close to Mayka's ankles, and Mayka appreciated that. It would be easy to be separated in a crowd like this. Looking up, she scanned the roofs for Jacklo and Risa. She thought she saw them perched at the top of a building on its gutter. At a distance, they blended in with the flesh-and-feathers pigeons.

Mayka and Si-Si kept asking stranger after stranger. But everyone seemed intent on making their own way into the city and had no interest in helping two stone creatures who looked like a young girl and an ornament.

Maybe we need to be farther from the gate before anyone will listen, Mayka thought. *Too many people here.*

Picking a direction at random, she joined the stream of flesh-and-blood people and stone creatures.

After several blocks, Mayka realized that the street had cleared, at least somewhat. Instead of the chaotic tumble of people, now she was part of a steady flow up the street. She was finally able to look around and see the city itself.

And it was beyond what she'd imagined.

Stone was everywhere: the buildings, the benches, the roads. Some of it was alive, and some of it wasn't, but it was all amazing to look at, with intricate patterns that seemed to swirl the longer she stared at them, elegant arches that looked as if a breath would break them, and soaring spires that rose so high, their points were lost in sunlight.

Father had built their house out of stone, and she'd thought it was the most beautiful place in the world, but these . . . these buildings were works of art. Alabaster spires spiraled up beside gold-leaf domes. Even the streets sparkled with quartz and mica and pyrite caught in the mountain granite.

Stop sightseeing. You're here for a reason!

Mayka picked the next person to ask: an older man who was carrying a stone turtle tucked under his arm. Maybe it was the presence of the turtle that made her choose him. Maybe it was merely that he was moving slower than others on the street. She caught up to him and walked alongside him. "Very sorry to bother you."

"Hmm? Yes? What is it, dear?" He squinted at her. His eyes were milky, and they didn't quite focus on her. The turtle didn't speak or move.

"We're looking for a stonemason," Mayka said. "Do you know where we can find one?"

"Ah, a tourist? You want the Stone Quarter, my dear. Head northeast three blocks, and look for the multicolored wall. Can't miss it. Prettiest wall in the valley."

She thanked him. *That was easy,* she thought. *Maybe I shouldn't be so afraid of people here. Maybe everything will be fine and we'll be home, with a stonemason, in no time.*

Humming to himself, the man continued on as the two birds dove down to rejoin Mayka. "What did you learn?" Risa asked.

Si-Si hopped from side to side. "He said northeast! Let's go!" Bounding ahead, she hurried across the square. Mayka jogged after her, while the birds flew.

Three blocks northeast, and she saw it: the Stone Quarter.

It was unmistakable, surrounded by a towering wall made of hundreds of brilliant, gleaming stones. "Don't touch it," Si-Si warned her. "It's probably alive." She trotted toward an archway carved with leaves and vines. The entrance to the Stone Quarter was much smaller than the gate to the city, only wide enough for one person at a time, and it was guarded by a flesh-and-blood man in a red uniform.

Mayka approached him.

He neither moved nor spoke.

"We'd like to go in, please," Mayka said.

Glancing at her, the guard said, "No one allowed without express permission of a stonemason until after the festival. Go back to your keepers and wait." As if he'd dismissed her from notice, he went back to watching the crowd flow up and down the street.

"We're not here for any festival," Si-Si said. "We're here to see a stonemason, on business." She puffed herself up to look bigger and more impressive, but she still stood only as high as Mayka's knees.

"All stone business is suspended until the conclusion of the festival," the guard said. He was as motionless as a tree and as wide as a bear, filling the gateway.

We can't slip by him, Mayka thought. *Maybe we can wait until he lets us through. How long could it be? An hour? Two?* "When is the festival?"

"It begins in four days' time," the guard said. "Move along. The Stone Quarter is closed."

Chapter
Nine

Tucked into an alleyway, Mayka and her friends plotted how to get into the Stone Quarter. Waiting was out of the question. Now that they were here and so close, the thought of waiting another moment made every inch of Mayka's stone body itch, an unfamiliar and uncomfortable feeling that she wanted to end as quickly as possible.

"When it's dark, maybe we can sneak in," Jacklo suggested.

Si-Si shook her head, her stone wings tinkling as they rattled together. "When it's dark, they'll replace the flesh guard with a stone owl or cat. My keepers did that on their estate — they used stone guards who could see in the dark."

She's probably right, Mayka thought. At home at night, Nianna watched over the chickens and the cottage from above, while Kalgrey prowled on the ground, keeping the foxes away. *So what can we do? There has to be a way in!* "We could climb over the wall where they can't see us . . ." But as the words left her mouth, she thought of the stone wall they'd encountered in the field and dismissed that idea.

The dragon snorted like a high-pitched whistle. "This is where the stonemasons live. They'll certainly have a living wall. The only safe way through is the gate."

"Or over it," Risa chirped. "Jacklo and I can fly over the wall and find our stonemason. Bring him out."

No, Mayka wanted to say. *This was my idea. It's my responsibility.*

But she had to admit that it was a logical plan.

The birds could fly over the wall with no problem, and they both could talk as well as Mayka could. There was no rational reason that they couldn't be the ones to find the stonemason.

But they shouldn't even be here! She was supposed to have come alone, so that only one of them would be leaving their sanctuary — Nianna had been right about that. They should be safe at home. "You have to promise to be careful," Mayka said.

"We are always careful," Jacklo said loftily.

Risa rolled her eyes. "You wouldn't know 'careful' if it marched up to you and introduced itself." To Mayka, she said, "Don't worry. We'll be fine. Come on, little brother." She flapped out of the alleyway, and Jacklo followed her.

A few seconds passed, then minutes. Mayka tried again to remember what it was like to wait for the setting sun or the rising moon, when patience was easy to come by.

"If my marks had given me a spectacular singing voice, I'd

sing to pass the time," Si-Si said. "Sadly, they didn't. How about telling me a story?"

"I can tell you a story about Jacklo and Risa," Mayka said. She knew several, some true and some not. Jacklo always liked the tale about how he'd saved their animals from a hungry mountain lion, which wasn't true, or the tale of how he'd flown through a storm to bring Father a strip of bark he'd wanted for his tea, also not true. "This one's a true story: once, long ago, a lizard named Etho had become lost in the woods. He had chased an orange-and-black butterfly across a meadow, through a stream, and between trees, and only when he was so deep into the forest that all the trees looked the same in every direction did he realize he was lost.

"As soon as his friend the bird Jacklo realized Etho was missing, Jacklo set out in search of him. But Jacklo was easily distracted, and when he too saw a pretty orange-and-black butterfly, he chased it. He became lost also, but the butterfly did lead him to his friend Etho. The bird and lizard wandered through the woods together for days, following more butterflies, until they found a patch of trees covered in hundreds of migrating butterflies.

"And when Risa realized that both Jacklo and Etho were missing . . ."

Si-Si interrupted with one raised wing. "Don't tell me. She followed a butterfly and got lost too."

Mayka smiled. "She didn't need to. She flew exactly to

where the monarch butterflies always rested on their yearly migration, which was less than a mile from home, and she found Jacklo and Etho within minutes."

Si-Si giggled. "If they were only a mile away, why didn't Jacklo just fly above the trees and see where they were?"

"Risa asked him the same question. He said he didn't want his friend to be lonely. Ever since then, Risa takes Jacklo and Etho — and anyone else who wants — to go see the butterfly migration every year, and when the final butterflies have flown south, she leads them back home." She remembered how beautiful it had been the last time she went, when hundreds of butterflies spiraled up toward the sky while the sun rose. They'd looked like flying jewels. "Risa is the one who looks out for all of us. She might seem prickly, but she has the biggest heart."

"Tell me about your other friends."

"Well, there's also Nianna the owl and Badger and —"

She heard a *thump*, like wood hitting stone, as if a tree branch had smacked against a nearby building. "Hey, come on out of there!" a voice, deep and male, called. "It's curfew!"

Si-Si whispered, "Does he mean us?"

Closer, the voice called. "Don't make me come in after you!"

He definitely means us, Mayka thought.

She inched forward, keeping to the shadows, until she could see out of the alley. Standing in the street was a man in a red uniform. He had three silver stars pinned to his shirt, near his neck, and a mustache like a caterpillar on his upper lip, and he was thumping a thick stick into one meaty hand. "Sunset. It's curfew for — oh, sorry, miss, what are you doing in that alley?"

"Waiting," Mayka said honestly. "I didn't want to be in anyone's way while I did it. The streets are very busy." Or at least, they *had been* busy. Stepping out to look past him, she saw they were emptying, as people flowed into houses. Only one stone donkey marched down the street, pulling a load. The cart's wheels clattered, the loudest nearby sound.

"You should head home. It's not safe for a little girl to be out at night —" He stopped, then frowned at her as she came into the low rosy light of the setting sun. "Oh. I thought you were real. Still, you should get home. Your keepers will be coming to me for reparations if anything happens to you. Get going."

"I'm waiting for someone," Mayka said. "I can't leave yet. It's important." She wondered how much of her story she should tell. So far, no one seemed to be interested in listening.

"Who are you waiting for?" the man asked.

"A stonemason."

"Which one?"

"Whichever one will come."

"No stonemason is going to do housecalls this close to the festival." He withdrew a notepad from his pocket. "Let me take the name of your keepers. Someone ought to tell them not to send you on fool's errands so close to stone curfew."

Si-Si bumped against her ankle. "Run?" she suggested, whispering.

Mayka hesitated — the man seemed friendly, in an official sort of way. She hadn't come here to be afraid of people. She'd stick to the truth, she decided. "My family lives far away from the city. We didn't know about the festival."

He paused, his pen poised above the paper. "Are you serious?" He looked from the girl to the dragon. "The Stone Festival. You must have heard of it."

Mayka shook her head.

Si-Si gave a shrug, which made a tinkling sound.

"Then why are you in Skye?"

"I told you: to find a stonemason." Mayka wondered if talking with city people was always this frustrating. She felt as if she'd said the same thing three times. "My family needs me to bring one back with me. He's needed to recarve their marks."

"Your 'family' can hire one after the festival — that's the whole point of all the demonstrations. It isn't just for the stonemasons' egos, even though it seems that way. They're showing off their skills and wares, so keepers can choose who to hire."

Hire?

She hadn't thought about hiring one. She'd planned to ask, explain their situation, and impress upon him or her the urgency. "How do I hire one?"

"*You* don't." He was frowning at her. "I think you'd best come with me. We'll find your keepers, and I'll speak to them about their responsibilities to you. Mighty careless of them to allow you to wander like this."

Si-Si bumped her again and whispered even louder, "Run now!"

This time, the man heard her. "Hey, now, no running!" He lunged forward to grab Mayka's arm, but Mayka was already in motion, and he grabbed her as if she were flesh — lightly, so as not to bruise her skin. Mayka twisted hard and broke free.

She pounded down the pavement.

He shouted after her, and she heard others take up his cry: *Stop! Come back!* She didn't listen. She headed to where she knew she could lose them: in the crowd by the city gates.

With sunset darkening the sky, the flow of traffic had slowed, but there were still a few wagons coming through the arch. The owl in the center of the entrance square was still directing people to the Inn District or the Festival Square or wherever they planned to go. *Except, apparently, to the Stone Quarter,* she thought.

Picking the thickest crowd, Mayka plunged in and then slowed as she was swept up in the swirl of traffic. Si-Si matched her pace. "Do you think we lost him?" the dragon asked. She craned her neck to see, and Mayka looked too.

"If we can't see him, then he can't see us, right? Besides, he must have better things to do than chase us all night. We didn't do anything wrong."

"I don't know," Si-Si fretted. "We look valuable. He has to

think we're precious baubles who've run away from wealthy owners. If so, he'll want the reward."

Stopping — the crowd flowing around them as if they were stones in a river — Mayka bent down so her face was even with Si-Si's. "I don't care what your markings say. You aren't a bauble." She'd thought their marks defined them, but she'd never met anyone like Si-Si before, who wanted to be more than her story. "And no one owns you. Is that what 'keeper' means? Owner? People can't own other people. You shouldn't have a 'keeper.'"

But instead of looking comforted, Si-Si looked wounded. "But I *want* to be valued! I want to be useful and never again forgotten."

"What your keepers did says more about them than it does about you," Mayka said. "You should be with people who appreciate you for who you are. You should come home with us, to the mountains, and meet my friends. You'll love it there! You can see the whole world laid out before you, and the sky — it's so close you'll feel like you know the stars personally. Every night, we lie on the roof and watch them cross the sky."

"Sounds dreadfully boring," Si-Si said.

Boring? It was the most beautiful place in the world! Mayka missed the sound of the wind through the pine trees, the warmth of the sun of the rocks, the rustle and chatter of her friends in the pens and garden. "It's perfect." *It's home!*

"Oh! Sorry! I was rude, and you've been so nice. It's just . . .

Now that we're separated from the birds, how are they going to find us, even if they do locate a stonemason?"

It was an excellent question. They should have had an emergency plan and picked someplace to meet in case they had to split up. Instead, they'd barreled in without any plan at all. *But how could we plan when we had no idea what was here?*

The owl on the pillar had changed his cry. Instead of welcoming visitors, he was squawking about curfew: all stone creatures were required to return to their homes, except for those with permits for night work. "All permits must be presented to the city guard!"

"What's a permit?" Mayka asked.

"Something we don't have," Si-Si said.

"Then I think we need to find a place to hide." Mayka didn't like saying it — if they were hidden, it would be even harder to be reunited with the birds. "We'll have to meet up with Jacklo and Risa in the morning, when it's safer."

She didn't know what the city guards would do to stone creatures wandering around without a permit, but she had a pretty good idea that they weren't treated nicely, if the encounters she'd had so far were any clue. At the very least, the guards would try to take them to their keepers — and would most likely be angry when they failed to find hers.

"It's not that I'm not brave, but hiding is a very, very good idea." The dragon peeked through the legs of the people in the crowd. "But where? That alley was discovered quickly, and all the buildings have their own guards."

Mayka looked through the arch, at the road that stretched away into dusk. "Outside the city?" They'd have to travel for a while to reach beyond the walled-off fields, but since they had no need of sleep . . . "We keep moving until we've gone half the night, and then we come back."

"*That's* your plan?"

"Can you see any problems with it?"

"It's . . . um, it's not much of a story, is it? When they retell our tale years from now, what will they think of us spending the night out roving across the countryside, rather than a fraught-with-peril night spent hiding in the city?"

Mayka stared at the little dragon. "That's your worry?"

"Well, this is the beginning of my story: how I became the hero of the valley, the fierce dragon defender of Skye who soars with the wind. Or, you know, whatever I'm going to be, once I can fly."

"Uh-huh. If it's anything, it's the story of how we saved my friends by bringing a stonemason to them, and they won't care about any of it except that we came back."

As the last of the sun dipped behind the mountains, the turtle gate began to close, his legs shifting and the rock creaking as two massive doors started swinging shut. Mayka noticed it first and began to jog toward the gate. Si-Si followed her. People blocked their way, but Mayka and Si-Si weaved between them. "Excuse us, excuse us, sorry!"

People glanced at her. Some moved out of the way, and some didn't. "Excuse us, please, excuse us." She and Si-Si reached the gate when it was open only a few feet. Mayka didn't hesitate —she plunged through it and turned back to see Si-Si squeeze out just in time.

The gate shut behind them.

And the sun vanished behind the mountains.

Chapter
Ten

Mayka and Si-Si ran all night, and at dawn, they were back at the city gate, in a line of people and stone creatures, all of whom were waiting for the gate to open. Mayka scanned the sky, looking for any sign of her bird friends. She saw a few sparrows and one hawk, but no Jacklo or Risa against the pale blue.

"Hi," a voice said beside her.

Jumping, she looked to her left. A flesh-and-blood girl, exactly Mayka's height, stood next to her with a wide smile on her face. She was dressed in brilliant yellow. Even her socks were yellow.

"Hello," Mayka said, cautiously.

"Are you here for the festival? What part are you excited about? I'm excited to see what new creatures the stonemasons have carved. And I'm excited for the music and the dancing. And

I'm excited to see the fireworks, because I think it's amazing we can set the sky on fire without setting the city on fire."

Mayka had never heard anyone talk quite as quickly as this girl. "Um, I've never seen fireworks. I've heard about them in stories."

"Ooh, do you know any good firework stories? I do. I know six." The girl held up six fingers. She gestured so much as she talked that Mayka wondered if she ever held still. "In one of them, the city gets half blown up. It's exciting."

"I don't know that one." A new story! Mayka prepared to memorize it, to tell her friends on the roof later, when she was home. "Will you tell me?"

"Really? You want to hear it? My parents are tired of all my stories. They say I talk too much, but I think if you have thoughts, you shouldn't hold them prisoner inside your head. You should let them walk free! Unless they're bad thoughts that are going to hurt someone else. Those shouldn't be free. Unless they *have* to be free, because you have to say them or else something *worse* will happen."

Mayka wasn't entirely sure what the girl was talking about, but she liked the way she talked, with a waterfall of words. "I do want to hear your story."

"Yay! Okay, it happened in Skye during the second Stone Festival. See, the first festival was meant as a punishment, and it was all dour and no fun at all. All the stonemasons had to prove that they hadn't carved anything dangerous, but by the *second* Stone Festival, some of the people of Skye decided that if they were going to have to watch a bunch of stonemasons show their wares, then it might as well be fun. But they kind of forgot to tell anyone else."

Mayka had so many questions: What was the Stone Festival? Why was it a punishment? For what? But she didn't interrupt — this was the girl's story, and she'd asked to hear it. Beside her, Si-Si was listening too.

"So they hired all sorts of acrobats and musicians, and when the stonemasons came out of the Stone Quarter, the revelers signaled for everyone to begin. And there was music and performances and so much excitement that the people of Skye began cheering, as if it were a parade, which it kind of was, just an unplanned one. But one stonemason thought they were being attacked, and he panicked." The girl waved her arms over her head, to mimic panicking. "He started running around and screaming, which caused all his stone creatures to panic and start running around, and they knocked over some of the food vendor carts — and one of the carts was roasting chestnuts, and when the hot chestnuts rolled out, they hit the confetti, which caught on fire, and then the fiery confetti blew all over the place until it landed on a firework-maker's shop, which was closed for the stonemason demonstrations. And *boom!*"

"All the fireworks blew up?" Mayka guessed.

"Exactly," the girl said. "Straight into the sky. And half

the city with them. But the best part was that since everyone in Skye was in the square for the demonstrations, no one was hurt. Afterward, everyone decided they loved it so much that they made it part of the event. And that's why we have fireworks at the festival."

Mayka grinned. That would be a fun one to tell the others. She could already think of ways to elaborate on it, with voices for the stonemasons and *boom* sounds for the fireworks. She'd never heard real fireworks before, just Father's description of them. "I can't wait to see them."

"Is this your first festival?" the girl asked.

"Yes. I didn't even know it was happening."

"You didn't? Wow, I thought everyone knew! We come every year. You're going to love it. Oh, we can watch it together! I mean, if you want to, if you don't have other plans. I'd rather see it with a friend than trail after my parents the whole time — they just want to shop and talk to people they know who will ignore me or, worse, tell me how much I've grown, as if I was going to stay baby size forever."

Mayka wanted to say yes to watching the festival — whatever it was — with this unusual, friendly girl. She knew stories that Mayka had never heard, and she chattered more than anyone Mayka had ever known. On the mountain, they all knew each other so well there were no surprises. But every word out of this girl's mouth was a surprise. "What's your name?"

"Oh! I'm Ilery. What's yours?"

"Mayka, and this is Si-Si."

Si-Si drew herself up taller. "Siannasi Yondolada Quilasa."

"So nice to meet you!" Ilery curtseyed to both of them. "I'd been hoping I'd meet someone I could talk to."

Mayka thought back to how she'd wished to meet another stone girl. This girl wasn't stone, but maybe that didn't matter. Ilery didn't seem to care whether Mayka was stone or flesh. "Me too. What's your story?"

"Mine?" Ilery's mouth opened and closed like a fish, and Mayka wondered if anyone had ever asked her to tell her story before. "I don't have much of a story."

"Everyone has a story."

"Even if it's pathetic," Si-Si said glumly.

"Okay, I guess mine starts with the day I was born. Except I don't really remember that. My mother says I cried a lot, but I was a baby, so I think that's to be expected. You probably didn't cry when you were born."

"I can't cry at all," Mayka said.

"That must be nice. It makes my nose feel all stuffed up."

"I don't know what that feels like either."

"Can you smell?"

"Not a thing."

"But you breathe?"

"Yes. But I don't think I have to. It's just . . . a thing we do, because we're alive."

Ilery blinked at her, as if trying to process that. "That makes no sense. You're stone, so you don't have any insides, so you don't have any lungs, so why would you need to breathe?"

"It's the way I was carved." Mayka pointed to a neat, tiny mark on her collarbone. "It reads 'Mayka is a twelve-year-old girl.' And it means I think, I feel, I breathe — I live as a twelve-year-old girl." She never thought to question *why* she'd been carved this way.

"Wow."

Mayka held out her arms to show more marks. "And these tell more about me and my life." She thought she should have another mark, about how she'd ventured out of the mountains and what she'd found. Maybe when they found a stonemason, she'd ask him to add it. She liked that idea. "How do you manage without your story written on you? How do you stay the same?" It was a question she'd always wished she'd asked Father. It hadn't occurred to her while he was alive.

"I've got my story inside." Ilery thumped on her chest, near where Mayka knew humans carried their heart. Father had had a heart. She remembered sitting on his lap, her head against his chest, and listening to his heartbeat as he told her stories or just looked up at the stars. Sometimes he sang to her, though his voice was low and he sang only a few notes. It had always reminded her of the crooning of wind through the pine trees.

"If I had marks, they'd say I'm a farm girl," Ilery continued.

"I live with my parents on a small farm far away from the city. Not many neighbors. No kids nearby. And my parents don't have much money, so they can't afford much help. They run the farm themselves, which means I'm alone pretty much all the time. So I made friends with the stones who work the fields. One of the horses loves to talk — he'll talk even if there's no one listening — and there's a stone dog who thinks he can predict the weather. He's always wrong. They're my friends."

Ilery went on to describe her life on the farm, and Mayka thought it wasn't so different from her life. Ilery fed the chickens and the goats. She planted seeds and weeded the garden. She helped keep the stone horses clean and ready to plow. From her description, Mayka gathered that Ilery's horses were a lot more alert than the ones Mayka had seen on the road.

When Ilery finished, Mayka talked about her home, about the cottage and her friends, about the fish in the pond, about the way they watched the stars at night, about how sunsets looked over the valley.

For the next hour, while they waited for the great turtle to wake, they traded more stories: things they'd done, things they'd seen, things they'd felt, until they heard a commotion from the front of the line, near the entrance to the city.

Jumping from foot to foot, the girl pointed toward the gate. "Look! He's awake! It's about to open!" She clapped her hands together.

On the arch, the turtle's eyes were open, and he was

surveying the crowd. "Good morning! Please form an orderly line. Welcome to Skye, home of good fortune!"

Ilery waved at a man in a purple cloak and a woman with a golden bird's nest, cradled in a purple hat, on her head. "Those are my parents. We're going to stay at the Marble Inn. Where are you staying?"

"Um, we aren't staying anywhere," Mayka said.

Si-Si jumped in to explain. "We don't sleep."

"But you need someplace to spend the night, don't you? Ooh, you should stay with us!"

"We have to meet up with some friends of ours," Si-Si said. "Other stone creatures."

"Maybe we'll see you again?" Mayka asked Ilery. As she said it, she knew it was unlikely. Once she found her friends and the stonemason, they'd leave for the mountain. This was her one adventure beyond the forested slopes.

"I hope so!" Ilery waved happily and bounded off toward her family. A man loaded her onto a seat on a cart, then climbed up next to her — the cart was pulled by two stone horses.

Mayka waved back.

At least there was someone here who treated her like a person. She wished they could have gone with Ilery, seen the city together, watched the festival like ordinary tourists. But Ilery's family was already swallowed by the crowd, separated from her by two other wagons and a string of stone donkeys.

Bells rang cheerfully from the spires of the city as the great gate swung open and the crowd pushed through. There were even more people than yesterday, coming for the Stone Festival. Most of them streamed toward the festival grounds or toward the inns, directed by the owl, but Mayka and Si-Si weaved through the people and creatures, aiming directly for the Stone Quarter.

Slowing, they saw it: the thick wall that gleamed with a thousand jeweled stones, and the arch of stone vines and leaves with a red-clad guard. The guard turned several people away. Even though she couldn't hear what he was saying, she could imagine it. *Closed until after the festival.*

"Now what?" Si-Si asked.

"We wait for the birds to find us." Mayka was sure they'd come out, sooner or later. They'd probably been searching for Mayka and Si-Si all night. "All we have to do is make ourselves visible."

Parading up and down the length of the wall, Mayka scanned the sky. She saw plenty of birds, mostly pigeons, and with each one, she called out, "Jacklo? Risa? We're here!"

She got lots of questioning looks, but no one stopped her, and she didn't go near enough to the wall to wake its defenses, or to the guard to attract his attention. As she called to her friends, she tried not to worry, but failed, as her imagination kept conjuring up images of the birds broken in the street, swept away with the trash . . .

At last, one of the birds overhead broke from the flock and aimed directly for them. Closer, Mayka saw its feathers were gray stone, and its eyes were black. "Risa!" She held up her arm, and Risa landed on it, then climbed up to her shoulder.

"Where were you?" Risa scolded.

"Did you find a stonemason? Where's Jacklo?" *Can we go home yet?* Mayka wanted to ask but didn't. She surveyed the sky, hoping that Jacklo would fly to them next. After an entire night and morning of worrying, she'd had enough of the city and adventure.

Risa ruffled her feathers, trying to make them lie flat, but they spiked back up, a clear sign she was upset. "I haven't seen Jacklo all night, and the stonemasons refused to talk to me — they'll only deal directly with my 'keepers' and only *after* the festival."

"Maybe Jacklo had better luck?"

Watching the sky, they waited for him until sunset, but he didn't return. Several times, Risa flew over the wall into the Stone Quarter, only to come back more worried than before.

"He could have become lost," Risa said. "Or gotten hurt and been unable to fly. Or gotten himself stuck somewhere." All of them stared at the darkening streets, as a stone ferret went from streetlamp to streetlamp, climbing up one and then using a knife against his body to strike a flame. Lights began to blaze from the lamps as the sun sank behind the mountains.

"We can't wait any longer," Mayka said. "There's a curfew. We'll have to leave the city before they close the gates. We'll return in the morning." *I shouldn't have let him fly away from us.*

Jacklo was too easily distracted. He lacked common sense. Anything could have happened to him.

"I'll continue to search," Risa said. "And when I find him, I'll wring his neck for worrying us." She flapped toward the Stone Quarter, while Mayka and Si-Si left the city to hide again in the darkening fields beyond.

Chapter
Eleven

S till no Jacklo at dawn.

Risa circled twice above Mayka's head before settling down on her shoulder. "This isn't right," she fretted. "I can always find him. Always. I know something's happened to him. He's not on any street. He's not on any roof. He's not in any alley. I searched them all."

Mayka stroked the bird's head and tried to think of what she could say to reassure her. But she couldn't find the words. She'd never felt like this before: as if something were gnawing on her, chewing her stone body. *Jacklo's gone.*

He's not. We'll find him.

"You couldn't search inside the buildings, right? He must be in one." Mayka tried to make her voice sound calm and reasonable. "All we have to do is find which one he's in and let him out."

Beside her, Si-Si rose up on her hind feet as if that would

be enough to let her see over the Stone Quarter's wall. "How can we do that? We can't even get past the wall, much less into the houses."

"Then we find someone who can," Mayka said.

Si-Si snorted. "Because we've had such luck with people so far." She dropped back to four feet and glared balefully at a woman leading a stone donkey laden with packages. The donkey didn't even glance at them, but the woman switched to the opposite side of the street.

Mayka thought of Ilery, who hadn't been like the other people they'd met. There had to be other friendly people in Skye. "Ilery talked about stonemasons at the festival — she mentioned they did demonstrations in a square."

"Who's Ilery?" Risa asked.

"A flesh-and-blood girl we met outside the city," Mayka said. "Maybe someone preparing for the festival can help us get into the Stone Quarter?" She was flailing for an idea, she knew, but it *felt* logical. The guard had said you needed permission from a stonemason to enter the quarter — what if they got permission?

"The owl on the stick talked about a festival square," Risa said. "Come on. He can tell us where to find it." Without waiting for a response, she flapped away from the Stone Quarter, and Mayka and Si-Si followed her.

Closer to the entrance to the city, it was even more crowded than it had been the day before. More and more flesh people and stone creatures were pouring through the city gates, all of them talking about the upcoming Stone Festival. The streets were clogged with wagons, and the sidewalks were filled with families and workers. Mayka felt like a fish swimming against the stream as she and Si-Si were forced to slow to a near stop, despite repeating, "Excuse me, excuse me."

Overhead, Risa flew above the crowd, directly to the owl on the pillar who was giving out directions. She returned to Mayka and Si-Si and reported, "It's east, just past the city mural."

"What's the city mural?" Mayka asked.

"Ooh, it's famous!" Si-Si said. "It's supposed to be the history of the valley. I've never seen it, but it should be a very clear landmark."

"Follow me," Risa said.

Joining the flow of traffic, they switched directions and, trailing behind Risa, made their way across the city, toward the Festival Square. Soon, they encountered the city mural, a vast tapestry of stone.

"We're on the right track!" Si-Si cried. "Come on!"

But Mayka slowed.

Other pedestrians flowed around her, but she ignored them.

Stretching across several buildings, the city mural was a mosaic made of shards of different colored stones and jewels carefully arranged into images, scenes, and landscapes. They weren't alive, but they were beautiful.

Mayka stared in wonder as she walked slowly down the street, drinking it all in. She hadn't ever seen anything like this. The colors were like the sunset, rich and deep. She saw the Dragons of the Mountains, depicted in all their splendor, and the great soaring glory of the towers of Skye. She saw the first stonemason carving a rock in the orchard — a story she knew. She saw giant stone creatures destroying a city — a story she didn't know. She saw other images from more tales: humans riding stone chariots in what looked like races, fields being plowed by horses that were led by a stone farmer, depictions of festivals, children playing, and then she saw a very familiar face, composed of topaz and diamond shards:

Father.

She stopped in front of it. There was a series of panels in this section, each with Father in the center. She reached out and touched the jewels that made his face. He was carving in this first one, and the image had caught his fierce concentration and joy with onyx for his eyes and red garnets for his cheeks. "He's here."

Si-Si hopped impatiently. "Come on! The Festival Square is just ahead!"

"Father, I miss you," Mayka whispered. She hadn't expected to see his image in Skye. Why was it there?

"I miss him too," Risa said softly. She landed on Mayka's

shoulder and then pecked at the next frame. "What's he doing in that picture?"

The next one showed Father with a mountain-size stone dragon. He appeared to be carving it. *But Father never carved mythical animals,* Mayka thought. *He only carved real ones.* Gently, she touched the stones that made his face. She then walked to the next picture.

In it, a monstrous six-headed beast was attacking a city, and Father was riding the stone dragon, fighting against the beast. Then in the following panel, men and women were rebuilding the city. A few people were celebrating, while others were bent over and looked unhappy, tiny blue stones on their cheeks as tears. She saw graves.

And she saw Father by two of the graves, one larger and one smaller. *Who died?* She touched the stones that formed the smaller one.

In the last frame, he was standing beside his dragon, but the dragon lay on the ground, eyes closed. His wings were broken. Blue stones depicted tears on Father's face.

"What does it mean?" Mayka wished she could talk to Father — ask him what happened, why the dragon had stopped, who was buried in the two graves.

Si-Si poked Mayka's knee with her snout. "What does it matter? It's the past. You still have a friend to find, and we still need a stonemason. Isn't that more important than staring at some old picture? Come on, let's go!"

Mayka shook herself. *Si-Si's right.* The mystery of why Father was pictured in a mural in Skye would have to wait. Jacklo needed them now.

Following Si-Si past the mural, Mayka felt her fear for Jacklo creep back in. *Risa must be even more worried,* she thought. The two birds hadn't been apart for more than a day in . . . well, years, not since the incident with Etho and the butterflies. According to family stories, Father made the pair of them at the same time: he'd carve the body of one, then the body of the other, the wings of one, then the wings of the other, the beak of one, then the beak of the other, so he'd finish them both on the same day. He finished Risa a few hours before Jacklo, a fact the bird took to heart. She was Jacklo's older sister and had taken responsibility for him from his first flight.

Mayka hadn't been carved yet, so she wasn't there to witness it, but the others all had their own memories of that disastrous flight. Father had woven all their versions together to create a tale of a string of accidents that resulted in a stampede of goats and the shattering of nearly every roof tile. That roof had been made of pottery tiles. After Jacklo learned to fly, Father had replaced it with stone.

She told that story once a year, on the anniversary of Jacklo and Risa's carving day.

As they drew closer to the Festival Square, they heard music, and Mayka felt as if the noise was enveloping her. She'd never heard musicians before. Singing, yes. She remembered

Father would sing while he worked sometimes, story songs with rambling tunes as he chipped and chiseled his stone creations. She'd listened to birds sing. She'd even tried it herself a few times. But this was *music*.

Coming into the square, she saw the musicians on a raised platform: drummers and flutists, plus a few plucking at strings on wood instruments that looked like crescent moons. She felt the music as well as heard it, vibrating through her entire self. Each drumbeat shook her, and each chord lifted her. Closing her eyes, she let it soak into her, surrounding her and bathing her.

Then the singing began.

There were three voices, weaving together, telling a tale of stonemasons.

One stonemason was kind, and he created creatures who could care for the sick, the very young, and the very old.

One stonemason was strong, and she created creatures who could build homes, plow fields, and dig graves.

One stonemason was clever, and she created creatures who could study the stars, measure the mountains, and solve the mysteries of life and death and immortality.

Each one claimed that their creations added more to the world and were more important than the others, and so they fell to arguing, and then challenged one another to battle, with their stone creatures as soldiers. But when it came time to meet on the field, the creatures refused to fight.

Fighting would hurt the sick.

Fighting would destroy the homes.

Fighting would bring only death.

But the stonemasons —

The singing stopped abruptly, the music twanged to a halt, and a man dressed all in black began to shout at the musicians to try again, watch the timing on the third measure, and obey the intensity notations.

Si-Si bumped her head into Mayka's knee. "Are you all right? You look transfixed."

"It was beautiful." She stared in awe at the musicians and wished she knew how to make such beauty. It must be so tremendous to create something out of nothing. Out of sound. Out of air. Out of movement and —

"Eh." Si-Si sniffed. "I've heard better."

"Well, I haven't," Mayka said, but she followed Si-Si into the square.

All around, stone donkeys, horses, and oxen were carting loads from one end of the square to the other. Stone squirrels were unloading wood, nails, hammers, and other supplies, and scampering with them to flesh-and-blood humans, who would then direct other stone creatures — beavers and badgers — to build. The sound of hammers hitting wood filled the air. Saws, chisels . . . *Chisels!* A stonemason's tool!

The familiar clink made her ache inside, in the hollows of her body, and she found herself thinking about Father again.

That sound used to fill their house. *Clink, clink, clink.* Mayka followed the noise, and the rest of the cacophony faded into the background.

She brushed past a woman who said, "Watch where you're going! Oh my, how exquisite! Deneb, did you see that stone girl? Find out who made her."

But Mayka didn't slow. She kept weaving through the crowd, heading for the clink of metal on stone, until at last she saw a boy wielding a hammer and chisel. His hair was tied back with a strip of cloth, and he had the same kind of leather gloves that Father used to wear. He was trimming the stone with a point chisel, and he was focusing so hard that he was biting his lip. She watched as the hammer hit the head of the chisel, and the stone chipped, a chunk popping off and skittering across the cobbles.

Before he could line up the next tap of the chisel, Mayka stepped forward. "Excuse me," she said, "but are you a stonemason?"

He was dressed like one, and he was working with stone. He even had a badge with an embroidered picture of a chisel and hammer. Si-Si had said stonemasons wore badges.

She startled him so much that he jumped.

"Garit, apprentice to Stonemason Siorn, at your service!" He dropped the hammer, narrowly missing his toes, and then clapped his hands together and faced Mayka and Si-Si. "How can I . . ." He trailed off and his eyes widened. Crossing the stage to her, he knelt as he reached out and touched her cheek. "Amazing!"

"Um, thanks?" She leaned backwards, so his fingers fell away. "We're looking for our friend, a bird named Jacklo. We were hoping you could help us find him."

He hopped off the stage and walked in a circle around her. She pivoted, watching him. "Wow!" He whistled through a gap in his teeth. "You're fully articulated. Full motion. Can you raise your arm, please?"

People here have strange manners, she thought, but she lifted her arm, then lowered it. "He's small, gray, and from a distance can blend with other birds. We think he's somewhere in the Stone Quarter, possibly inside a building. But the guard won't let us in."

"Us?" He seemed to notice Si-Si for the first time. Squatting down in front of her, he admired her. "You're a beauty. Who carved you?"

"Master Lison of Skye," Si-Si said proudly. "I was inspired by —"

"The Dragons of the Mountains. Of course." His attention flicked back to Mayka. "But *you* weren't made by Master Lison. He didn't carve granite. I can recognize one hundred fifty carvers by their signature style. It's part of my training. But you . . . I don't know who carved you, but whoever it was was clearly a master." He contemplated her some more. "Don't tell me. Let me guess . . . Hmm . . . It has to be someone well established, who doesn't care what other people think. Sure, it's not illegal to carve a human, but no one does it. No market for it. So your carver has to be someone who —"

Risa landed on Mayka's shoulder. "We don't have time for games! Jacklo's missing!"

Risa was right. Mayka could tell him all about her father, if he wanted, and how Father carved them. But later! "Please, can you help us enter the Stone Quarter? Could you help us find our friend? He's been missing since yesterday, and we're worried."

Now he was staring at Risa. *Honestly, he's as easily distracted as Jacklo,* Mayka thought. He opened and shut his mouth several times, before pointing at Risa and saying, "Everyone says flying stone is impossible! I always thought if you could figure out the balance of weight and determine the exact right marks . . . But no one's ever done it. I mean, there are legends saying it was done once, but there's no record of the marks and no one has been able to do it since, and believe me, many stonemasons have tried." Blinking, he shook his head. "My master needs to see you!"

Mayka seized on that. Yes, a master stonemason! Exactly what they needed. "Is he in the Stone Quarter?"

"Yes, of course, that's where all the stonemasons live. It's the law."

"Can you take us to him?" Maybe whoever he was would

listen to them and help find Jacklo—and maybe he would be willing to come recarve her friends. This could be the perfect answer to both problems!

"Sure! Oh wait, no. I'm supposed to finish this." He frowned at the half-chiseled stone block, then looked at them, then over his shoulder at the corner, and back at the stone. Like Ilery, he seemed to wear every thought he had on his face, and right now he was clearly waffling between finishing his task and escorting them to his master.

"Take us now and finish it later," Mayka suggested.

"But he was very insistent. It all has to be finished. The festival is in two days!"

Again with the festival! "Okay, what do you have to do to finish?" Maybe it would be quick.

"I'm to make the pedestals for his creations to stand on. He wants them visible to the audience during his demonstration." Waving his hand, Garit indicated the area where the stone beavers were building with wood, and she realized they were making a series of benches, each higher than the next. *Seats for an audience*, she thought.

"So you aren't making real carvings? No creatures? Just pedestals?" She studied the chunks of rock. She'd helped Father before, with the rough preparations, and she knew the techniques, at least the basics. She was certain she could hold a point chisel steady and wield a hammer. "What size and shape?"

He told her the dimensions, about half her height and twice

her width, with a flat top. "It will take me about four more hours to complete them all."

"I can help you halve that." She held out her hands. "If you'll share your tools?" Father had never liked anyone to touch his tools, except with his supervision. This boy might say no, and then she'd have to wait hours for him to help her.

"You? But . . . you can't be a stonemason. You're stone!"

"I'm not a stonemason," Mayka agreed. "If I were, then I wouldn't be here in Skye looking for one. If I were, I'd never have left home. If I were, Jacklo never would have gotten lost, and we wouldn't be having this conversation. But I *can* make a block with right angles. Now, are you going to let me help you, or are you going to make me stand here and wait? Because on this journey I have discovered something new: impatience."

Wide-eyed, he held out an extra hammer and chisel, but then he drew back when she reached to take them. "Be careful. If you chip yourself before my master sees you . . ."

"She'll be careful," Risa said. "I'll watch her. We all take care of each other."

We're not taking good care of Jacklo now, Mayka thought. But she'd fix that soon. As soon as Garit led them to his master, she'd convince the stonemason to help.

She took the tools.

It felt strange to be holding a hammer and chisel. Except to clean them, she hadn't touched Father's tools since he died. There had been no point. The house was complete, and she was no stonemason to try to do what he did. Father often said he'd been born to the art. His mother told him that as a baby, he had preferred a hammer to a rattle. He saw a block of stone, and he saw the shape within it — his job was to set that creature free. She, on the other hand, saw stone, and it was stone. *I'm no stonemason*, she thought.

But I can turn a chunk of stone into a pedestal.

She heard Father's voice, in her memory, as she stepped up to the chunk of rock. See the shape within the stone, he'd say. Parallel cuts. Angle the chisel, aim the hammer, and hit from the inside out, away from the heart of the stone. Carve around the heart. The trick was to find its weak points. Identify the impurities, the places where the stone would naturally split, and then you can cut the stone the way it wants to be cut.

She'd been the last living statue that Father had carved, but he hadn't stopped sculpting. He'd continued to add to the house — the petal-shaped roof tiles, the kitchen table, the bathtub. He'd carved the sluice for the fish to water the goats, cutting their channels straight into the mountainside. He'd cut and piled rocks for the wall. She'd helped him, any way he needed. Carrying stone. Sharpening tools. Even roughing out the shapes, which was all she needed to do now. Carving a pedestal was no different than shaping a block for the stone wall, and it didn't take long for her hands to remember how to hold the chisel steady and how to swing the hammer at just the right angle.

The musicians were playing again, and the drums thudded

in a steady beat. She matched her strikes to the rhythm and let the melody pour over her. Dust from the stone flew in clouds, and the square looked as if she were seeing it through a fog. She struck again and again, chipping away at the block until it was roughly square, then she picked up a rasp and began to smooth away the chisel marks.

Risa perched on top of the block, watching her.

Switching to a tooth chisel, she bent over the top of the block. She chipped at the grooves, and then changed back to the rasp to smooth again. She polished with sandpaper. Stepping back, she examined it. *Bit more polishing on the left* . . . Kneeling, she finished the pedestal.

"Wow, nice work!" Garit said.

She beamed at the compliment, and then moved on to the next block of stone. "Tell me about the Stone Festival. Everyone seems to be talking about it."

Garit returned to carving his pedestal. "You don't know about the Stone Festival? It's only the most famous and important festival in the entire valley!"

"This is my first time in the valley," Mayka said. "We live on a mountain, and we've never left before. Which is why I'm so worried about my friend. He's not used to all of this. He's probably caught somewhere and scared."

Risa drooped. "Terrified."

"Your friend is stone too?"

"A stone bird. Like Risa." Mayka suddenly realized she'd

never properly introduced herself. "I'm Mayka, and these are my friends, Risa and Si-Si."

"Siannasi Yondolada Quilasa," the little dragon said. "Is your stonemason master any good? Because we are looking for the very best."

"He *is* the very best," Garit said automatically. "He carved the gates of Skye, or at least he would have, if his commission had been chosen. His work is seen in the most important houses and with the highest families. He's an innovator and a genius. You'll be awed by what he presents at the festival."

He sounded as if he was repeating something he'd memorized, but at least the words seemed promising. A genius would easily be able to recarve their marks. Maybe even help Si-Si.

"And the festival?" Mayka prompted.

"It's where all the stonemasons showcase their skills. Reveal new carvings. Demonstrate new marks. And people can then choose who to hire for carvings and recarvings. It happens once a year, but this is the first time I will be attending as a full apprentice. I was just a kid last time."

He still seemed like a kid. She guessed he was about twelve years old. He was her height, with a slight pudge to his cheeks. He was sweating through his shirt. She was glad she couldn't sweat. It would be unpleasant to be damp all the time.

"We set up all around the square. This is my master's stage. Other stonemasons will share it at other times, but he has it on the first afternoon. He plans to amaze everyone."

"How?" Si-Si asked.

"Uh, well, I'm not supposed to talk about it. Surprise, you see." Then he brightened. "But you can ask him yourself, if you want! He won't tell you any secrets, of course, but maybe he'll show you a hint."

Together, they finished the rest of the pedestals, and then Mayka handed him the hammer and chisel. "All right, then," she said. "Let's go."

Chapter
Twelve

G arit strode toward the entrance to the Stone
Quarter. Pointing to the badge on his leather apron,
he announced, "They're with me! Bringing them in."

Behind him, Mayka and Si-Si stuck close. Mayka tried
not to look as nervous as she felt. Holding up one hand to block
them, the guard squinted at Garit's patch.

Chest puffed out, Garit said, "I'm taking them to see my
master, Master Siorn — those are his colors, see? I'm his apprentice!"

The guard grunted. "Never heard of him. But you're clear."

Garit flushed, his cheeks and neck pinkening. Mayka
stared in fascination at his slightly red ears and wondered what it
would be like to change colors with your emotion. *Must be a bit
inconvenient.*

He shot a glance at her. "He really is a good stonemason,"

Garit said to her and Si-Si. "One of the best. That's why my family apprenticed me to him."

Mayka opened her mouth to ask about his family.

Si-Si nudged her, prompting her to walk forward, through the arch. Overhead, Risa had already flown in and was perched on the gutter of a nearby house, waiting for them. As they passed through the wall, the bird leapt off, spread her wings, and glided down to land on Mayka's shoulder.

"Jacklo must be so scared," Risa said into her ear.

"We'll find him," Mayka promised.

"What if we don't?"

"We will."

Stepping onto the street, Mayka saw the Stone Quarter for the first time. And she halted and stared, jaw dropped and eyes wide. She'd thought the city was incredible, but this . . . It was . . . It was . . .

Si-Si squeaked, "Oh wow, it's beautiful!"

Spinning in a slow circle, Mayka tried to look in every direction at the same time. She felt as if she'd walked into a dream. Everything, everywhere, was stone, and it was all alive!

Both sides of the street were lined with palaces carved out of every color marble in the world, and decorated with more sculptures than Mayka had ever imagined. Stone turtles, stacked one on top of another, held up the corner of one portico, while two stone herons flanked a door of another palace — the door itself was carved with images of the mountains. By another, a stone bear held a cauldron overflowing with stone flowers. As Mayka watched, a second bear lumbered up to the first bear and shouldered its load. The first bear shuffled away.

"Keep walking," Risa told her.

As she stepped forward, Mayka felt stones shift beneath her. Looking down, she saw the street itself was *moving*. With each step they took, the stones shuffled their positions to smooth the path ahead of them. Looking around, she saw it was doing this for everyone, and no one else seemed to notice. *Maybe they're used to it.* She certainly wasn't.

The street was surprisingly busy, given that the quarter was "closed." She noticed that, unlike in the rest of the city, most of the crowd was made of stone, not flesh. Also, there were more different kinds of creatures here. A moose trotted down the street beside a pair of otters. A pink quartz snake slithered by. Little bejeweled lizards clustered on one wall, and an oversized stone beetle trotted across the street, carrying a load of wood on its back.

"I thought no one was allowed in the Stone Quarter until after the festival," Mayka said, swiveling to see more. Even the trees were stone, and they didn't budge in the wind. Not a leaf stirred. A stone owl sat on one branch, watching them as they walked by.

"These all belong to the stonemasons." Garit waved his arms grandly.

Si-Si's red eyes were wide, and she craned her neck right and left, as if she too wanted to see everything all at once. "This is a treasure trove!" Si-Si said. "My keepers had the most extensive collection in our region, but it didn't compare to this!"

"I know! It's magnificent. Can you believe this place was originally set up as a punishment? Look at it now!" Garit said. "When I was a boy, I used to try to climb over the wall to see inside. And then when I was old enough, I'd beg anyone I could think of to let me run errands for them inside the Stone Quarter. That's how I met Master Siorn. I was delivering chicken necks. He likes them in stews."

Mayka thought of their chickens and shuddered. Perhaps they could hide them when Master Siorn came up the mountain. "What do you mean it was a punishment?"

"Well, after the Stone War, all the stonemasons were rounded up and moved to this part of Skye, and the city council ordered a wall built around the district. For the first few years, stonemasons were only able to leave on the Day of Demonstration, when they had to display everything they'd carved and prove it was all harmless. Over the years, of course, the Day of Demonstration became the Stone Festival, and the wall also keeps tourists from sneaking in to see the miracles before they're presented. But it still serves its original purpose: keeping new carvings away from people until they're approved as safe."

His story about the Stone Festival was similar to Ilery's, except hers said it turned into the festival after only one year. It was close enough, though, to make Mayka think the basic story was true.

"Do you think your master will be willing to help us?" Si-Si asked. "Even though he's preparing for the festival?"

"We're worried about our bird friend," Mayka explained. "If he could help us —"

"Master Siorn knows about every stone creature in the quarter. If your friend is here, my master will have heard," Garit said confidently.

A few flesh-and-blood men and women were out in front of their mansions, corralling the stone creatures. One woman was loading up a cart, pulled by a stone . . . Mayka didn't know what it was. It was larger than a bull, with a long nose that looked like a snake and broad ears that looked like leaves. "What is *that?*" Mayka pointed.

"That's an elephant," Garit said. "She's debuting him at the festival. Beauty, isn't he?"

"He's huge," Mayka said. She'd heard a tale once about an elephant and a mouse who become friends with a lion — it was a silly little fable that Dersy liked. She wondered if a flesh-and-blood elephant would be this enormous.

"They're said to live beyond the mountains," Garit said. "Master Trenna claims he's strong and gentle and can replace a team of two oxen in a field. She predicts they'll be very popular after her demonstration at the festival." He pointed across the street. "That's Master Suba's workshop. He's been working for fifteen years to invent new marks for stone mice that will make them smart enough to solve any maze."

Instead of a garden or a lawn, the front of his palatial house was consumed by a stone maze laid into the earth, with walls that wove in intricate patterns. Mayka could see stone mice running back and forth through the maze, navigating the passageways. "But . . . why? Are there a lot of mazes around?"

"Um, well, no . . . Actually, I don't really know why. Just that no one's ever done it before. Stone mice usually figure out mazes at about the same rate as flesh-and-blood mice, because, you know, they're mice, but Master Suba thinks he can improve their problem-solving skills."

"Good for the mice," Mayka said. How strange it must be to be the one to decide how smart or skilled a creature would be. She glanced at Si-Si. Someone had decided that the dragon was decorative. The stonemason who had carved her could have given her a different story, but he chose to define her by her limitations.

She'd never thought about it before, but it was a lot of power for one person to have over another. *Father chose my story.* Opening her palm, she studied the mark of the reading eye. *Except this one.* She'd asked him to carve it. She considered what that meant. *It means I grew. I changed.* "What if the mice decide they don't want to run mazes anymore?"

"No one's making them run," Garit said. "Look at them."

She watched the mice race through their passageways, their

tiny paws scrabbling on the stone and their tiny noses twitching. She had to admit they did seem to be happy zooming through. They'd make it to one end, pop out, and then dive back in to begin again, as if this was their sole purpose and joy.

"Up ahead is Master Zillon." Garit pointed toward a flesh-and-blood man in front of a mansion made of polished black marble. "He specializes in doors."

Master Zillon was directing two stone bears, who carried slabs of granite, then leaned them up against a wall. Each slab was a door, elaborately decorated. One had leaves carved all around a man's face. Another was covered in stone scorpions, their tails poised. As Mayka watched, the scorpions moved, running around the edges of the door.

"He's been working nonstop on tons of new designs. That scorpion is one of them — it will protect your home when you aren't there. And there's supposed to be one where the door knocker can actually leave the door and go tell his keepers who's there, then return to the door to be ready for the next visitor."

"If he can leave the door," Risa asked, "why would he stay on it?"

"Because he's a door knocker," Garit said, as if that answered everything. "Oh, and look over there! Master Pria is experimenting with legendary creatures too. That will make my master happy. He's always saying we need to stop limiting ourselves and our imaginations. The laws place enough limits on us already. You should see some of the creatures Master Siorn has carved!

Mixes of animals and birds and serpents. No one wants them, of course — everyone wants 'practical' creatures — but they're really cool."

Mayka saw a woman with two girls dressed the same as Garit — more apprentices, she guessed. They were helping the woman, Master Pria, subdue a three-headed stone dog. Two heads were already drooping down, as if in submission, but the third was snapping ferociously. The stonemason rapped the snapping head on the nose, and it whined. She scratched behind its ear, and it licked her with its stone tongue, nearly knocking her over.

"Um, maybe we should walk on the other side of the street, just to be safe," Si-Si said, trotting away from the three-headed dog.

"Don't worry," Garit said. "Stonemasons haven't made dangerous creatures since the Stone War. Of course, there are sometimes accidents. Like the Disaster of the Oxen. That was embarrassing. Did you hear about it?"

Mayka shook her head, continuing to look all around her. Every building here belonged to a stonemason — each one bore a sign above the main door, etched with its owner's name — and each one had its own magnificent wonder. Jacklo could have been distracted by the sights here and gotten himself lost.

"Risa?" Mayka said in a low voice. "He could be inside any of these houses."

Her beak in Mayka's ear, Risa said, "They're all too well

guarded. I tried a few, but . . ." She shuddered, and her stone feathers clinked as they ruffled together.

Mayka hoped Garit's master would be able to ask his neighbors and friends if they'd seen a stray stone bird, though everyone seemed so busy she wondered if anyone would have noticed him. Poor Jacklo!

Garit had launched into his story already: ". . . the stonemason set about making as many stone oxen as he could. He took on dozens of apprentices and hired even more workers to haul the stone and make the rough cuts. The city of Skye had never seen anything like it. Instead of handcrafted beautiful art, he was churning out creature after identical creature. The stone wasn't polished, the faces weren't crafted—but the farmers coming to the festival wouldn't care, he thought. They didn't want art; they wanted their fields plowed.

"By the time of the Stone Festival, he and his workers had crafted three hundred oxen."

Mayka hadn't imagined there were that many stone creatures in the world. But then, she'd never imagined as many as were in this city either. "Wow."

"I know, right? But the problem was, he worked so quickly to be done in time that he was sloppy with the marks. He'd had some workers do it, and they weren't so skilled, and well . . . the festival came, and everyone rushed to the Festival Square to see all the masterpieces . . . And the oxen panicked. There was a stampede. People lost their lives. Houses were destroyed. As punishment for his carelessness, the stonemason was forced to recarve all three hundred sculptures by himself and then give them to the families he'd hurt. It supposedly took him the rest of his life."

"What happened to the oxen?" Mayka asked. When they'd recovered from their panic and realized what they'd done, they must have been heartbroken. "They must have been so upset after going through all of that."

"I guess so," Garit said, as if he'd never considered it. "I don't know. It happened a long time ago. Anyway, between catastrophes like that and the Stone War, every stonemason knows it's important to be careful. And that's why the city council insists we all live in the Stone Quarter, for their protection and ours." He said it as if she was supposed to know what the Stone War was, but Father had never mentioned any kind of war with stone. She wondered what other common stories she didn't know. "Master Siorn says we don't really have to worry so much about obeying the letter of the law — he says the people will never get rid of us. We make their lives easier, with supplying everything from farm workers who don't need to be fed to transportation that doesn't need to rest. But stonemasons still abide by the rules, to be safe."

"What kind of rules?" Mayka asked.

"You know, practical ones," Garit said. "Like no carving any marks that could hurt people. No making any fighting creatures or giant monsters or anything dangerous like that. We have to show all our work at the Festival, as I said, and we have to live in the Stone Quarter, where new kinds of creatures can be contained until they're approved at the festival."

"What kind of creatures have you carved?" Si-Si asked. "Anyone like me?"

"No one shaped like you," Garit said. "But I've worked on your kind of stone before. Firestone. It's amazing stuff. I can show you a snake I made, if you'd like."

"I'd be happy to see it," Si-Si said politely.

"Snakes are harder than you'd think," Garit said. "I had to sand it for days and days to get the curves right, and even then it ended up being a little bulgy around the middle, like it just ate a mouse."

"Better not let it near Master Suba's maze," Mayka said.

"I don't think . . . Oh! You were making a joke! You have a sense of humor. Ha! Amazing. I've never met a stone girl before, you know. It's just . . . not done often. People find it unsettling." He added quickly, "But I don't think you're unsettling at all. I think you're great!"

"Thanks," Mayka said, uncertain if she'd just been insulted or complimented. *Maybe both*, she thought. "So there aren't any other stone people here?" She was disappointed to hear that. She'd been hoping to meet another like her sometime. She'd imagined there would be lots in the city.

"Not that I know of," Garit said. "You can ask Master Siorn, if you'd like. He knows all the stone creatures —"

"Yes, you said that," Risa interrupted. "But we're really only interested in one: Jacklo. Are we there yet?"

"Just up ahead." Garit pointed.

The building was . . . not impressive. Or rather, it was impressively large, but it was also ugly. It was shaped like an eggplant, with a crown of stones for a stem, and its walls were made of a purple stone the likes of which Mayka had never seen. Hemmed in by a stone wall with a gate, the front yard was littered with boulders and chunks of rock with gouges in them, as well as piles of chipped stones and shards, and the backyard was dominated by an enormous domed structure stuck to the rear of the eggplant and towering over its "stem."

"There's nothing like it in all Skye," Garit said.

Mayka tried to think of what to say. "I'm . . . sure that's true."

Garit strode toward the gate, which was flanked by two stone lizards clutching a shield. The shield was emblazoned with the stonemason's sign. Slowing, Garit said to Mayka and her friends, "Master Siorn is as unique as his house, and he's, um, sometimes very focused on his projects."

"We'll catch his attention," Risa said. "This is important."

Mayka found herself getting nervous. This man could be their answer to everything: finding Jacklo, fixing her friends, helping Si-Si be who she wanted to be. Or he could reject them like almost everyone else in this city had.

Garit spoke to the lizards. "Hey, it's me. I've brought friends. Can you spread the word they're not to be trapped, crushed, or mauled?" He shot a look back at Mayka. "Master Siorn values his privacy. He wants to surprise everyone at the festival, so he's increased security to keep out spies and busybodies. He'll probably swear you to secrecy once you're inside. Not that you'll be able to guess from what's visible. Don't go in the back workroom. Front workroom is fine, but the back one, his private workroom, is off-limits to everyone. Also, don't comment on his hair."

Si-Si peeked around Mayka's legs. "What's wrong with his hair?"

"Exactly what you shouldn't say," Garit said.

"What's in the back workroom?" Mayka asked.

"Again, not a good idea to ask. Even I don't know."

The stone lizards swung open the gate and stood at attention on either side of it. Garit passed through, and Mayka and Si-Si hurried after him.

He held up a hand. "Step where I step."

Hopping, he jumped from stone to stone. They followed him. There didn't seem to be any specific reason for why they had to step on one stone versus another. Mayka couldn't see any marks on them.

On the third stone, Si-Si's back foot slipped, and her claws touched the next stone.

"Down!" Garit shouted.

Mayka ducked, and several rocks flew over her head and

smashed against a boulder. She heard chittering, like angry squirrels.

"Stop it!" Garit called. "These are friends!"

A stone face peeked over one of the boulders. It looked like an otter's face, with stone whiskers etched in its cheeks and bright sapphire eyes inset above them. "Aw, Garit, let us have a little fun! Come on, Garit!" A second stone otter joined the first. "Yeah, they stepped out of line! That means they're ours to play with!" A third popped up and barked, "Play, play, play!" A fourth and then a fifth appeared.

"Your idea of play leaves scars." Garit flipped up his hair to show a finger-long mark near his ear. "Go back to hide-and-seek!"

"Yes, yes, yes! I hide; you seek," one otter said.

"No, I hide; you seek," the second said.

"We all hide," the third said.

"Yes, all hide," the first otter agreed, and then all five dropped down behind the boulders out of sight.

"Just watch where you step," Garit said to Mayka and Si-Si, and continued across the last of the stones, until they stood on a broad patch of dirt. "Okay. Safe now."

Unlike the other houses in the Stone Quarter, Master Siorn's had a blank, smooth boulder in place of an ordinary door. No face. No knocker. No handle, or any way to open that Mayka could see.

Garit waited.

"Why are we —" Mayka began.

Risa squawked as two eagle-like talons wrapped over the top of the boulder. The boulder-door rolled to the side, and, outlined by candlelight, a stone creature filled the entrance. He had the head and talons of an eagle, and the body of a lion.

"Ooh," Mayka breathed. She'd never seen a creature like this.

Si-Si made a chirping sound that was almost a sigh. "A griffin!"

The griffin lowered his head to examine the little dragon. Si-Si held still as the griffin studied her. "Hmm, a dragon." Rising back to block the door, the griffin said, "Garit, I presume you have an explanation?"

"Master Siorn will want to meet them."

"That is an excuse, not an explanation."

"They need help," Garit said.

"Master Siorn does not engage in charity. Especially not before the festival. You had best be certain what you ask of him, before you bring this dragon and her keeper to see him."

"I'm not her keeper," Mayka said. "I'm her friend."

"Friend or not —" Actually looking at her directly for the first time, the griffin broke off what he was saying and reared backwards. "Extraordinary! Yes, indeed, bring them inside."

"Thanks, Kisonan." Garit scooted in and waved for Mayka and Si-Si to follow. Risa swooped in with them, flying right in front of the griffin.

Seeing Risa, the griffin exclaimed, "Oh my!"

"I know," Risa said. "You've never seen a flying stone bird before. Blah-blah-blah."

"Actually, I expressed astonishment because you are the second flying stone bird I've encountered this week," the griffin said. "The first is the master's guest."

"He is?" Mayka cried.

With a squawk, Risa darted forward through the house. "Jacklo! Jacklo, are you here? Where are you?"

Mayka ran after her. "Jacklo!"

Chapter
Thirteen

Mayka ran from room to room through the stone-mason's house, with Garit and the griffin shouting after her to stop, slow down, wait for them, but she couldn't wait anymore. Jacklo was here! She heard a noise up ahead — the clink of metal on stone — and ran toward it.

She burst into the workroom only seconds behind Risa.

The room was vast, with half-finished carvings everywhere, boulders piled in one corner, and slabs of stone resting against the wall. In the center of it was a man wearing a leather apron. His beard was white, with curls poking out at odd angles, and his hair was a cylindrical patch in the center of his head that grew straight up like a plant in a vase. He blinked owlishly at them. "Garit, you're back early. And not alone, I see?"

Garit skidded to a stop behind Mayka. "Yes, sir," he panted. "I brought them. They wanted to meet you, and I thought you'd want to meet them."

"Where's my brother?" Risa cried, as she circled the workroom.

Master Siorn squinted at her, and then he smiled broadly and clapped his hands together. "Ah-ha! Excellent! This must be Risa." He beamed at his apprentice. "Garit, my boy, stupendous work!"

Garit gulped. "Really? I mean, thank you, sir! I mean, you know her name?"

Mayka hurried forward, passing by a half-carved heron, a block of stone shaped into the rough form of a bear, and an ornate vase with figures sketched in chalk, ready to be sculpted. "We're been looking for our friend, a bird named Jacklo. Is he here?"

Master Siorn stared at her. "Garit, what's this?"

"I found her by the festival stage. Or, more accurately, she found me, sir. She's searching for a stonemason, as well as a second stone bird. You really have him here? You, uh, didn't tell me."

Grabbing a monocle, Master Siorn positioned it over one eye. He peered at Mayka, shoving his face up to hers. He lifted one of her arms then released it.

Cradling her arm, Mayka took a step backwards. "Jacklo?"

"Yes, yes. Kisonan, would you please fetch our newest addition?" As the griffin bowed and backed out of the workroom, Master Siorn continued to examine Mayka. "Stunningly exquisite. The level of craftsmanship. The choice of detail. The way the strands of hair are carved to mimic the appearance of wind tugging at her braids. Even down to the texture of the fabric of the 'clothes.' I haven't heard of this quality of work since . . . Could it truly be?"

Kisonan returned to the workroom with a cage dangling from his beak. The cage was covered in a thick cloth. Plummeting from the rafters, Risa darted for it. "Jacklo!" She caught the fabric in her beak and yanked it away from the cage.

Inside was a stone bird.

He was lying limply on his side, his head tucked under his wing. But before Mayka could speak, he raised his head and blinked. "Hullo? Morning already? Risa?" He hopped up onto his feet and then onto the bar that stretched across the center of his cage. "Risa!"

Mayka ran across the workroom. "Why is he locked up? Let him go!"

The griffin twisted, putting his body between Mayka and the cage.

Risa dove at him, pecking at his face. "Let him free!" she screeched.

"It's okay!" Jacklo cried. "I'm okay!"

"You misunderstand," Master Siorn said, his hands out as if he could calm them all.

Kisonan set the cage on a workbench and then snapped his beak at Risa. "Quit your feeble attacks. Your brother is quite well."

Mayka tugged at the cage door. "Why is he caged?" She

found the latch and opened it, but Jacklo didn't fly out. "Jacklo, what did they do to you?"

He held up one wing. "He fixed me."

Mayka saw a crack through it, sealed with a white streak.

"Please, please, don't overreact," Master Siorn said soothingly. "This is a peaceful place! A place of creation and healing, not of anger and fear. You have nothing to be afraid of." He crossed to them and patted the top of the cage. "We found him. He'd been injured trying to enter one of my fellow stonemasons' houses. Fell afoul of their security systems. Luckily, my otters recognized him for an injured victim rather than an intruder and brought him to me. I've done my best to repair the damage, but he must not attempt to fly for at least another day. He's caged in case he forgets—he's already forgotten once, which was why we took this measure. It's for his own safety, you see."

"Master Siorn saved me!" Jacklo said.

Risa flew into the cage and hopped in a circle all around him, studying him. "Jacklo, your marks! They're deeper!"

"He recarved my marks too," Jacklo said proudly. "I'm not fading anymore, Risa, Mayka. He fixed me!"

Mayka wanted to cheer or dance or explode from joy. Jacklo was not only okay—he was better than okay! And this stonemason had fixed him! This stonemason could fix all of them! "Master Siorn, thank you so very much!"

Si-Si hopped forward. "You *are* a great stonemason! You can help us!"

He smiled at the dragon and reached down to pat her on the head. "Ah, a Master Lison creation. Very nice." Turning to his apprentice, he said, "Garit, you may observe as I examine the second bird and the stone girl. Take notes for yourself too. But I think the findings will confirm what I suspected: these, all of them, with the exception of the decorative dragon, are the work of Master Kyn."

Mayka jumped when she heard the name Kyn. He knew Father?

"Wow!" Garit said. "But I thought all of his work had been destroyed."

"So say the stories." Master Siorn circled Mayka again. "Clearly, they were exaggerated, for here is proof." He waved grandly at her and the birds.

"What stories?" Mayka asked. "You knew my father?"

"*Of* him, child. I knew *of* him. All stonemasons do. But I was born well after his time. My grandfather used to talk of those days."

She'd lost track of how many years had slipped by on the mountain.

"He's quite famous, one of the greatest masters ever known. Perhaps *the* greatest. And to think, three never-before-seen masterpieces are here in my workroom!" He clapped a heavy hand on Garit's shoulder. "Well done, my boy, bringing them here. Shows good judgment."

Garit's cheeks turned pink. "Oh! Thank you!"

Master Siorn rubbed his hands together. "Make some room. I want to study them." The griffin waddled forward and began to shove workbenches to the side. Garit scurried to pull candlesticks as tall as he was into a circle. He lit them, creating an amber flicker on the walls.

"What do you know of Father? You said his work had been destroyed. Who would do that?" The idea that there were others like her . . . She'd never imagined he made anyone but her friends on the mountain, but of course he must have. She'd known he was a stonemason in the valley before he climbed the mountain to be alone, but she hadn't thought of what that would mean. *I could have brothers and sisters!* There could be others like Risa and Jacklo, like Turtle, like Nianna. *Like me!*

"Garit, answer her questions, please," Master Siorn said. "I need to focus." He pulled out a notepad and began sketching. Examining Mayka, he drew her form in rough lines with a charcoal pencil that shed black dust all over the paper and his hand.

Garit looked suddenly nervous, shifting uneasily and fiddling with the collar of his shirt. "Uh, I've heard a couple stories. Master Kyn was the most famous stonemason in the valley. It was said that he carved the moon one night when it forgot to shine."

Master Siorn snorted. "Nonsense."

"It was also said he carved birds that could fly and fish that could swim."

"Clearly not nonsense," Master Siorn admitted, "though I would have said it was. No one has ever carved such masterpieces before or since."

"No one?" Si-Si chirped. "But surely a stonemason of your skill —"

"Everyone assumed the secret of how to carve birds that could fly died with him," Master Siorn said, talking over the dragon. "Others have been trying to invent flying marks for decades without success. As to human-looking sculptures . . . Such finesse! Never seen its equal."

"No one else can make creatures fly?" Si-Si spread her wings and looked at them sadly. "But I hoped . . . I want to fly. I'm *made* to fly. Just not . . . precisely made to fly. Yet."

"Our friend Siannasi Yondolada Quilasa is looking for a stonemason who can make her wings functional," Mayka said, speaking up for her. Si-Si gave her a grateful look. "And we are looking for a stonemason who will come home with us, to the mountains, to recarve the marks on myself and our friends. We are beginning to fade. Our friend Turtle has already stopped."

Master Siorn's head shot up, his hand freezing mid-drawing. "There are more of you?"

"Yes." Mayka pointed toward her mountain, even though it couldn't be seen through the walls. She knew which direction home was, as surely as the sun knew which direction to rise. "High above, at the treeline. We promised to bring a stonemason back with us. You would not have to stay long. Just long enough to recarve us, like you did Jacklo."

Master Siorn stared in the direction that Mayka had pointed, drawing forgotten, pencil fallen onto his lap. "Incredible. How many more of you did he carve?"

"Jacklo and Risa are our birds. Dersy and Harlisona are rabbits. There's also Turtle, Badger, the cat Kalgrey, the owl Nianna, Etho the lizard, and the fish. All of us need the kind of help you've given Jacklo, if we're to continue to survive. Will you help us?"

Garit cleared his throat. "The stories say that Master Kyn swore he'd never carve again, broke all his masterpieces, and fled to the mountains, to live out the rest of his days as a recluse. It was believed he'd died . . ."

"He did," Jacklo said. "We were all very sad."

"It was some time ago," Risa said, folding her wings and lowering her head. "All of us helped bury him, under rock, the way he wanted."

Mayka remembered it as clearly as any story: the way the dirt had felt in her hands, the sound of the wind as if it were moaning, the feel of the sun as it rose her first morning without him. It had taken years before she faced the sunrise without expecting him to wake.

"I don't understand," Mayka said. "Why would he swear never to carve again? Father loved to carve. He made our cottage. Shaped the pond and the streams. He made *me!*"

"He'd suffered a tragedy," Master Siorn said.

Garit nodded and said, "He fought in the Stone Wars. In fact, he —"

The stonemason cut him off. "We don't talk about that time." He spat on the floor twice and snapped his fingers to ward off bad luck. "Especially not before the festival."

"But he —"

Master Siorn held up a hand, stopping Garit midsentence again. "Great artists have sensitive hearts." He thumped his chest with a fist. "His family — his wife and his twelve-year-old daughter — both died. Crushed to death by stone, during the time we won't speak of. And the loss broke his heart."

Mayka thought of the mural and the picture of the two graves, side by side, and Father with blue stone tears on his cheeks.

"They died instantly," Garit said, "and even though Master Kyn sent every stone creature he could to help clear the rubble as quickly as possible, it was too late. All told, about two hundred deaths that day, I think. Maybe more."

"Or just as likely less," Master Siorn said with a wave. "The story has grown in the retelling. But the event broke his spirit. He destroyed his workshop that night and was last seen walking toward the mountains. Many searched for him, but none found him. Ah, to see where he spent his final days! To see his final masterpieces!"

"Then you'll come with us?" Mayka asked. "You'll help us?"

"Of course! I would be honored," Master Siorn said. "As soon as the festival is over, I will join you in your mountain home."

Jacklo and Risa cheered. Mayka smiled so hard that her stone cheeks felt as if they'd harden in that position. "Thank you, Master Siorn. On behalf of all of us, thank you!"

In a tiny voice, Si-Si whispered, "But will he help me?"

Chapter
Fourteen

Mayka tried to be patient as Master Siorn studied her and the birds. He sketched them. He measured them. He instructed her to raise her arms, then touch her toes, then turn her head, then sit and stand and walk and even demonstrate how well she could use her fingers to tie a knot in a ribbon. All the while, he murmured praise about her father, which was nice to hear but *not* why she'd come.

Every time she tried to ask a question — about Father, about Skye, about the Stone War — he shushed her absent-mindedly, his attention clearly on his notes, not on her words.

She gritted her teeth and managed not to complain, though, because he'd promised to save her and her friends, and he had fixed Jacklo. Risa spent the entire time next to Jacklo's cage, scolding him about being reckless and irresponsible and worrying her so badly that she wanted to molt, which was impossible because she was stone. All the while, Jacklo hung his head and promised to be more careful.

At last Master Siorn put down his pencil, and Mayka thought, *Yes! Now we'll talk about recarving us.* But instead he said, "Garit, continue with your notes. Measure the birds carefully and record copies of their marks. As fascinating as this discovery is, I must work on my masterpiece."

"Yes, sir," Garit said.

Before Mayka could ask any questions, he bustled toward a heavy door covered in iron decorations at the back of the workroom. He swung the door open, and Mayka caught a glimpse of a massive mound of rocks inside a cavernous room — before she could see anything else, he'd shut the door behind him.

Si-Si waddled over to the door, sat, and stared at it forlornly. During all this time, Master Siorn had barely noticed her. And now they'd all been deserted, in favor of his "masterpiece." Morosely, Si-Si curled into a ball next to the door and rested her head on her front paws.

Mayka realized the stonemason had never answered the little dragon's question. Si-Si didn't know if he would try to fix her, now that he knew it could be done. *I should have asked again for her,* Mayka thought. But Master Siorn hadn't been paying attention to anything but studying them.

"He forgot about me," Si-Si said.

Garit shot an apologetic look at her. "I'm sure he'll help

you when he gets a chance. With Master Kyn's birds to study, it should be possible to replicate his marks for flight."

Springing up, Si-Si danced in place. "Oh, oh! You think so? Me, flying! Could it really happen?"

"Just not until after the festival," he cautioned. "That's his priority right now. Master Siorn cares deeply about his work. He believes he's the one who will restore the reputation of stonemasons to what it was before the Stone War. Stonemasons used to be revered."

"What was this Stone War?" Mayka asked.

He glanced at the door to the workroom. "Bad luck to talk about it before a festival. And I'm supposed to finish his notes. So . . ." He scurried across the workroom to the stack of notes, straightened them into a neat pile, and then shuffled their order and straightened them again.

"Are we supposed to just wait?" Risa asked. "Our friends are expecting us!"

"Master Siorn said I need to wait another day to heal," Jacklo said. "But truly, I feel stronger already. I could —"

"Stay still," Risa instructed him.

Garit spread his hands, palms up. "I'm sorry. The festival's important. Especially for Master Siorn this year. He's debuting a new mark. I'm sure he'll help you after it's over."

Sighing, Risa folded her wings around herself. "Then we wait."

"Make yourselves at home," Garit said. "You can look around, if you like. Meet the other stone creatures. If you're hungry, you can visit the kitchen . . ." He smacked his head with the heel of his palm. "No, obviously, you can't be hungry. Sorry."

"There are more stone creatures here?" Mayka asked. She'd seen the otters outside and the magnificent griffin, but she hadn't paid attention to anything as she'd raced through the house. She'd been too focused on Jacklo.

"Lots," Garit said.

I want to meet them! All of them! She'd seen plenty of other stone creatures in the city, of course, but here was a chance to talk to them and hear their stories. She glanced at the workroom door, then at the birds and Si-Si, then at the door again. Given that Jacklo was fine and the stonemason was busy . . . "I'll be back soon," she promised the birds.

"We'll be here," Risa said. "Waiting."

Leaving Garit with the others, she went to explore the rest of the stonemason's house. She'd passed through so quickly before that she'd barely looked. Now she wandered slowly. It was strange and beautiful, with mosaics on the floors, walls, and ceilings. Made of shards of stone, they showed flowers, vines, woodland animals, sea creatures, and dozens of kinds of birds. Every doorway was trimmed with stone swirls and flourishes.

As she peeked into dining rooms and sitting rooms, she heard a *thunk, thunk, thunk* sound. She followed the sound until she reached a stairway made of rolling boulders. Each boulder *thunked* as it fell onto the next one. It was like the street outside but more complex.

As they tumbled, she read their marks: "I roll. I carry. I . . ." The third mark was one she didn't recognize — it was another verb but with flourishes all around it. "Curious he didn't name you." The marks were all verbs, which wasn't the same as an identity. She looked up the stairwell. *Am I supposed to ride on them?*

She supposed she was.

"Do you mind if I walk on you?"

The moving steps didn't answer. She hadn't really expected them to — their story was so simple that all they knew was a life of constant motion.

Stepping onto the first boulder, she held out her arms for balance as it rolled beneath her, carrying her up the stairwell. She stepped off at the top and looked back down at it, as it continued to roll along, not speaking, not reacting, just rolling. *What an odd thing to carve*, she thought. It wasn't necessary or even very useful. She hadn't risen to any great height, and she could have easily walked up ordinary stairs.

She wondered what other oddities the stonemason's home held.

Upstairs, the walls were of polished blue stone with flecks of mica. They glittered like the night sky, and she found herself looking for constellations as she walked along.

The walls murmured as she passed, as if talking about her, but she couldn't hear any clear words. It was more like the babbling of a brook. She found their marks: "'Walls that watch.' That's it? Where's the rest of your story?"

Searching the corridor, she found more marks: "Protect against the rain and cold. And . . . huh, there it is again." The mark on the boulders she hadn't recognized. She wished she could draw and dissect it. It seemed to be a mix of other marks. Staring at it, she thought it reminded her of the mark for "lead" but it was backwards.

Up ahead, she heard a noise like a brushing sound and went toward it. Rounding the corner, she faced a stone creature that looked . . . well, she'd never seen anything like him. Sculpted from sandstone, his body was bulbous, with eyes set into either side, and he had eight smooth . . . tails? Each tail held a brush or a broom, and the creature was maneuvering through the hallway, dusting and sweeping everything he could reach.

"Hello? I'm sorry to bother you, but . . ."

The creature halted. "You aren't tracking dirt into the house, are you?" He stuck to the ceiling as he climbed over her to examine the floor behind her; then he swept.

"Sorry," she said again. "But . . ." She didn't know what to ask without being rude. "Were you made by Master Siorn?"

"Yes, I most certainly was. Lift your left foot."

Mayka obeyed, and the creature rubbed the bottom of her foot with a rag. "Um, would you mind if I read your story?"

"Right foot."

Mayka lifted her right foot. She held her arms out to balance. "It's only that I've never seen anything like you."

"Octopus," the creature said. "See the eight tentacles? Master Siorn saw an illustration on a map drawn by a sea captain, and he decided to replicate me. I was shown at the last Stone Festival, but there wasn't any demand for me, so Master Siorn kindly decided to keep me. He gave me a purpose here in his home." He lifted two tentacles (*Not tails*, Mayka thought) to expose his stomach, which was etched with a spiraling circle of marks.

She spotted the mark for "octopus" quickly. Even though she hadn't seen it before, it was a clear representation of the creature. The story went on to talk about how the octopus loved cleanliness and order and . . . *And there's that same mark again. Curious.*

Why would the stairs, the walls, and the octopus all have the same mark?

"Excuse me, but I must continue my work." The octopus lowered his tentacles and continued down the hallway, not touching the floor but instead suspending himself between the walls and cleaning beneath him. Mayka watched him go.

The mark was a mix of two other marks, she was sure, judging by the way the indents curved, but which marks? And could that really be an actual creature? She'd never heard of an octopus.

Still mulling over the marks, she peeked into rooms:

bedrooms and bathrooms, and then she went down again—using a second rolling boulder staircase—and found the kitchen.

The kitchen was curved like a cave but an open one with stone tables down the center and hearths on either side. A fire danced in the fireplace, with pots and pans and kettles hanging over it from an iron rod.

It was a marvel.

Not so much because of the room itself, but because of the creatures in it.

Six stone creatures bustled between the tables. One would chop a vegetable and toss the slices into the air, another would fling a pot across the room, and a third would catch the pot, then catch the vegetables. The other three were playing by the fire, tossing a glowing ember back and forth as if it were a ball. Once in a while, they'd pause to scrub a pot or fold a piece of laundry.

All of them looked like mishmashes of other creatures: one was half hedgehog and half lizard, one had a deer head with antlers but a body like a turtle. Another had human hands but a snake's body covered in stone scales. Another looked like a cross between a duck and a rabbit. These were the creatures that Garit had mentioned—the ones that Master Siorn had carved but no one wanted. *They're incredible*, she thought.

Careful not to interrupt what looked like a choreographed dance, Mayka picked her way between them, studying them and looking for their marks.

Oddly, on all of them, she saw the same mark she'd seen

on the stairs, wall, and octopus. It was improbable for so many vastly different creatures to all bear the same bit of story.

Seating herself on an unused stool, she began to draw the mark in flour that had been spilled on a table. Sketching the various lines, she separated them into essentials.

Two different marks — combined into one — that much was clear.

One was the verb "lead" inverted.

The other . . . It didn't resemble any word she ever knew — it was structured like a noun but not a familiar one. The fact that the two marks were intertwined had to be important. Rubbing her hand across the flour, she wiped out her experiments.

"Stone girl," a voice grated.

She looked up to see the griffin, Kisonan, filling the arched doorway into the kitchen. All movement and sound ceased as everyone turned to look at Mayka.

"This household functions best when everyone focuses on their duties, without distraction," Kisonan informed her, then barked to the others, "Go about your tasks! The master requires his dinner in his private workroom. Leave it outside the door."

Crossing the room, Mayka smiled and nodded at the strange creatures, who all ducked their heads and resumed chopping and mixing and stirring. A few smiled back at her. "Sorry for bothering you," she said.

One — the half headgehog, half lizard — waved its paw. "No worries. Not a bother." The creatures all returned to their slicing and stirring and cooking, chattering to one another in a low murmur.

Reaching Kisonan, she asked, "Do you have the same mark?"

"Excuse me?" He ruffled his neck feathers as if she'd just asked something rude.

Mayka was growing tired of trying to guess what passed for manners here in the valley. It wasn't an unreasonable question. She was curious. All of them wore the same story, yet they were all so different. It didn't make sense.

"The one that looks like a verb and a noun tied together. May I read your marks?" Mayka stepped toward him, eager to see what was written on the griffin.

"My story is mine alone," Kisonan said. "Now, if you would allow me to escort you back to the workroom. The master would not want you poking your nose into matters that don't concern you and upsetting the balance of his household. You are here as his guest, and if the master wants —"

An idea occurred to her, and what had seemed to be merely an interesting mystery now suddenly seemed alarming. *No, it couldn't be.* She interrupted him. "How does your master write his name?"

The griffin broke off his scolding. "Pardon?"

Mayka hurried past him — she didn't need him to answer. She knew where Siorn's name would be. All the stonemasons had had signs in front of their houses. She hadn't paid attention to

Siorn's, but if she was right . . . *Please, don't be right.* She reached the boulder that served as the door.

Kisonan squeezed between her and the door. "I do not believe the master wants you to leave. He wants to study you and help you. If you'll wait here while I inquire —"

"I'm not leaving." *Not yet,* she thought. *And not without my friends. But if I'm right . . .* "I only wish to see his sign. Could you please step aside?"

He hesitated a moment, then scooted sideways. "It is heavy. You seem agitated. Perhaps if you told me your concerns, I could assist —"

"It could be nothing," she said. "Overactive imagination."

Bracing herself, Mayka pushed the boulder. It rolled sideways, opening a gap. Outside the stone otters popped up around the yard. "Play, play, play?"

"Not now," Mayka said.

She stepped out, careful where she put her feet, trying to remember the exact pattern that Garit had walked. An otter popped up from behind a boulder. Watching her, it chittered to its friends. She stopped walking and called, "Lizard? Hello? Could you please turn around?" She hoped she was wrong. Garit seemed so friendly, and Master Siorn seemed so nice. Absent-minded and focused on his work, perhaps, but no more than Father had been. When Father had been in the middle of a carving, it would have taken an earthquake shaking the mountain to catch his attention.

One of the lizards at the gate swiveled its head to look at her.

"The shield you hold. May I see it?"

He turned, facing the stone shield toward her.

Oh no.

She was right.

This was it, the noun she hadn't recognized, beside the mark for a stonemason. It was Master Siorn's name. The mark she hadn't recognized was his name, combined with the inverted sign for "lead," which could be read as "obey."

Obey Master Siorn.

He'd made that a part of all of the creatures' stories. *Obey me*, he'd written on their bodies. She was certain she was reading it correctly, and equally certain they had to leave. Right now.

Chapter
Fifteen

Mayka did not run.

She was proud that she didn't. She walked, calmly, under the eye of the curious griffin, back through the halls, past the kitchen, and by the octopus, who clucked at her and cleaned the floor where she stepped, to the door of the workroom.

Hurrying past her, the griffin blocked the doorway. "You cannot disturb Master Siorn. He's in his private workroom, which means he wants no interruptions."

"I won't bother him," Mayka promised. "I just need to speak with Si-Si and my bird friends." She pushed past his wing —Kisonan was larger, but she was made of stone too, and he wasn't trying to keep her out of the main room.

Inside, Risa was perched on top of Jacklo's cage, talking to him, while Si-Si was still huddled by the door to the back room. Garit was next to her, and they were deep in conversation. Seeing him, she hesitated. Once she announced her intention to leave, the apprentice might try to stop them. *Don't be so untrusting*, she told herself. *It's not as if he captured me. Coming here was my idea.* Garit had only been kind.

She hurried over to Risa and Jacklo.

Reaching into Jacklo's cage, she scooped the bird into her arms.

Jacklo squawked. "I'm supposed to rest!"

"You're supposed to stay still," Mayka told him. "I'll carry you, and you can stay still. Come on, Risa, on my shoulder."

"What's going on?" Risa asked.

"We're finding a new stonemason," Mayka asked, keeping her voice level, calm, and low, as if every instinct weren't screaming at her to *run*. "I don't like this one's style."

"But he helped me!" Jacklo said. "He saved me!"

"Hush," Mayka told him.

"He's a genius and a hero," Jacklo continued.

"She said hush," Risa said, and snapped her beak at him. He subsided and curled himself against Mayka's chest. Cradling Jacklo, she crossed the workroom.

The boy looked up from the dragon. "You're back. Did you meet the others? What did you think of the octopus? And the stairs? Did you ride the rolling stairs? The first day I was here, I must have ridden them up and down twenty times."

Mayka made herself smile and say in a casual, friendly voice, "Hello, Garit, thank you so much for your hospitality, and please thank your master for us for helping Jacklo. We very much appreciate it, but it's time for us to leave now. Si-Si, you should come with us too."

"What? Why?" Si-Si got to her feet. "I can't leave! Garit has offered to fix me!"

"*Try* to fix you," he corrected. Standing, he twisted his hands in his apron nervously. "I'm going to study the dragon, in conjunction with the bird, to see if I can figure out how to adapt the bird's marks and structure so that the dragon can fly —I know it's never been done before, but no one has ever had Master Kyn's original work to study. I've already started to make notes."

"I believe in you!" Si-Si cheered.

He smiled at her, a wavering, hopeful kind of smile.

"Apprentice Garit, I'm sure you're a wonderful person who means well, and I'm sure you're a very talented stonemason, but we need to leave. There's a mark on every stone creature in this house that I believe is . . . Well, we can't stay."

Garit's smile faded. "What mark?" From his expression, she had the sense he knew exactly what she meant. His shoulders had tensed, riding up beside his neck, and his breath had quickened. But Si-Si had a mulish look on her face. It was clear she wasn't going to leave until Mayka explained, and Jacklo wouldn't be happy either.

Mayka turned to the griffin. "You have it too, don't you? Show them."

The griffin drew himself taller. "You do not understand —"

"I think I do," Mayka said.

He studied her for a moment and then slowly he lifted one wing to display a mark on the side of his chest, tucked up under where the wing bone met the shoulder. It was the same mark she'd seen on the others.

"Obedience," Mayka said, pointing to it. "That's what it means. It means his story is owned by Master Siorn."

Risa gasped, and Si-Si let out a whimper. "You're wrong," the dragon pleaded. "You have to be reading it wrong."

Mayka tried to keep her voice calm. It was horrible, the worst mark she'd ever seen, a corruption of what stories were supposed to be. Stories were supposed to set you free to be whoever you could be, but this . . . it constrained instead of freed. "We need to leave, because anyone who would carve a mark like that is *not* someone I want carving into my friends."

Kisonan lowered his wing.

Garit was staring at her, shock clearly on his face. "You can read it?"

"Can't you?" Mayka countered. He was a stonemason-in-training. He should be able to. Given that it was on every creature in the house, he couldn't have missed it. The question was, why was he okay with it? "It took me a while to decipher, because I've never seen a mark used like that. It's not right."

"Master Siorn said . . ." Garit looked uncomfortable, as if ants were crawling on him and he wanted to shake them off. "He said it makes them part of his household. It makes them safer, because they're his."

Si-Si perked up. "Does that mean she read it wrong? This is my best chance at my dreams, and I don't want to run away because Mayka misread a story."

"I didn't misread it," Mayka said. "That's what the mark says."

"You said yourself that the marks are just guides," Si-Si said. "I'm sure there's a reasonable explanation that isn't . . . this. The obedience mark doesn't exist. It's a legend! The stories say that in the Stone War, a stonemason used an obedience mark to compel stone creatures to fight. But no one believes it."

Mayka shook her head. Even if she was reading it wrong . . . *I'm not*, she thought. Regardless, there were plenty of other stonemasons in the Stone Quarter. They could simply pick another one. Maybe the one with the mice and the maze. Or the one with all the doors.

"He's making their lives his. Their stories his. Don't you see? With ordinary marks, *we* choose how we act and react, based on our stories. But with this 'obedience mark,' Master Siorn chooses." She fixed her gaze on Kisonan. "He controls your story."

"He does," Kisonan said quietly.

"He could control us all, if we let him carve us," Mayka said to Si-Si and the birds. "We need to leave. Garit, you understand, don't you? You can't tell me you think the mark is right."

"I . . . I . . ." He looked like a rabbit caught by the gaze of a hawk. "It was the best choice for his sculptures. He doesn't mean harm. He wants what's best, for everyone."

"Best?" Si-Si squeaked. "*Best?* An obedience mark? We used to tell stories about such a mark at my estate late at night, to scare the new stone creatures." She scurried to Mayka and hid behind her legs. "I was about to trust you to recarve me! I *wanted* to trust you!"

"I know, but . . ." Garit ran his fingers through his hair. He glanced at the door to the private workroom. "There's something you should see, and then maybe you'll understand." He spoke quietly and led the way across the workroom to a nondescript door tucked between two boulders. The door itself was wooden and shut with a single latch.

He lifted a lantern from a hook on the wall, and then opened the door and held a lantern inside so that amber light fell over the jumble of shadows. "This is the Scrap Room, where Master Siorn stores failed carvings."

Risa flew in and then darted back out to cower behind Mayka. Si-Si peeked in and then slunk out. Gathering her courage, Mayka took the lantern from Garit and stepped inside.

What she saw was a graveyard of broken sculptures.

"If a sculpture doesn't turn out the way he wanted, if it doesn't behave the way it's supposed to, it's destroyed, and the fragments are kept here," Garit said. "We then reuse the stone for other works."

Mayka knelt next to one. It was half a face of a fox. Another was a chunk of an arm. All of this would have been fine, except for the next piece she found: it had marks on it, scratched out but still partially visible.

This stone creature had once been alive.

"How does he decide if a creature deserves to be destroyed?" Mayka asked. She was surprised that she was able to keep her voice steady.

"A lot of the scraps here are just from practice work. Inert stone. But this . . ." He picked up a stone chunk that was curved with feathers carved into it. "She was a whimsical creature, made for a commission. A family wanted a stone creature to keep their daughter company. Watch her during the day. Make her laugh. Tend to her needs, when necessary. But she didn't turn out right, and the family rejected her. She lived here for a time. She . . . made me laugh. She would make the oddest observations and prattle on and on. I liked her. But he said she was broken."

Mayka didn't know what to say.

"I cried when he discarded her, and he told me it was foolish. But now that Master Siorn has invented his new mark . . . No one will ever need to be discarded. If he'd created it sooner, she would have been saved. How could I tell Master Siorn not to use the mark, when *this* is the alternative?"

She stared at the scraps. He wasn't even making sense. There had to be a hundred other marks that Master Siorn could have used to help his friend. "Broken" wasn't the same as "disobedient." "An obedience mark wouldn't have saved your friend. All it could have done is enabled Master Siorn to destroy your friend's true self."

"What . . . what do you mean?"

"He would have ordered her to change, right? And she would have had to obey. And the friend you knew would have been just as destroyed as she is now."

He looked as shocked as if she'd slapped him. "But . . . but Ava would have been alive!"

"Ava wouldn't have been Ava anymore." *That* was the true horror of the obedience mark. If Master Siorn chose to, he could destroy a creature's entire personality. His mark could override other marks, effectively giving him the power to rewrite all stories and making him the narrator and sole interpreter. *Obey me*, the mark said. *Not yourself.* "We should never have left the mountain. Risa, Si-Si, come on. We're going." Carrying Jacklo, she hurried out of the workroom and to the front door, which was still open. She stepped outside.

The otters popped up. "Playtime?"

She tried to remember what stones she'd stepped on earlier . . . Holding Jacklo tightly in her arms, she started forward. She was aware that Kisonan and Garit had followed her and were watching from the doorway. They hadn't fetched Master Siorn, which was good—that meant, she thought, that they weren't going to try to stop them.

Jacklo squawked. "No, I don't want to leave!"

She held him tighter. "We can't stay. Shhh, Jacklo."

Flapping over them, Risa chirped at him. "Don't be an idiot. You heard what Mayka said about that horrible mark. You saw the Scrap Room! Settle down. You'll hurt yourself."

"You're wrong about him! He'll help us!" He writhed in Mayka's arms, trying to escape. She loosened her grip, afraid he was going to injure himself. Splaying his wings, he burst out of her arms and darted back into the house. Once across the threshold, he crashed onto the floor, his wing drooping down.

Garit knelt to examine him as Mayka rushed back.

She dropped down on his other side, looking at the wing. His struggle to get airborne had torn it again, cracking the white cement. "Jacklo, why did you —" She stopped.

She saw it.

The new mark, the obedience mark.

He'd carved it into Jacklo.

"Oh no," Mayka said.

"What is it?" Risa asked, hovering over them. "Did he hurt himself again? Jacklo, you should have let Mayka carry you. You knew you weren't ready to fly. What were you thinking?"

"I can't leave Master Siorn," Jacklo said. "It wouldn't be right. He wants to help us! He's good and noble and wise! You've just misunderstood. If you talk to him, he'll explain. Please, if we leave now, we'll lose our best chance to save our friends."

"He did this to you." Mayka glared at Garit. "Did you know?"

"I didn't!" Garit backed up. "Well, I mean, I'm not surprised. He's added it to all the creatures in his household —"

"Jacklo isn't in his household! He's with us! He belongs on the mountain!" *Where I belong! I never should have left! I should have listened to Nianna and come alone. This is my fault.* "Jacklo, I'm sorry. We'll fix this. I promise."

"Master Siorn believed he was a stray," Garit said weakly. "Making him part of our household was an honor. It grants him protection."

"Well, now that he knows Jacklo's not a stray, he'll just have to remove the mark." Standing, Mayka scooped Jacklo into her arms again. He shouldn't have tried to launch himself into the air. The strain of takeoff had been too much. "Take us to him?"

Garit looked at Kisonan.

The griffin's expression did not change. "Very well. I have not been ordered not to."

On the short walk back to the workroom, Mayka had barely enough time to think of what to say. She was so angry that she felt as if she was vibrating. This stranger had carved his mark onto her friend! How dare he?

She stroked Jacklo as she cradled him. "It will be okay. We'll make him fix you."

Jacklo shivered. "I want to go with you, but I want to stay too. Can't we all just stay here? You're wrong about him. He saved me and healed me, and I want . . . I want—"

"Shhh, it's all right."

Kisonan led them to the workroom. "You must wait. I will see if he is willing to speak with you." The griffin crossed to the massive door to the private back room. He spoke in a low voice to the door, and then he stepped inside, closing the door behind him.

They were left to wait.

"Master Siorn will explain," Garit said. "The new mark is his invention, for the festival. No one has ever created a mark like this before, at least not outside of legends."

"He never should have done it."

Garit looked uncomfortable again. "He didn't think the bird belonged to anyone—"

"The bird *doesn't* belong to anyone," Mayka snapped. "Except himself!"

Emerging from his private workroom, Master Siorn removed his gloves and protective glasses and smiled at all of them. "Here now, what's this fuss about? You should be letting your bird friend rest and heal. It's too soon for him to be up and about, after a breakage that severe."

Si-Si waddled up to Master Siorn. "Please tell us you didn't create an obedience mark!"

He frowned at Garit. "You know the importance of secrecy —"

"The girl can read!" Garit yelped. "She read it herself. Master . . . Tell them it will help. It's supposed to keep stone creatures from hurting people. And that will keep stone creatures safe from us."

Kisonan spoke. "It is a promise between flesh and stone, binding us together." His voice was flat, and Mayka thought, *He doesn't believe it.* She peered at him, wondering what he really thought of the mark, but his eagle face was unreadable.

"Precisely!" Master Siorn said happily.

"*You* aren't wearing a mark," Risa said to him.

Master Siorn chuckled. "Of course not. I can't. Believe me, if there were a mark I could wear that would ensure the safety of all people, I'd carve it into my skin myself. But since there isn't one —"

"Master Siorn, I'd like to ask you to please remove your mark from my friend Jacklo," Mayka said as politely as she could. "I would like to also ask you to remove it from your other creatures as well. It's not right."

"It's beyond right," Master Siorn said, looking startled, as if she'd suggested something ridiculous. "It is necessary! It's the solution that people and stone creatures have been looking for since the first stone creature walked among us: a way to have peace."

"There's already peace."

He shook his head. "Sadly, that is not always true. For now, yes, we are in a time of peace. You have been in isolation, up on your mountain. Perhaps I *should* tell you the tale of the Stone War."

Garit gasped. "Master —"

"This is important," Master Siorn said. "She doesn't understand. My mark will transform the world for the better. It will inoculate us against destruction and chaos."

Mayka didn't think there was any story that would change her mind. But she wanted to know what he meant. "Tell me."

"Many years ago, the stonemasons were in a race, each to carve the most magnificent, monstrous creature they ever could. They made fabulous giants that stomped over forests, great dragons that seared the sky with their fire —"

Si-Si perked up at the mention of dragons.

"— and sea serpents that filled the sea. Giant worms that dug through the earth. Mighty stone trees that shaded half the valley."

Mayka tried to imagine a world like this, filled with stone giants. She thought of the fallen giants that Jacklo had seen and the images in the mural. Was this a true story?

"But the stonemasons had given no thought beyond the majesty of their creations. They failed to respect the power of the creatures they were making. And so when the creatures turned on them, they were unprepared."

Jacklo gasped. "Stone creatures wouldn't do that!"

"They could, and they did. They crushed villages, destroyed fields, and wrecked harvests. Winter came, and people starved. They fled to caves in the mountains and lived in fear as the stone creatures hunted them down."

She thought of the tale of the sky brothers. Father had told her that story, but not this one. *Maybe because it doesn't make sense. Why would stone creatures attack?* In the song the musicians had played in the square, they sang of stone creatures who *refused* to fight — she'd rather believe that story.

Mayka opened her mouth to ask about this and what it had to do with Jacklo, but Master Siorn wasn't done. "But one brave stonemason ventured out of the caves, carved his own giant creatures, and used them to defeat the monsters. Legend says he used an obedience mark. Legend also says his name was Master Kyn."

"Father?" Mayka cried.

"He saved the valley. But after he achieved peace, he turned his back on our craft. He destroyed the very creatures who had helped him, and he erased the obedience mark so thoroughly that it was lost to history. And then he fled for the mountains, abandoning stone and flesh alike." He sighed heavily. "Worse, the people of the valley turned against us as well. There were some who advocated outlawing stonemasons, or worse. But even with all their fear, people still covet our creatures — they want stone workers to plow their fields and carry their goods and guard their houses. So they tried instead to control us. They confined all stonemasons to the Stone Quarter and built a wall to contain us. Anyone with knowledge of the carving arts was forced to register and wear a badge at all times, and once a year, the stonemasons had to display all they had carved for the people to see and judge. To this day, this is why you see stone creatures who mimic flesh and blood animals, or doors and other household items. You don't see the giants of old."

"But *why* did the giants turn on the flesh people?" Mayka asked. "And how do you know Father used an obedience mark?" He'd never do that! Her father would never have stolen a creature's freedom.

He shrugged. "Who knows? Something went wrong in the carving, and they went bad."

"It must have been more than that," Mayka said. "Did anyone ask them?"

"Ask? You don't argue with monsters. You flee." He held up one finger. "Unless . . . the monsters have bound their loyalty to you. Unless they bear a mark that makes it impossible for them to harm a human. Do you see?" He beamed at them, as if surely they'd agree with him now that he'd explained.

She folded her arms. "I don't see what that has to do with Jacklo." And she didn't believe it. She thought of the mural she'd seen, with Father and the dragon. It seemed to support Siorn's story . . . *I refuse to believe it.*

"At this year's Stone Festival, I will prove that it is possible to create masterpieces again, because I have found a way to ensure they will not harm us: I've perfected the mark your father once used to save us all. I will prove that stonemasons should not be mistrusted. I'll restore our reputations. The wall will finally be torn down, and there will be no one in the valley who will have any reason to fear us — or to fear stone."

He seemed to believe every word he was saying. He was gesturing wildly, and his voice was soaring. "It will revolutionize what's possible in stone. It will change things for everyone! We will be able to trust stone creatures with our very lives, and working together, flesh and stone, we will be able to accomplish miracles. Can't you see it? The possibilities are extraordinary, for you as well as for us. The laws against what we can create, what stone creatures can be and do, will be repealed, and you will have freedom!"

"I don't think you know what that word means," Risa said.

Sticking her head out from behind Mayka's legs, Si-Si nodded vigorously. "No stone creature wants to be controlled!"

"It's not about control. It's about safety! Yours and ours! Right now, stone creatures aren't trusted. You know of the curfew, don't you? If humans weren't afraid of you, it would be lifted. Stone creatures would be free to go where and when they wished."

"You're afraid of us?" Mayka said. "But we're just like you, in all the ways that matter. We think, we feel, we live!"

He shook his head. "Your father carved you with such innocence."

She glared at him. "My father carved me to be *me*. You have no right to deny creatures control of their own stories! Everyone has a right to —"

"Not to kill! Not to harm! No one has that right! Because of me, the Stone War will never happen again. I've created peace that will spread to the entire valley!" He then sighed. "I'm saddened that you don't see it my way."

"I don't," Mayka said. "So if you'll *please* remove your mark from Jacklo, we will all be on our way." She wanted to tell him to take back what he'd said about her father too. It had to be a lie. Father had believed in peace that came from family and love and trust, not from coercion and control and dominance. *And so do I.*

He made gentling motions with his hands. "I cannot spend any more time convincing you. The festival is coming, and I need to be ready. This is more important than one bird. This is about the future of all stonemasons. And the future of the valley. Garit, please tend to the bird's wing."

"Yes, Master," Garit said, and reached to take Jacklo from Mayka.

"No!" Mayka cried. She clung tighter to him, and Jacklo wriggled and squirmed.

Risa swooped down. "Mayka, release him. He'll hurt himself." She glared at Jacklo. "Stop it, you idiot. She just cares about you."

Jacklo strained with his unbroken wing toward Garit. Risa was right — if she held on, he'd hurt himself worse. Grudgingly,

Mayka loosened her grip, and Garit lifted Jacklo out of her arms. She watched him carry her friend to a worktable on the opposite side of the room and lay him down beside a collection of chisels and hammers.

"You'll understand after my demonstration," Master Siorn said. "Watch how the people react. Once they understand that stone can be trusted, everything will change! I am going to make the world a safer place, a better place." To the griffin, he said, "See that they don't disturb me again."

"Yes, master," the griffin said.

Retreating into his private workroom, the stonemason shut the door behind him. Mayka heard it lock, and Kisonan positioned himself in front of it, guarding his master and whatever secrets he hid.

From the workbench, Jacklo whimpered.

Chapter
Sixteen

You're going to fix his wing, not add any more marks to him," Mayka said to Garit. She didn't phrase it as a question. She wouldn't *let* him add anything else.

"Yes, of course, that's the plan." He picked up a tub of white goop. "This is the cement glue we use. It will bind the stone. All I need to do is fill in the cracks with it. But he'll have to wait until it dries before he tries another takeoff, or he'll just need to be fixed again."

She studied it. Father had used a similar paste. "All right. But I'm watching."

"Great." He muttered, "That won't make me nervous or anything."

Risa glared at him. "Don't mess up. This is my brother. Maybe you should let Mayka do it. She has steady hands."

Mayka held her hand out, palm up. She'd helped Father

with tasks around his workroom before, and this didn't seem difficult.

Garit clutched the glue tighter. "I can do it! Look, I know you don't have any reason to trust me after . . . Well, I just want to help. Let me fix his wing. Please. The bird . . . he didn't ask for the mark that Master Siorn carved, and I . . . didn't realize someone might not want it." He looked first at Kisonan, then at the Scrap Room where the pieces of his friend lay, and lastly back at Mayka.

She stared at him, trying to read his thoughts in his eyes.

I wish humans wore their stories on their skins, she thought. He must have been willfully delusional not to realize a living, thinking being wouldn't want to be controlled.

She let him keep the glue, but she watched as he opened it, dipped in a brush, and painted the cracks in Jacklo's wing. He did it painstakingly slowly, only a drop here and a drop there, careful not to allow the glue to drip in between the feathers.

He pursed his lips as he concentrated, and Mayka had the feeling he'd forgotten she was there. She didn't speak. Merely watched. Perched on her shoulder, Risa watched too.

Jacklo was quiet as well, which worried Mayka more than anything else. The bird was more vulnerable to the mark than Kisonan was, because he was naturally so trusting. Already Jacklo was changing, incorporating the mark into his personality, letting it rewrite him into a creature who belonged here with

Master Siorn, rather than with Mayka and Risa on the mountain.

"He's good," Si-Si said, as Garit added another drop of cement, filling in a fissure. "Steady hand. Eye for detail." She lowered her voice, speaking softly enough that the griffin guarding the private workroom wouldn't be able to hear. "He could remove the mark."

Garit flinched, answering in an equally soft voice, "I can't."

"You could," Si-Si corrected. "You won't. You have the skill."

Jacklo spoke for the first time since Garit began. "Of course he has the skill! He's learned from one of the best stonemasons the world has ever seen." The worship in his voice rang out clear and strong.

"Shhh," Risa ordered.

"Master Siorn is *not* the best," Mayka said. "He plans to control all stone creatures. Rewrite their stories. Look at what the mark has already done to you! You've always loved our home — it's part of who you are — but now you don't want to leave this place."

"Stone creatures have always belonged to keepers — that's how the system works. Keepers pay, and stone creatures work," Garit said. "This just formalizes that." But she heard the uncertainty in his voice.

He doesn't believe it, she thought. *He's only repeating what Master Siorn must have said to him.* If she could convince him to remove the mark now, while Master Siorn was locked away in his private workroom . . . Garit wasn't meeting any of their eyes. Instead, he was spending an inordinately long time sealing the lid of the cement glue. "By choice," Mayka pressed. "This takes away any choice. Don't you see how wrong it is? See this?" She thrust her arm in front of him, forcing him to look at it. "My story says I'm a girl who lives on the mountain, surrounded by my friends. But because it's my story, I got to decide what part of that tale is important. To me, it's my friends. So I chose to leave the mountain and come here to try to save them. If I had Master Siorn's obedience mark, though, he could have ordered me to abandon my friends. Or even to stop caring about them at all."

Looking at her own arm, she had the startling thought that she really had done everything she'd described: she'd changed her own story. She wasn't just a girl on the mountain anymore. She'd come to the valley, to Skye.

Shifting away, Garit mumbled, "It will improve the lives of both people and stone creatures. It will ensure peace and enable innovation without fear."

Mayka continued to study his reaction, certain she was getting through to him. "You don't believe that. You're just repeated what he said. What do *you* think?"

"You're asking *me*? I'm the apprentice. My opinion doesn't matter."

"It matters to me," Mayka said.

He stared at her.

She stared back, and waited. *Please, understand.*

The silence stretched long, as if he were considering a dozen thoughts and then discarding each one. She did not rush him. This was too important. Softly, Mayka said, "Tell me your story. Why are you here?"

"I . . . I don't have a story."

Funny—Ilery had said almost the same thing. Did all flesh creatures deny their part in their own story? Doing that didn't exempt you from having a story; it just meant other people would shape your tale for you. *You have to seize your story,* Mayka thought. *That's what stone creatures do. We make our marks our own.* And that was part of why the obedience mark was so horrific—it hijacked that process. "Of course you do. Everyone does."

"It's not very interesting. I'm from outside of Skye. A farm. I have twelve brothers and sisters and . . . well, it's hard on the farm. Bad weather killed our crops for a few seasons. And there's been flooding in the pastures. With a family so large, there's not much money for food and clothes and everything we need. My parents brought me to the city, found me this apprenticeship . . . I'm very lucky. It's hard to find a good apprenticeship. My family has such high hopes for me." He held her gaze, as if pleading with her to understand. "I need to keep this apprenticeship. So I can't . . ." He trailed off.

"You'd sacrifice the freedom of stone creatures like Jacklo because of your family's hopes?" Mayka tried to be angry with him. He *knew* the mark was wrong, and yet he wasn't going to help them! But his family . . . She thought of her family back on the mountain. *I came here to help them,* she thought. *He did the same thing.*

"He's right that if stone creatures had the mark, the laws would change," Garit said. "Stone creatures would be trusted more. Given more responsibility and more opportunities. Treated better." He sounded as if he was trying to convince himself as much as them. "With his new mark, Master Siorn believes we could do great things together."

"And what do *you* think?"

He was silent for a moment. "I think if I defy Master Siorn, I'll lose my apprenticeship, and no one else will take me on, and I wouldn't be able to help my family."

Si-Si growled. "Coward."

"Would you take the risk, if you had something to lose?" Garit countered.

Si-Si fidgeted, hiding her face behind her wings. "Yes," she said in a small voice. "I already did." Lowering her wings, she glanced at Mayka. "I lied to you. I wasn't forgotten by my family. I ran away. They thought of me as a decoration — that much was true — but I didn't want to be just a useless toy. *That's* what my story means to me: I yearn to be like the great dragons of legend, to soar on the wind and save the day!"

"You aren't just a useless toy," Mayka told her.

"The point is," Si-Si said, glaring with her fiery eyes at Garit, "if a mere bauble can choose to be brave, so can you."

Garit shot a look at the door to the private workroom, and the griffin stared back—too far away to hear but close enough to watch. Under Kisonan's expressionless gaze, Garit fidgeted as if he wanted to bolt. "I . . . I . . . can't. You don't understand."

Maybe if Mayka *could* understand, she could convince him. "Tell me about the creature you lost. Your friend that he broke."

"What? But she's gone. It doesn't matter anymore."

"Of course it matters." Mayka sat down on a stool, ready to listen. She felt certain that this was the key to Apprentice Garit. Everyone had a story that mattered most to them, that defined them. For her, it was the mark that made her part of a family. For Si-Si, it was the mark that made her want to be like the flying dragons of legend. "What was her story?"

"Uh, well . . . she was nice. And I didn't expect that, because most of the stone creatures that Master Siorn carves just do their job. They clean or cook or guard or carry. They don't *listen*. But she listened. When I messed up on a carving . . . or when I couldn't find the right tool or the right stone that Master Siorn wanted when he wanted it . . . or when I was missing home . . ."

"You miss your family?" Mayka prodded. "I miss mine."

"I still see them on holidays, but it's not the same. I miss having breakfast with them. I miss sleeping under the same roof as all of them. I miss the sounds at night. Crickets in the field. The cows. Sounds stupid, doesn't it? Here I am in the greatest city in the valley, with an apprenticeship that helps my family . . . I should be grateful. That's what my parents say when I tell them I miss home. But Ava, my stone friend, didn't say that. She just . . . listened. And it was nice. She might have been terrible at everything else, but she was good at that."

"Did you ask him not to destroy her?" Mayka asked.

"He doesn't listen to me. Doesn't listen to anyone. He's always absorbed in his work — it's his life. Truthfully, I'm surprised he even talked to you. Guess it's because you look so much like a person but you're not."

Mayka scowled at him. "Thanks."

"Sorry! I mean . . . You're offended by that? Really?"

"Yes, really." She poked him in the shoulder. "How would you like it if I said you weren't a person because you're made of mostly water, hmm? How would you like it if I said you weren't real because your body changes all the time, and you aren't made up of the same parts from one year to the next? Your blood changes, your skin changes, your whole body gets swapped out for new bits — it's happening all the time. But I don't say you aren't real, even though your very existence is ephemeral. You are no more real than a cloud. You're here, you live, you die, and the world goes on. You're a breath of wind. Of the two of us, I am more real. I am stone, eternally unchanging." *Except that I'm fading.* She stopped herself. She *wasn't* eternal or unchanging. She simply would last longer than he would.

His mouth was hanging open.

"It doesn't matter whether I was born in a mess of blood and goo, or whether I was shaped lovingly and carefully in a workroom with chisel and hammer. I exist now, and so do Jacklo and Risa and Si-Si. And so did your stone friend. Master Siorn has no right to our existence."

He stared at her.

She crossed her arms and glared at him.

At last, he said, "You're right." There was a note of wonder in his voice, as if he were seeing the world anew. He took a deep breath. "I'll help you."

Uncrossing her arms, she smiled. "Thank you."

Garit placed a monocular over one eye, and he examined Jacklo's marks.

Mayka waited. Risa fidgeted. And the griffin stood guard at the door, silent and motionless. *I wonder how much of that he heard*, she thought. *And what he thought of it.* She stroked the crest of stone feathers on Jacklo's head, to keep him calm.

Garit made *humph*ing noises, as if he'd seen something he didn't like, and Mayka leaned in to see what he was looking at.

The new mark was glaringly raw against the old, worn stone, and to Mayka, it looked like a cut in flesh. She wished she could seal the stone closed again. Master Siorn had carved it right in between Jacklo's other marks, intertwined with them, so it all became part of the same story.

"It won't be easy to remove," Garit whispered. He pointed

to the lines. "Look how it's bridging the other lines. I don't even know what all these symbols mean."

"I can read it for you," Mayka offered.

He looked at her oddly but moved aside.

Leaning over Jacklo, she began his story: "Once upon a time, the sky was empty of laughter. The sun shone in the day, and the moon and stars decorated the night. Rain fell. Wind blew. Clouds formed and fled. And a stonemason looked up at the sky and thought it was lacking. So he carved a bird and filled it with delight and wonder. This bird is Jacklo, full of innocent joy, and laughter on the wing. He soars through the sky and" — she stopped, because there was where Master Siorn's ugly mark cut across his tale. She swallowed hard — "*obeys Master Siorn. He loves the air above the mountains, the trees, and his sister, Risa.*"

"I do," Jacklo said solemnly.

"I don't see all that in those symbols," Garit complained. "I see sky and laughter — but how did you connect them like that? How did you know that's how to read it?"

"Because of how the symbols are drawn touching." She pointed to the lines that linked them, like vines lashed around a tree. "And because I know Jacklo, and that's what his story is. He loves to fly. He loves the mountains. And he loves us. Master Siorn had no right to add *that*" — she jabbed at the obedience mark — "to his tale. It doesn't belong. He's supposed to be a bird who lives with us on the mountain, not a bird who serves a stone-mason in Skye."

Garit leaned over him again.

"Can you do it?" Risa asked.

"I . . . I don't know. It's between his other marks," Garit said. "If I were to try to chip it out . . . Look how close it is to the words that grant him flight. If I try . . . It's possible he won't be able to fly anymore."

Si-Si squawked. "Don't do it!"

Jacklo raised his head. "Not fly?"

From across the room, the griffin guard shifted, and Garit gave him a weak smile and a wave, as if to say all was well here and the griffin needn't concern himself. Kisonan didn't move again.

"I'm sorry," Garit whispered to Mayka and Jacklo. "I wish I could promise that it would be fine, but the way the lines are positioned . . . I don't know. I have to be honest. I'm not good enough to be sure I can get the mark out without damaging the marks on either side."

He seemed genuinely sorry.

She turned to Jacklo. "It's still your decision — do you want to take the risk?"

"He's going to do it," Risa said.

Mayka held up her hand. "Jacklo's decision only."

"How can he make a proper decision when that mark is interfering with his brain?" Risa asked. "He can't think straight

when it's on him. Otherwise he wouldn't have hurt himself trying to keep from leaving the stonemason."

That was true. But still . . . "Jacklo? What do you think?"
It was too big a decision to be made for him: flight or freedom.
He defined himself by flight. It gave him joy. It made him a bird,
himself, Jacklo. Only he could decide whether or not to risk it.

"I . . . don't know. I don't want to disappoint Master Siorn,
but I don't want to upset you and Risa either," Jacklo whispered.
"I don't like how I feel. I feel so torn. Why do I feel this way?"

"It's because of the mark," Mayka said. "You understand
that, don't you?"

He didn't answer, and for a moment, she thought he wasn't
going to. But then he said, in a voice so soft it sounded like a puff
of wind. "I want to think for myself again. Please do it, Garit. I
trust you."

Looking at Garit and remembering his lost friend, Mayka
thought, *I do too.*

Chapter
Seventeen

I t will take time," Garit cautioned. "And I'll need the tools in the workroom. So it will need to be done when Master Siorn is away." He shot another look at the locked door.

Mayka nodded. This would have to be done secretly. *Funny, I've never kept a secret before.* She'd never needed to. She'd told Father everything she thought and felt, and she'd assumed he did the same.

He kept secrets from me, though. She hadn't known he'd been in a war, or that he'd lost his family. Or even that he'd had a daughter before her. He hadn't talked much about his life in the valley. Maybe because those stories hurt too much to tell.

Or maybe because he'd used an obedience mark and knew how I'd feel about it? No, she didn't believe that. He'd made her the kind of person who would hate such a mark, so how could he be a person who would carve one?

She wished she could have asked Master Siorn more. If he were a different sort of man, the kind who would never think to create such a mark, then she would have happily spent a week or two staying here, listening to tales about Father. There must have been more to tell, if he was famous enough to inspire legends and a mural.

"How do we get your master to leave?" Risa asked.

Garit considered it for a moment, chewing on his lower lip as he thought. "The trick isn't getting him to leave; it's me being able to stay. He needs to oversee preparations for his festival stage. He'll have to leave the Stone Quarter so he can make sure everything's in place and exactly like he wants it. Usually, I take notes for him and run errands."

"Tell him you need to stay here to work," Risa said.

Mayka pointed at the dragon. "Tell him you need to work on Si-Si."

"That's . . . not a bad idea," Garit said. "I can start to carve her, and then when Master Siorn says it's time, I'll say that I'm at a delicate point and can't stop. He'll want me to finish what I started. It's brilliant!"

Excited, Si-Si danced in place. "Yes!"

Mayka beamed at Si-Si. "And then we'll be able to leave, and Si-Si will be able to fly! Everyone gets what they want."

He held up both his hands. "Well . . . not just yet. I can prepare her wings — I've been thinking about how to do that — but

I'll need to study the birds more to replicate what Master Kyn did with the marks."

Si-Si hopped up onto a stool and then onto a workbench. "So, study quickly."

"While you were exploring the house, I sketched out some preliminary ideas for how to carve her," Garit told Mayka. "Come on, I'll show you!" He bounded across the workroom with an enthusiasm that would have confounded a rabbit. Si-Si hopped after him, and Mayka, holding Jacklo, walked behind, with Risa on her shoulder.

He led them straight to a workbench that was covered in rolls of paper, all piled up on one another, like pine needles on a forest floor. He selected one and unrolled it. "No, not this one." Tossed it over his shoulder. Picked out another one. "Hmm, better, but no." Chose a third one. "Ah, this is it!" He unrolled it and then pinned the corners down with bits of rock. "Look!"

They gathered around. He'd drawn a sketch of Si-Si, with parts labeled and numbered. Several sketches, from different angles, as well as versions of her wing.

Si-Si rose up on her hind feet and poked her nose closer to the sketch to see. "You were thinking about this? Really? I thought . . . I'd been forgotten again." Softly, she said, "One of the worst parts about . . . leaving . . . the estate . . . was the fact that I don't think they noticed I left."

Kneeling, Mayka hugged the little dragon.

"See, there are two problems: the weight of her body, and

the shape of her wings. They're not balanced. So I'm thinking . . . make an incision and hollow her out." Grabbing a nub of charcoal, he drew onto the sketch.

Si-Si shrank back.

Quickly, he said, "It won't hurt! You're stone!"

"Yes, but . . ." She wrapped her tail around her body. Her fiery eyes flickered to the locked door, to the workroom door, to Garit, to Mayka, to Jacklo, and then at last to Risa, who fluttered over to the worktable.

Risa poked at the sketches with her beak. "You want to take away pieces of her torso? Won't that show?" The dragon was translucent stone. Any change within would alter how she reflected light.

Si-Si studied her stomach. The stone had swirls of orange and red, which Mayka thought was beautiful. She looked like the heart of a fire. "All right, do it," Si-Si said. "I'm ready to change." She held up her wings and closed her eyes.

"Are you sure about this?" Mayka asked. "What if he fails?" She wondered if the little dragon had thought this through. It was a major recarving, and you couldn't add back stone that had been taken away. Once gone, that piece of her would be lost forever.

"Then at least I'll have helped the bird." Si-Si lay down on the workbench. "Mayka, don't you see? I'm being useful!"

Jacklo turned his head away. "Tell me when it's over."

Flying back to him, Risa patted his shoulder with her wing

but didn't speak. She kept her wing around him, as if she could shield him with it.

Silent, the griffin continued to watch.

Garit picked up a piece of chalk and began to draw on Si-Si's torso. "The idea is to redistribute the weight so that your wings can hold you. I'm going to carve away here" — he drew a sweeping line across her stomach — "and shape it smooth, then drill holes here and here, to remove some of the weight from the remaining stone." He laid out his tools beside him, and then took a deep breath.

As Garit fiddled with his tools, Mayka laid her hand on his. "Can I help?"

Startled, he looked at her. "Um, really? But you're . . ." He stopped. "I'm sorry. You *did* carve the pedestals."

She picked up the chisel she knew would be right for Si-Si's stone type. It would make a clean strike without chipping. "This is the one you want to use."

He looked at it and said, "Yeah, it is." Taking it, he bent over Si-Si.

Si-Si reached out one paw, and Mayka took it in her hand. She squeezed, as Garit began tapping lightly with the chisel on the dragon's torso.

They continued that way, with Mayka holding the dragon's paw with one hand and passing Garit tools with the other. He tapped carefully, chipping away bits of her stone and then sanding it smooth, changing her shape. One shard of stone fell off the workbench and landed on the floor where Si-Si could see it. She let out a yelp. "That's a part of me!"

"We're making a new you," Garit reminded her. She started to sit up. "Don't look yet. I'm not finished. Long way from finished."

Si-Si settled back down.

From the doorway, Master Siorn said, "Oh, splendid! You've taken on quite a challenge." He bustled to the workbench to stare over Garit's shoulder. "Go on. Make the next cut."

Garit positioned the chisel. Mayka could see his hands were shaking.

Master Siorn clucked his tongue. "Not like that, all limp. Hold it steady, boy! And lift that angle up."

Concentrating, Garit obeyed. Sweat had popped onto his forehead. But he held his hand steady and tapped the chisel with the hammer. A sliver of red stone broke off. It tumbled off the table onto the floor, sounding like a bell as it bounced.

"Good," Master Siorn grunted. He watched for a while longer. "You stick with it. I have to speak with the festival organizers and check on the preparations."

Eyes wide, Garit looked up. "But don't you need me for that? I can leave this —"

"Ah, I can handle it without you, my boy." The stonemason patted Garit's shoulder with his beefy hand. "The best carvings happen when you're in the moment, focused on the task at hand, not distracted by details. If I need you, I'll come back."

"As you wish, master," Garit said, and bent over Si-Si again.

Very nice, Mayka thought. Maybe Garit was smarter than she gave him credit for. She suddenly realized the stonemason was looking at her. She shrank back, as if that would hide her from view.

He plucked a hammer out of her hand. "Be careful when you handle an artist's tools. These are what make us storytellers, not merely carvers."

She nodded, not trusting herself to speak. She would have said their imaginations made them into storytellers, not the tools. Besides, she knew how to handle tools. She'd always helped Father with his carvings, taken care of his tools, kept them organized and polished and sharp and whatever else they needed. She knew them very well. But she didn't argue.

"And please don't interrupt Apprentice Garit. He needs his concentration." Beaming at Garit, he swept out of the workroom with Kisonan trotting behind him.

Garit exhaled loudly, as if he'd been holding his breath the whole time.

All of them listened as the rock door was rolled open and the stone otters outside cheered and then fell silent when Master Siorn barked at them. They heard the door roll back into place.

"You should fix the bird now," Si-Si said.

"But I haven't finished you!" Garit said.

"Him first," she said. "Then me. He needs his freedom more than I need my wings."

Mayka squeezed Si-Si's paw — one of the few places on her body that Garit's chisel hadn't touched — before she rushed over to Jacklo. She laid him out on the workbench and gently spread open his wings.

"He gouged the mark deep," Garit said. "If I sand it out . . . even if I don't affect the other marks, it will change his shape and weight. It could still affect his flight."

Jacklo closed his eyes. "Do it."

Mayka wished she could cry. She stared at the marks, at the ugly gashes that the stonemason had dug into Jacklo's body, slicing through the delicate lines of the feathers.

She heard the otters screech from outside, and she heard the front rock being moved again. Kisonan's voice drifted through the house, "Welcome back, Master."

"Quick! Put him in the cage!" Garit whispered.

Mayka ran with Jacklo to the cage, while Garit carted the tools back to Si-Si. The stonemason stomped into the workroom, while the griffin followed behind him. "Garit, I need you. Those fools put my podium on the wrong stage!"

"But I don't want to wait!" Si-Si cried. Her distress seemed so real that Mayka almost believed her. She began to wail, a high-pitched nose that sounded like a kettle whistling. "Look at me! I'm hideous! You can't leave me like this!"

"Shush," the stonemason told her. But his voice was kindly. *He believes he's good,* Mayka thought. *He believes he's helping.* "You'll be worked on soon enough. I'll even assist Garit, once I've completed my own work."

"I can finish tomorrow," Garit told Si-Si, though he glanced at Jacklo as he said it.

Master Siorn shook his head. "Tomorrow I'll need you at the Festival Square, working on final preparations. It'll have to wait until after the festival."

Si-Si wailed louder.

"Cheer up! It will be over in a few days. We'll have you flying through the sky in no time! And then I'll present you at next year's festival! I'll unveil miracles two years in a row and secure my place in history!" Beaming at his idea, Master Siorn waddled out the door. *He has no idea how evil he is,* Mayka thought. *He thinks he's the hero of his tale, rescuing the poor stonemasons from unfair laws and bringing peace to the valley.* "Come along, apprentice. Kisonan, the door."

Garit shot Mayka a helpless look.

They waited in silence as Garit and the griffin followed the stonemason out. They heard otters chirp as Kisonan opened and shut the stone door.

"We have to leave," Risa said. "You heard him! He wants to make Si-Si one of his! If he comes back and puts the mark on her too, she'll be trapped."

But they couldn't leave, not with the mark still on Jacklo!

Mayka hurried over to Jacklo. Carrying him to the workbench, she studied the mark. *I don't know how to remove it without hurting him.* If she tried to chip it out, she'd risk damaging the story around it and changing the very essence of who he was.

"Changing..." she mused out loud. The word gave her an idea, a crazy just-might-work kind of idea.

"Mayka?" Jacklo asked. "Did you say something?"

What if there were a way to *change* the mark, instead of removing it? "Risa, is there paper here? And something to write with?"

"Of course. Look at all his plans." Risa flew over to Garit's mess and plucked out one.

Bending over it, Mayka began to draw. She started with the obedience mark. And then she added lines and swirls. When that didn't produce the shape she wanted, she crossed it out heavily and began again.

"What are you doing?" Risa asked.

"You're right — we have to leave. But we can't while Jacklo has the mark," Mayka said. "And Garit isn't here to remove it. I'm not skilled enough to do it — even with all his training, he said it would be tricky. But I'm thinking... I could *change* it." A few more lines and Master Siorn's name could be transformed into Master of the Sky... But what about "obey"? She kept drawing.

Risa cleared her throat. "Mayka?"

"What?" She almost had it. If she added an additional symbol, the one for wind, it would read as the "Master of the Sky obeys the wind," which was a lovely summary for their travels, far from the mountain. He'd flown on the wind, sailing high and low. *It could work*, she thought.

"Mayka, audience," Risa whispered.

Mayka looked up.

The griffin, Kisonan, was back in the workroom, watching them.

"Um, hello," Mayka said. She didn't know if they could trust him. From what he'd said and done, she thought he didn't always agree with his master, but she didn't know how far that went.

"I have only been instructed to let the master in when he returns, and the otters will alert me when he is here." Kisonan sat, seeming to anticipate her questioning. "Until then, I may go where I please and do as I please."

Good enough, she thought. She didn't have time to worry about him. She turned back to her friend. "Jacklo, I have an idea, which might work and it might not." She told him about how she could change the mark. "It will certainly have an effect, and I'm not sure what kind. It will be up to you and how you interpret the new story."

"It has to be better than what's there," Risa said. "But are you sure you can do it?"

"I've helped Father," Mayka said. "And I know how to write. I've done that often enough." She gestured at her notes.

"Do it!" Jacklo said.

This is crazy, a part of her whispered. *You can't change his story: you aren't a storyteller!* Carving a pedestal wasn't the same as shaping a story. But she knew the tools, she knew the words, and she knew stone. She whispered back to herself, *You can do this.*

Chapter
Eighteen

*J*ust like writing *on paper,* Mayka told herself. She knew the strokes and the lines. She could visualize it exactly. Bending over Jacklo, she held the chisel steady. *A light touch. That's all it needs.* She tapped the chisel with her hammer.

It barely dinged him.

"Your time shortens," Kisonan said. "The master is rarely gone for long, especially so close to the festival. He must work on his masterpiece."

Jacklo looked up at her. "I trust you," he said. "And whatever happens, I won't blame you. This is my choice."

Those words gave her the courage. She positioned the chisel, tapped it, and made a line. Concentrating, she continued, adding line after line.

"How do you feel?" Risa asked, anxious.

"Shhh," Jacklo told her. "Mayka needs silence."

"Never thought I'd hear *you* ask for silence," Risa said, but then she was quiet.

Mayka didn't know how much time passed before she was finished. But at last, she was. Leaning back, she studied the mark. "'Master of the Sky obeys the winds.' That is your new story, Jacklo. Use it as you will."

"I'll use it to soar," he promised, as he spread his wings.

"Not yet!" Risa cried. "You aren't healed! You don't want have to come back for more glue, do you?"

He folded his wings, and Mayka scooped him up. She turned to Si-Si. "Ready?"

The little dragon let out a hiccup-like sigh as she looked down at her body, once perfectly polished but now flecked with chips and roughly chiseled gouges.

Gently, Mayka said, "We'll find another stonemason to finish you." She didn't know who, but that was a problem for later, after they were far away from here.

Cradling Jacklo, she hurried toward the doorway — and the griffin who blocked it. Caught up in carving, she'd forgotten he was there watching them. He'd been standing so still that he'd blended in with the half-formed sculptures that filled the workroom.

Risa flew toward his face. "Are you going to help us leave, or keep us here?"

Kisonan didn't flinch. "You should know that Master Siorn will pursue you."

"Oh?" Risa flapped her wings and raised her talons. "Is that a threat?"

"It is a warning," he said. "There is something you must see, if you are to take the right precautions to protect yourselves and your family." He crossed the workroom to the back door, and Mayka, curious, followed him. "There is no length to which he will not go. He has broken the law already, in his quest to restore the reputation of stonemasons. Ever since the Stone War, stonemasons have been forbidden to make giants. But that is what Master Siorn makes in secret."

Si-Si skidded to a stop. "But . . . but he can't!"

"He can and did," Kisonan said gravely.

"But . . . but . . . how do you know?"

"I am his obedient servant," Kisonan said, bitterness in his voice. "It is I who brought him the stones. It is I who cleared the space in the back room. It once housed raw supplies. Now it houses his masterpiece."

Si-Si shook her head. "But . . ."

"He believes that once he has demonstrated that the obedience mark works with ordinary stone creatures, the law will be changed, and stonemasons will once again be revered. It is then he plans to unveil *this*." He unlocked the door and swung it wide open. Mayka stepped forward and peered into the private workroom.

And she saw a monster.

There was no other word for what he was. Mayka had never seen a creature so massive. Crouched over, he filled the room, as if he were his own mountain. His muscles were boulders, with huge arms that looked designed to crush and bash.

His stone eyes were closed.

She didn't see any marks.

For now, he was inert stone.

"He's not finished yet," Kisonan said, behind her. "But if Master Siorn's plan goes as he intends, the law against stone giants will be abolished, and he will have this behemoth at his command. He may send it after you if he wishes, and I believe he will wish to possess Master Kyn's last creations. He will justify it, of course, in talk of the betterment of man, and claim that he and the monster are acting in the best interests of Skye, but the result for you and your friends will be the same: the loss of your freedom. You must be prepared to hide."

Mayka stared at the griffin. Surely, she'd be safe on the mountain . . .

"And now you must flee, before it is too late for warnings to save you." Kisonan led them out of the workroom and to the rock at the front of the house. He rolled it aside, and Mayka saw that it was nearly sunset. The fat sun looked as if it were about to drip onto the distant mountains.

We'll have to hurry, she thought. *Curfew begins soon.* "Thank you," Mayka said, "for not stopping us and for the warning."

The griffin fixed his eyes on Mayka. "If it works, if the bird is able to leave, if what you did truly changed the mark . . . I wish you to return someday, when it is safe, and do the same for me. The mark is . . . a source of shame. I would have been loyal to him without it, but he took that choice from me. He did not, though, tell me how to feel about it, and I want it gone."

"I will change your mark right now," Mayka said. "Let me see —"

"There is no time," Kisonan said. "You must be gone before he returns. Otherwise, he will issue orders, and I will not be able to allow you to leave." He gestured to the yard. "Step on every third stone, and the otters will not touch you. Duck after the fifth."

Hurrying, Mayka hopped from stone to stone. She felt the otters' eyes on her, and after her fifth step, she ducked. Stones sailed over her head. She glanced back at the griffin, but he wasn't looking at them. He was standing like a sentry by the door, looking into the distance.

"Ready to leave?" she asked Jacklo.

"Beyond ready," Jacklo said.

And Mayka stepped between the two stone lizards, through Master Siorn's gate. Jacklo lay in her arms, not trying to get back, not needing to obey. She hurried through the Stone Quarter with Risa flying above and Si-Si hopping beside her.

"Walk," Risa whispered from her shoulder, as they approached the gate to leave the Stone Quarter. "You look like you're fleeing someone."

"I am," Mayka said, but she slowed down to a brisk stroll, matching the pace of the apprentices and stonemasons who were scurrying to and from the gate. The cobblestones smoothed beneath her feet, leading her through the crowd. She hoped it wouldn't be a problem to leave the Stone Quarter without Garit to speak for her. She wished she could tell the truth: *Master Siorn has created an abomination, a mark that steals stories.*

But she couldn't be certain the flesh-and-blood gatekeeper would see it that way.

If it hadn't been for Ava, the apprentice's stone friend, Garit might not have sided with them. Mayka thought back to the way people had treated her from the moment she'd entered this city. *No, it's not safe to tell the truth. Better just to leave without saying anything.*

"Lie to the guard," Si-Si advised. "You must tell him you're obeying your keeper."

"I can't say that," Mayka said. It was one thing to omit the truth, but to say she had a keeper ... The very idea of claiming someone owned her made her feel as if bugs were burrowing into her stone arms.

"You must."

You can do it. It's only words.

Except there's no such thing as "only words." Words are every-thing.

And then another voice in her head said, *Yes. And the right words can give you freedom.*

For the first time in her life, Mayka deliberately concocted a lie. She practiced it in her head, and when she reached the gate, she smiled at the guard and said, "My keeper, Stonemason Siorn, asked me to take these sculptures to him at the festival grounds. He plans to use them in his demonstration." The lie burned on her tongue, but she didn't waver.

"Huh, that one looks unfinished." He pointed at Si-Si. "She's a mess."

Si-Si tucked her wings against herself and hunched over. "I'm in the middle of a metamorphosis. Caterpillars in cocoons are probably ugly too."

The gatekeeper's eyes widened as he saw Jacklo. "Wow, a stone bird! So that's what he's been keeping secret? Has he found a way to make it fly?"

"He can't fly," Mayka said. Another lie. "He's only for deco-ration."

The guard's face fell. "There are stories of a stonemason who could create flying sculptures. All of them were destroyed when he lost his family in the Stone War."

Did everyone but her know about Father's past? "Do you mean Master Kyn?"

He beamed. "Yes, that's him! Those were the days, huh? Stonemasons lived like kings, and we all benefited from it. Stone marvels everywhere, doing all the work. Until the stonemasons got too big for their britches." Squinting, he glanced up at the sky — the sun was setting fast, melting like hot butter. "Eh, I shouldn't keep you with my babbling. It's nearly curfew. Best make your way to your keeper before it's fully down. You'll have a bit of a grace period since it's so close to the festival, but best not to push your luck." He shooed them forward.

She wanted to ask more, to hear another story about Father, but he was right: in a few minutes, it would be dusk. They needed to be beyond the city gates before they closed. She nodded politely at the guard and walked through the archway. She made it ten paces before she heard a shout: "Wait! Stop! That's my stone girl!"

Master Siorn.

He was coming from the Festival Square, toward the Stone Quarter, toward them.

Above her, Risa shrieked, "Run!"

The guard lunged for her, grabbing her arm.

Si-Si shouted in a shrill voice, "He's lying! He stole us from our keepers! He's a thief!"

The accusation made the guard hesitate, and it was enough for Mayka to break away from his weak, meaty hands. She ran, her stone feet pounding on the pavement, while Risa flew overhead and Si-Si raced beside her. She held Jacklo tight against her and didn't look back.

The streets were packed with people: workers setting up and families who were strolling by, gawking at the sights. Mayka weaved between them. "Sorry, sorry, excuse me!"

A few called out to her: "Are you all right?" "Is anything wrong?" "Who's chasing you?"

I'm drawing too much attention, she thought. She scanned the area and saw other children, skipping as they played, and so as she rounded the corner, she switched to skipping. She painted a bright smile on her face and hoped she looked as if she was holding a toy instead of a live bird. No one shouted at them. She kept turning down different streets, each time choosing the most crowded.

Risa flew lower. "You lost them, as far as I can tell."

"Now it's time for us to get out of the city," Jacklo said. "Please, I want to go home."

Me too, Mayka thought. She wished they'd never come to the valley. It was a terrible place. No wonder Father had left it. *Why didn't he tell me what it was like? Or about his family? Or about the Stone War?* He was famous, yet she'd had no idea.

Everyone here knows his story but me. If only his story had been written on his skin, instead of hidden, written on his heart.

"Which way is the gate out of the city?" Si-Si asked.

Mayka halted. They'd run down so many streets, and she

hadn't kept track of the turns. She'd been concentrating only on getting away. "Risa, can you fly above the buildings and see which direction we need to go?"

Launching upward, Risa soared toward the tops of the spires. The sky was a deeper blue than it had been moments ago, and a faint star shone above. *Oh no*, Mayka thought.

The sun had set.

The gate . . .

Risa plummeted toward them and then swooped up at the last moment. "The gate!" she cried. "It's closed!"

Si-Si began to panic, chasing her tail in a circle. "What do we do? Where can we hide? Oh, he's going to find us! Oh, we're doomed! He'll catch us! He'll change us. He'll destroy us!"

Mayka knelt on one knee, even though she wanted to run in a circle and shriek too. "Shhh, Si-Si, calm down. We'll find a place to spend the night, and then we'll leave the city at dawn."

"Where? There's nowhere to go, no one to turn to!"

"I have an idea: we're going to walk calmly and purposefully to the Inn District, and we're going to find Ilery." She'd said she was staying at a place called the Marble Inn.

Si-Si paused. "But she's flesh! She may have been friendly while she was waiting and bored, but do you really think she'd hide us?"

"I think we have to find out," Mayka said. "Come on."

Leading the way, Risa flew with the city birds, blending

in with the pigeons, and Mayka had trouble keeping her eye on which one was Risa. She was glad Father had made the birds so lifelike. It made them easier to hide. She wondered if he'd ever thought about that as he carved them.

She had so many questions she could never ask him.

She wished she had asked him to teach her how to carve. She'd watched him and helped him. But she'd never thought that she too could create a sculpture like he did, complete with its own stories. He seemed as if he'd been born knowing exactly where to place the chisel, exactly what kind of shape to coax out of a stone.

But Garit hadn't been born with those skills. She'd seen him learning, trying, experimenting, failing.

And she herself had changed the mark on Jacklo.

She could carve.

It was such a revolutionary thought that it almost stopped her in her tracks. *I can carve. I am a storyteller.* She could, if she practiced and tried, recarve her friends.

We don't need a stonemason.

We only need me.

She could read Father's marks, and she'd watched him carve. In a way, though she hadn't known it and he may not have intended it, he'd been her teacher. She had his knowledge. All she needed, like Garit, was practice. And time.

I have time. Plenty of it, until my marks fade. And I have

Father's tools, up on the mountain. We've got to go home. I want to begin!

But first, they needed to leave the city.

And before that, they needed to make it through the night.

Chapter
Nineteen

The Inn District was very different from the other parts of Skye. For one thing, it was full of flowers. Real flowers, not stone. Everywhere, there were flowers in gardens and planters, their blossoms closed for the night. Mayka knew many of them were out of season, but they'd been grown here anyway. Trees with blossoms lined the sidewalks, and their petals coated the hardened dirt street.

By now, the stars were scattered all over the sky, but there were still so many people in the streets that it was easy to blend into the crowd. *We need to find the Marble Inn before our luck gives out*, Mayka thought. *And hope that Ilery is there, not roving around like everyone else.*

In Mayka's arms, Jacklo fidgeted. "Are you sure we can trust her?"

She wasn't sure of much, except that they had very few

options left, in a city full of people who were hostile to stone, with a stonemason actively searching for her. But her instincts said they could trust Ilery.

"I'm sure we need a place to hide for the night."

The Marble Inn was up ahead. Carved out of white and rose marble, the inn was three stories tall, with pillars sculpted to look like trees. *I hope I'm right about her, and I hope she meant her invitation.* For all Mayka knew, Ilery befriended everyone she saw and didn't mean any of it. Mayka hadn't made enough friends to know what was real and what wasn't.

Walking up the steps, she stopped at the door, unsure what she was supposed to do.

She didn't have to decide — the door swung open, and a stone badger stood on his hind legs in the doorway. He was carved out of dust-gray marble, with onyx eyes and claws. But while her friend Badger was an exquisite replica of a flesh badger, this badger was carved with every feature exaggerated: his eyes were bulbous, his claws blunt, his body polished smooth instead of painstakingly carved to resemble fur. "Welcome to the Marble Inn! Rooms available to let."

Mayka shot a look back to where Risa perched on another building. She'd stay hidden with the flesh-and-feather birds and keep watch, in case Master Siorn showed up.

As they entered, the badger stared at Mayka. "I didn't know any of the stonemasons had begun making people."

"I'm a rare case."

The badger peered closer and noticed Jacklo in her arms. He squinted at the bird, squinching his stone face until his eyes nearly disappeared in folds of marble. "You're all stone. This *is* unusual, especially after curfew. Where's your keeper?"

Slipping past him into the lobby, Mayka pretended she didn't hear the question. "We're looking for someone who's staying here. A girl named Ilery?"

"I can check the guest list. One moment." The badger waddled inside and hopped himself up onto a stool. He flipped through a ledger and ran his claws lightly over a row of marks.

"You can read?" Mayka asked, watching his lips move as he scanned the ledger. After Garit and Master Siorn's reaction, she'd thought she was the only one.

"Contrary to the opinion of *some*, stone creatures can be quite intelligent and capable." He sounded miffed. "Ilery . . . Ilery . . ." He ran his claw down the ledger. "She is checked in."

Yes! She shot a look out at the street again. No Master Siorn, and no guards. "Where can I find her?"

He closed the ledger. "I'm sorry, but my keepers do not want me to share room numbers with nonguests. She is at this inn, but that is the most information I'm allowed to give you. You could leave a message for her, if you'd like."

Mayka tried not to slump. *So close!* she thought. *And it was such a good idea.*

The badger was peering at them again, leaning so close that

his nose almost touched Jacklo's tailfeathers. "If you don't mind me asking, which stonemason carved you?"

Mayka hesitated. Could she trust anyone here? *I refuse to think of everyone as an enemy.*

Before she could answer, Jacklo piped up. "We were made by our father, Master Kyn, the best stonemason who ever lived."

The badger blinked. "It was said that all of Master Kyn's works were destroyed. It was also said that he carved birds who could fly."

She wondered what else he knew about Father. "You know about him?"

"Everyone knows about him! He was a hero. As the bird said, he was the greatest stonemason who ever lived. I assume you've seen the mural? The mural doesn't tell the whole story — it was done by stonemasons, and they have a skewed view of the past. On one thing we all agree, though: because of him, there is peace in the valley."

"What is the whole story?" Mayka asked. She glanced at the window again — they were safely inside at least, and Risa was keeping watch. She could take a moment for a story, especially one about Father. *And maybe while he talks, I'll think of a way to reach Ilery.*

"A group of stonemasons were working to enslave our kind, make us fight their battles. They pitted us against one another, for wealth, for land, for power. But Master Kyn believed this was wrong. We should not be fighting their wars. We are creatures of peace! And so he carved a giant stone dragon and marched him into Skye to defeat the corrupt stonemasons."

She thought of Master Siorn's version of this story. "I heard he used an obedience mark, and that the stone creatures were attacking the flesh-and-blood people."

"Bah! You've been talking to stonemasons. No, Master Kyn was a friend to stone. He'd never compel our kind to obey. Such a mark is a myth, and certainly nothing he needed."

Jacklo chirped. "See! I never doubted Father."

She felt as if her stone knees had weakened. *I knew it! Father wasn't like Master Siorn.*

"He was noble, but many stonemasons were not. Unbeknownst to him, the evil stonemasons had kidnapped his wife and daughter and placed them in the city. When the city was destroyed in the great battle, so were his wife and daughter. He was, unwittingly, responsible for their deaths. It was a terrible tragedy."

Poor Father. She wished he'd told her about them. He'd hid his sorrow inside.

Si-Si sniffled. "Oh, that's so sad!"

"But he was victorious nonetheless. The evil stonemasons were stopped, their work destroyed, and everyone — stone and flesh — was saved. Master Kyn himself helped write the laws to keep stonemasons from ever achieving so much power again. All was not perfect, of course. He could not eliminate all his enemies, and before they were at last caught, they destroyed every bit of his work they could find, including his great dragon, and he was forced to flee for his life. There are tales that say he destroyed his creations himself to keep them from falling into the wrong hands, but I don't believe that for a moment. He'd never destroy the creatures he loved."

I don't believe it either, Mayka thought.

"But all tales agree he left the valley. Some say he died. Some say he lives on."

"He did die," Mayka said quietly. "But not for many years."

"You truly knew him?" the badger asked. "He was the greatest hero we've ever had, among both stone and flesh. What happened to him?"

"He made himself a new family," Mayka said, "and he was happy."

The badger sighed. "That's lovely. If I could cry, I would. Thank you for sharing that with me. In return for that news . . ." Lowering his voice to a whisper, he said, "Room thirty-three. Up the stairs. Third floor."

"Thank you!" Mayka said.

She climbed the stairs two at a time until she reached the third floor. Sconces on the wall had already been lit, and she read the numbers on the doors easily. "Here it is."

"Are you sure about this, Mayka?" Jacklo whispered.

"Yes," Mayka said. "There are good humans. Father and Garit prove that. Don't let one bad man make you scared of people. Don't change that much, Jacklo — your story isn't about distrust." Cradling Jacklo in one arm, she knocked on the door with her other hand. She waited, listening, and heard footsteps shuffling toward the door. Si-Si ducked behind her.

"One minute!" a cheerful voice called.

The door opened to reveal Ilery. She was grinning as widely as she had when they first met, but she'd changed clothes. She now wore billowing purple pants, a blouse with a star on it, and several strands of necklaces. If it weren't for the smile, Mayka wouldn't have recognized her at all — she'd forgotten that flesh people could so easily change their outsides.

But the second she spoke, it was clear this was Ilery. She flung her arms open, as full of enthusiasm as before. "Oh! Mayka, Si-Si, you came! And you found your friend!"

Mayka smiled. "We did. May we come in?"

"Of course! I'm so glad you're here. It's been so boring cooped up here while my parents work — they're looking for more help for the farm this year, but our budget is limited, so it's tricky." She waved them inside and then shut the door.

The room was tiny, with flowers everywhere: painted on the walls, in vases on the tables and dressers, sewn into the quilt on the bed. A trunk was open on one table, and it overflowed with dresses and other clothes — clearly all Ilery's.

"We . . ." Mayka began, then stalled, unsure how much to explain or how to ask if they could hide here, but before she could say more, Ilery was talking again.

"Aw, look at you!" She leaned in and touched Jacklo's chin. "You're so cute! And wow, those look like real feathers."

"I know," Jacklo said. "I was perfectly carved."

"He's modest too," Mayka said.

Ilery laughed. "He has no need to be." She plopped onto the bed. "Are you excited for the festival? Two days until it begins! What do you think of Skye so far?"

"It's nothing like what I expected," Mayka said truthfully. "Ilery . . . we need a safe place to spend the night. Stone creatures aren't supposed to be out after dusk, and there's someone . . . We seem to have made an enemy, and we don't want him to find us."

Ilery sat up straighter. "A dangerous enemy?"

"You're not in danger," Mayka said quickly. *I hope.* It depended on what the stonemason told the guards. If he was smart, he'd continue his story that they'd run away . . . *but then Ilery will look as if she's stolen us.* "Or maybe you will be, if we're caught."

"Then we won't get caught," Ilery said firmly.

Mayka smiled and exchanged glances with Si-Si and Jacklo. *I knew we could trust her. We'll be safe here tonight.* "Thank you."

Si-Si inclined her head in a bow. "Yes, thank you."

"What happened to you?" Sliding off the bed, Ilery squatted to examine Si-Si, frowning at the gouges in her torso. "You look half carved. Who did this to you?"

Si-Si lifted her head proudly, though her mouth quivered. "It was necessary, in order for all of us to escape."

Not all, Mayka thought. They'd left Kisonan and the other stone creatures.

"Escape from who? Who's your enemy?"

"An evil stonemason," Mayka said, thinking of the badger's story. Checking the door to make sure it was safely latched, she told Ilery everything: why they'd come to Skye, how they'd lost Jacklo, what had happened with Garit and Master Siorn. Then she plunged on and told her about the obedience mark, and she was relieved when Ilery gasped in shock.

"But that's terrible!" Ilery cried. "Stone creatures work for their keepers in order to pay back the fee for being carved, and so that their keepers will pay to have their marks recarved. It's a working relationship. Not . . . not . . . He can't just . . ." She was waving her arms so emphatically that Mayka had to hop backwards to avoid being accidentally swatted.

"Exactly," Si-Si said. "Even when we serve a keeper, we have choices about what we do. With a mark like this . . . a stone creature could be ordered to do horrible things."

"Like in the Stone War," Ilery said. "But, Mayka, how did you escape?"

"We had help. And the stonemason had tools." She told Ilery how she'd removed the obedience mark from Jacklo — and how she'd promised to return to remove it from the griffin who had helped them.

"We can't return," Risa said, from the windowsill. Mayka turned to see that the bird had swooped down from the roof and now perched on the sill, next to a vase filled with marble flowers. "If you go back to the Stone Quarter, you'll be caught."

"Two birds!" Ilery clapped her hands together in delight. "And you really can fly!"

Risa didn't seem interested in being admired again. She fluttered her wings, ready to launch from the window if necessary. "Who's this?"

"My friend Ilery," Mayka said. "Ilery, this is Risa. And the bird you already met is Jacklo." To Risa, she said, "I know it's impossible, but I hate leaving knowing the mark is out there. It's not just wrong; it's dangerous." As the words left her mouth, she realized, with growing horror, how true that was. She'd been so busy escaping that she hadn't thought through the consequences, not really. If she left the obedience mark on Kisonan and the others, Master Siorn would demonstrate its power at the Stone Festival — and all would know stone creatures could be compelled to obey flesh-and-blood people.

And then the freedom of every stone creature in the entire valley would be at risk.

I can't leave.

But Risa was right — it wasn't safe to go back. Guards could be looking for her, thinking she'd run away from Master Siorn. Still . . . *I wouldn't have to go near any guards to find Garit.* At some point, he was bound to be in the square preparing for the demonstration — she remembered that Master Siorn had said he was needed to finish preparations. If she could find him there, ideally without Master Siorn, he could help her sneak back into the Stone Quarter.

There were a lot of *maybe*s in that plan.

But it wasn't terrible.

"You could disguise yourself!" Ilery hopped off the bed and hurried over to her trunk. "Borrow some of my clothes! Then the only thing that will look stone is your skin, and if you don't get too close to people, they won't know."

"You don't mind?" Mayka followed her to the trunk. They were about the same size. She could put on a fabric dress over her stone dress. Ilery pulled out one, and Mayka held it in front of her — it seemed like it would fit.

"Here, you could wear a scarf too! Hide your stone hair."

"What about Jacklo?" Risa asked. "He still won't be able to fly until the glue finishes hardening."

"Ooh, I have an idea! Mayka can carry him in a basket. If you cover him with a cloth, everyone will think you're carrying food from the market." She clapped her hands together. "It's perfect! If you're disguised, you'll be able to go anywhere you want, including the front gate of the city whenever you're ready to go, even if that stonemason or any of the city guards are looking for you." She pawed through her belongings until she found a basket, then held it up proudly.

It was more than just an idea; it was a *good* idea. "Thank

you." Mayka impulsively hugged Ilery. She hadn't hugged a flesh person since Father, but it felt right.

At dawn, she'd free Kisonan and the other stone creatures, and then while the gate was still wide open, they'd leave Skye and never return.

Chapter
Twenty

Mayka watched dawn rise over the city. Lemon yellow licked the spires and towers until they gleamed. It truly was a beautiful city. She wished their adventure here could have gone differently. If Master Siorn hadn't invented his mark, if Jacklo hadn't fallen and broken his wing . . .

"How are your wings?" she asked Jacklo.

He stretched out his wings and twisted his head to see them. "All better."

"No flying yet." Risa pecked him on the shoulder.

"Hey! Don't do that!" Skipping sideways, he folded his wings back against his sides. He shook himself, and his feathers clicked together until they lay flat.

Jacklo's squawk woke Ilery. Rubbing her eyes, she sat up. Her hair had tangled in the night, and half of it was plastered against her cheek. Mayka's hair would never do that, no matter how she lay or how long she lay there. It would always look the same. She wondered what it must be like to have a body that changed all time. You'd wake up wondering how much you'd grown, and whether you'd function the same way that you did the day before. *How strange*, she thought.

"It's time for me to be going," Mayka said.

"Oh." Ilery sounded sad. "Will I see you again?"

"I don't know," Mayka said honestly. "I hope so. You could come visit me someday." She pointed in the direction of her mountain. "Climb the highest mountain, and when you get to the cliff with the waterfall, call to Jacklo and Risa, and they'll guide you the rest of the way. I'll ask them to fly out once a day to look for you. Jacklo, Risa, will you do that?"

"Of course," Jacklo said.

"If we make it home," Risa said.

"Don't be such a pessimist," Jacklo told her. "Mayka will get us home. She got us away from that stonemason, didn't she?"

"We haven't left the city yet," Risa pointed out. "And she's planning to go back."

"You don't need to come," Mayka told the birds. She could do this alone. She was the one who'd made the promise to the griffin.

Swinging her legs out of bed, Ilery stepped into a pair of slippers and dragged her fingers through her nestlike hair. "You can all stay here. You'll be safe with me."

"We stick together," Jacklo said. "We're family. That's what we do."

"And I'm not going to be left behind!" Si-Si piped up.

"Ilery has a point," Mayka said. "You will be safer if you stay here with her. Si-Si, you've already done so much to help us escape. And, Jacklo, you might want to lie low until you can fly."

Raising his wings up, Jacklo stood taller. "I can fly now!"

"No risking it," Risa insisted. "You might fall again."

In a small voice, Jacklo said, "I didn't like falling."

"How *did* you fall?" Mayka asked. "It's not like you." He hadn't told the story of his accident. She'd assumed he'd crashed into something — got distracted and flew into a wall. Or tried to break through a window — hadn't Master Siorn said Jacklo had been trying to enter someone's house? She wondered if she could trust anything Master Siorn said.

"It happened fast. I was flying along, trying to see through windows, when something hard hit me. I heard a crack, and suddenly couldn't control my wing." He studied it sadly. "I didn't see what it was. It's not much of a story, I know."

"Something hit you? Something thrown?" Mayka thought of the stone otters. Master Siorn could have ordered them to throw rocks at all intruders, even aerial ones. Under the control of his mark, they wouldn't have been able to resist. They even seemed to like throwing things. She shuddered. No one should be forced to hurt another. "Like a rock?" That would have been enough to damage him, and it would also explain where he fell.

"Maybe. Probably?" He shuddered.

"You'd think it would have taught you caution," Risa said.

Mayka smiled at Jacklo. "It's okay. I like you just the way you are." It was good to see him acting like himself, not worshiping Master Siorn.

"Can he learn caution?" Ilery asked. "I thought stone couldn't change."

Mayka used to think that too. "I already have." She'd left home — that was something she'd never expected to do. Since she'd come to this city, she'd learned how to lie, she'd learned how to sneak, she'd learned how to carve, and she'd learned how to be brave. All of that was new. "We should go, before I lose my nerve."

Crossing to a trunk, Ilery picked out a blue dress dotted with stars. She also chose a pair of black shoes and a yellow scarf.

With Ilery's help, Mayka dressed. It felt strange to have fabric encasing her. For her whole life, her clothes had been stone, but now layered over the stone was this cotton. She touched it and then looked at herself in the mirror. Already she looked transformed.

"You look like flesh," Si-Si said.

"Good," Mayka said. It was funny that simple clothes could change what others saw as her story. She'd become someone else with a different past and future. She wondered if clothes were a way for flesh people to wear a kind of mark. These clothes, for instance, marked her as a girl like Ilery, from a farm in the valley.

Ilery tied the scarf around her hair. "This is the style I wear mine in back home." She looked at Mayka in the mirror, standing next to her. "We could pass for sisters."

"I'd like you for a sister," Mayka said.

Ilery beamed. "I'd like that too. Did you really mean what you said? That I can visit you someday?"

"Yes, absolutely. I'll miss you." And she meant it.

"It might not be for a long time," Ilery said, her smile fading. "I'll live with my parents until I'm grown. You might not even recognize me."

"Then wear a scarf around your hair, tied like this." She waved at the scarf that Ilery had knotted around her stone hair. "I'll know you that way."

Ilery's smile came back, as bright as the rising sun.

Sitting on the edge of the bed, Mayka slid her bare stone feet into shoes for the first time. She giggled. It felt so strange! She wiggled her toes, and they hit against the top of the shoe. "You wear these all the time?"

"Otherwise we'd cut our feet."

Standing, Mayka practiced walking across the room. It would feel strange to run in them, but if she were running, that would mean something had gone wrong, and she could just kick them off.

Ilery fetched the basket, and Mayka laid Jacklo in it. Cooing at him, Ilery tucked him in with another scarf so he wouldn't be seen. She put an apple on top to further disguise him and then turned to Si-Si. "I don't know how to disguise you."

Si-Si folded her wings. "Don't worry. No one ever notices me anyway."

Ilery laughed. "You're a firestone dragon! Everyone will notice you! You're the reason I talked to Mayka in the first place, you know — I thought any girl who'd befriend a dragon had to be worth knowing."

"Really? But my keepers —"

"Didn't deserve you," Mayka finished for her. "You are extraordinary, Si-Si. You chose to help us. You are brave and selfless, even though your story doesn't say whether you are or aren't. You *chose* to be who you are."

"Also, you're really bright red and orange, so you can't come with us," Risa said. "Not to the Festival Square, and not to the city gates. You'll give us away."

"But I . . ." Si-Si blinked, and Mayka thought if the little dragon weren't stone, she would be crying. "I want to come with you! I want to keep being . . . me. This new me. And you . . . help me be that me."

Mayka and Ilery looked at each other. "I'd give her a dress, but I don't think that would fool anyone," Ilery said, and both of them grinned at the image of the little dragon in a dress. "I didn't pack any dragon disguises."

Jacklo poked his beak out of the basket. "Can't she just hide like me?"

Risa snorted. "She won't fit, silly."

Ilery brightened and then rummaged through her trunk again. She produced a pack with two shoulder straps. "You could carry her in this! I think it's large enough. But I don't know how heavy she is."

"Very," Mayka said, and then she smiled again. "But I'm as strong as stone." She took the pack and opened it. Si-Si climbed in and curled up with her wings around her. Bracing herself, Mayka lifted the pack onto her shoulders, and Si-Si made a chirping-chime sound as she bounced on Mayka's back. "Are you all right in there?"

"Yes." Her voice was muffled. "Let me know when you need me to come out and be brave."

Mayka smiled. "I will." She checked her costume one more time. "I might not be able to return any of this," she said to Ilery.

"Give it back when I visit," Ilery said.

Mayka hugged her. "Thank you for everything."

"Good luck," Ilery said, hugging her back.

Risa flew out the window toward the roofs, and Mayka left the room and then the inn. The badger at the front desk glanced at her with a squinting frown, and Mayka took that to be a good sign — he didn't recognize her. Stone creatures never wore cotton clothes.

Carrying Si-Si and Jacklo, she walked through the streets, past the mural, toward the Festival Square. Before she reached it, she heard the sounds: voices shouting orders, hammers hitting wood, chisels on stone.

The square was even more crowded than it had been before — the festival was tomorrow. Jugglers and acrobats were practicing. Dancers twirled one another in complicated steps, their skirts flowing around them as they spun and tossed ribbons into the air. Musicians, all playing at the same time, rehearsed. Food vendors were setting up carts and opening colorful umbrellas. She weaved her way toward Master Siorn's stage and hoped that Risa was keeping an eye out. If Master Siorn was there, then Mayka could blend in with the crowd and wait until Garit was alone.

But luck was with them: Master Siorn wasn't there.

Neither was Garit, though.

On his stage, she saw the pedestals she and Garit had made, decorated with wreaths of stone flowers — the flowers weren't alive, but they were beautiful, with petals carved from stones and jewels of every color of the rainbow. It looked ready.

He has to come!

Other workers and apprentices were at their stages, adding final details. One stonemason had shaped his entire stage like a clamshell, with seaweed made from green malachite and pearls shaped from alabaster. Another had etched geometric patterns in such fine detail that the lines seemed to spin as Mayka looked at them. A different stage was drenched in diamonds and rubies and guarded by two stone wolves who had emeralds for eyes. Yet another was bare, except for a perfectly formed stone sphere in the center, a marvel in its perfection.

Where is he?

Poking his beak out of the basket, Jacklo said, "I see him!"

"Shhh," Mayka said.

Through the crowd, she saw Garit squeezing his way to the stage, his arms full of firewood. Climbing up onto the platform, he piled the wood near the pedestals.

Slipping between two workers who were carrying armfuls of flowers, Mayka approached him as he climbed off the stage. "Hi, Garit. It's me."

He startled and then peered at her. "Mayka?"

"Did you get in trouble?"

"I'm fine. He was furious, but . . . I'm fine. You shouldn't have come back! I thought you'd be miles away by now."

"I can't leave, knowing what Master Siorn plans. I have to at least try to erase the mark from Kisonan and the others."

Garit shook his head. "I can't help you. Master Siorn will be even more furious! Look, I agree with you — what he's done and what he plans to do isn't right. I hate that I ever trusted him, and if I could leave my apprenticeship, I would be gone in a heartbeat. But I'm as bound to him as the stone creatures he's enslaved. I can't disappoint my family by acting against the man who is giving me a future."

"We'll keep you blameless," Mayka said. "Take me into the Stone Quarter, and then bring Master Siorn back here. Stay with him the entire time. That way, he can't blame you, because you'll have been with him."

"That's brilliant," Garit said.

"Thank you."

She waited while he looked at her.

"So you'll help us?" Jacklo chirped from within the basket.

Garit jumped. "Um, yeah."

"You're about to be heroic," Si-Si said from within the bag. "You should say yes with more conviction."

"Yes, I'll help you."

So many people and stone creatures were at the entrance to the Stone Quarter that there was a line that wound around the corner. Keeping her head down, Mayka held her basket tight to her chest as they shuffled forward in the line until they reached the guard. "Apprentice Garit," Garit said. "This is Apprentice . . . Bird. She's with me."

It wasn't the same guard as before, Mayka was relieved to see. This man had tufts of hair on his head, as if he'd torn out other clumps. He looked overwhelmed by the flood of people coming in and out through his gate. "Yes, yes, move along. Keep it moving."

In the Stone Quarter itself, there was chaos everywhere as stonemasons and their workers rushed to prepare. Mayka slipped closer to one of the houses, hoping to blend in with the various apprentices, while Garit went to persuade Master Siorn to join him on the festival stage.

Hidden in the crowd, Mayka watched as a stonemason tried to push a stone ox onto a cart. The ox didn't budge. Instead it stood still, watching a butterfly that flitted over a flowering bush. The woman looped a rope around the ox's neck and pulled, but it didn't work. She called over three helpers, and they all pulled.

The ox swung his head over lazily to look at them, then returned to studying the butterfly. At last, the stonemason called to the workers to stop. She asked for something from one of them — Mayka was too far away to see what — but the worker produced a cloth, which the woman then wrapped around the ox's eyes.

The ox walked docilely onto the cart.

Would these people recognize that the obedience mark was evil?

Or would they just see that it made their work easier?

I have to stop Master Siorn, she thought.

If she didn't, every stone creature here — every stone creature everywhere — would be in danger. She watched Master

Siorn's house anxiously, hoping he'd come out soon. If Garit couldn't distract him . . . If she couldn't change the marks . . .

At last Mayka heard a tweet overhead as a gray bird flew low — a signal from Risa. Mayka stepped behind a cart and watched through the slats as Master Siorn and Garit strode away toward the exit of the Stone Quarter.

She darted across the street and danced over the stones, ducking beneath the otters' rocks. "Kisonan," she called through the door, "we came back."

The rock rolled open, and the griffin filled the doorway. "You took a great risk in returning," Kisonan said, in a tone that implied he didn't approve.

"I made you a promise."

He snorted, and she expected him to send her away or at least argue. But he didn't. "There is limited time. You must begin."

She nodded and hurried to the workroom. *I hope I can do this.* So far, she'd carved only Jacklo. She wasn't sure she could carve the griffin the same way, since their stories were different. *But I have to try.*

She set down the basket with Jacklo and then lowered the pack with Si-Si to the ground. The little dragon emerged. "Hello again," she said.

Kisonan humphed. "You *all* took a great risk."

Mayka found the tools she'd need. The griffin stood still, his chest out and his wings displayed. She studied his marks.

This . . . looked possible. "If I change the left curve . . ." It should be a much simpler alteration than she'd had to do on Jacklo, primarily due to the size and placement of the mark.

The griffin's story said he was noble. It retold a tale of a long-ago prince who had become lost. Beset by wolves, with winter snows on their way, the little boy should have died, but a wild creature — part lion and part eagle — defended and protected him. *Kisonan is loyal, brave, and strong,* the story read. *He defends his prince.* And then: *He obeys Master Siorn.* Mayka understood why Kisonan had felt so offended. It wasn't just that the obedience mark took away free will, but he was already loyal — to have that questioned must have hurt his pride.

"Carve quickly," Kisonan said. "There are others who wish for your services."

Glancing at the workroom door, she saw several stone creatures had crowded inside.

"Master Siorn gave no order against this," Kisonan said smugly.

She smiled. "Si-Si, can you tell them that I'll help them all? And Risa, can you please fly outside and watch for Master Siorn? I'll carve as fast as I can."

And then she got to work.

Taking up her chisel, she reshaped the curve that formed the stonemason's name and added several more strokes so that it now read *He obeys his conscience.*

The next creature, an otter, rushed in and jumped onto

the workbench. "Me next!" He lifted one arm to show his mark, neatly tucked beneath it. Changing this one would be a little trickier because of the ripples in the stone that served as his fur.

"Your story says you were born playing and laughing." She touched the marks. "You're an acrobat of the river who once made the fish laugh so hard that they fell onto the shore and fed a family of flesh-and-fur otters for an entire winter. You came to land with your family to —" And here the stonemason had written his obedience mark. She set about changing it from "obey" to "lead" and linked it to the mark for laugh, obscuring the stonemason's name. "To lead them in laughter," she finished.

Grinning hugely, he hugged her, and the next otter scurried up, replacing him on the workbench.

"Watch for Master Siorn's return," the griffin instructed the second otter as Mayka finished her. "We will not have forever." The two completed otters scampered away to stand guard as Mayka sank herself into her work on the rest of the creatures.

She wasn't a master carver, or even an apprentice, but she could make the simple lines that were required to alter the words. The more marks she did, the better she got at carving them.

On one of the lizards who guarded the gate and had a story that spoke of stubbornness, she changed the mark to "obeys his own wishes." On the other, whose story told of loyalty, she made it "obeys his own heart." She wanted to give each creature its own unique tale, so that its revised story would mesh with all its old stories.

"Speed, little storyteller," Kisonan said. "You must finish."

On one mishmash creature, after a string of marks that talked of his love of silence, she made the obedience mark a part of his past but not his future. On another, she read about his love of the kitchen and preparing food — on him, there was enough room to add the mark for choosing so she wrote he could choose to obey or not. He could follow his love of cooking, or find another passion if he wanted.

The workroom was hazy with stone dust that floated in the air, and the sound of chisel on stone filled her ears. She grew used to the feel of the hammer and the way the impact shook her arm.

The griffin paced back and forth in the workroom, while the others watched either her or the door.

At last the final stone creature was done.

Her fingers ached, as if she'd been battering them against a wall. "You're all invited to come with us to the mountains — my family would welcome you. Or you can go wherever you want in the valley, or even beyond the valley. But we need to leave now, before Master Siorn returns. We'll tell the guard that we're all going to the Festival Square, and then we'll head for the gate to the city."

"We are not leaving," Kisonan said. "Master Siorn cannot be permitted to carve the obedience mark on any other creature, and he cannot be permitted to share his invention with any other stonemason. We must stop this abomination from spreading."

The two otters who weren't already on guard bobbed their heads in unison.

I know he's right, Mayka thought. It wasn't enough just to free these creatures. Master Siorn could simply carve the mark onto a new creature and show it at the Stone Festival. And if other flesh people learned that the mark worked, all stone creatures throughout the valley would be in danger. "But how do we stop him?"

Kisonan opened his beak and shut it. The other creatures whispered to one another. A few whimpered, and the octopus coiled his tentacles as if trying to curl into a ball.

Sticking his head out of the basket, Jacklo piped up. "Maybe we could trick him?"

All of them looked at him.

Before he could explain, an otter raced into the workroom. "He's coming back!"

Chapter
Twenty-One

The griffin turned to Jacklo. "Trick him how?"

"Make everyone think it didn't work," Jacklo said. "The obedience mark. He's going to demonstrate it at the festival, right? In front of everyone? Make them all think it failed. Make him look foolish. Then no one will believe him, and no one will believe the mark could ever work."

Everyone gawked at the bird.

"Jacklo, that's a great idea!" Mayka said.

Kisonan nodded. "Indeed, if we —"

Squawking three short chirps and one long, Risa swooped through the door. "Why are you still here? Get out, get out! He comes! He's on the path! In seconds, he'll be inside."

"Is there a back door?" Mayka asked.

"There is not," Kisonan said.

"We'll hide you," one of the mishmash creatures said. They scurried around her, and Mayka scooped up Jacklo in the basket and hurried with them. Si-Si hurried alongside her. She heard Kisonan shuffle toward the front door to greet Master Siorn, and she ran down the hall.

"Here, here, here," the creatures whispered as they shoved her into the pantry. Clutching the basket with Jacklo, she wedged herself between a barrel of potatoes and a stack of plates, and Si-Si squeezed in with her. She was sure Risa would have the sense to hide herself.

They listened as Master Siorn stomped into the house. He shouted for Garit to join him in the private workroom, all the while bemoaning the amount of work that needed to be finished before tomorrow's festival. Then he called for food to be delivered to the workroom and for no other disruptions. "Garit, what are you waiting for, boy? Grab your chisel and carve!"

She heard Garit's voice: "But it's your masterpiece! You want *me* to carve —"

"Yes, yes, you're skilled enough, and I don't have the luxury of complete secrecy anymore. There's no more time! I must be ready to reveal my masterpiece as soon as I've won over the public, so that all can see the glory that an unrestricted stonemason can accomplish. Join me, my boy, and be a part of history!"

"But, Master Siorn —"

"Enough, boy. Come! This is the most important moment of my career, and I will not have the day ruined because I didn't finish in time due to your dithering."

Your day will be ruined anyway, Mayka thought. *We will ruin it.*

She heard a door slam, and then she waited. In a few moments, one of the stone otters sped into the kitchen. "He wants lunch!"

The mishmash creatures sprang into action. Chattering to one another, they stoked the fire, sliced vegetables, and began preparing a soup.

Mayka came out of her hiding place, but stayed close to it in case she had to dive back in. Jacklo poked his head out over the lip of the basket and said, "Hey, you don't have to obey anymore, remember?"

One of the creatures paused, uncertain.

"It's okay," Mayka told them. "Just make lunch. We don't want Master Siorn to get suspicious before the festival begins." But it was a little worrying that they'd leapt so quickly to obey. Was it force of habit, or had she carved them wrong? *Maybe it just takes time for their new stories to sink in*, she thought.

"So what do we do at the festival?" the otter asked. "How do we trick him? We don't even know what he has planned!"

Kisonan appeared in the kitchen doorway and squeezed himself inside. "I do. He intends to use a number of us in his performance, making us perform a variety of tasks that anyone with common sense would balk at."

"Oh no," one of the mishmash creatures moaned.

"What do we do?" another asked.

"Refuse," Mayka said. "Show the audience that the mark doesn't work."

Kisonan nodded. "Wait until the audience is as large as possible, and then reject his orders. He'll be undone. No one will take anything he says seriously. If his humiliation is severe enough, the city council could revoke his stonemason badge. He could be forbidden from ever carving another creature."

The octopus waved his tentacles nervously. "But are you sure it will work?"

"He's trying to tell a story about how he's created an obedience mark," Mayka said. "But we're telling the story about how the mark doesn't work. Once *that* story spreads, no one will believe the obedience mark is real. He'll be the fool of the tale, not the heroic brilliant genius he thinks he is."

"I love it." One of the otters sighed happily.

"Yes," Kisonan said, "this is what we'll do. This time, *we* will shape the story."

Dawn plucked with prying fingers at the kitchen windows. At Master Siorn's command, all the stone creatures assembled in the front yard, while Mayka stayed behind, hidden with Jacklo in the kitchen — they'd slip out once everyone was gone.

"Do you think it will work?" Jacklo asked, after they were alone.

Yes. Maybe. "He's trying to sell a story to the crowd," Mayka said. "We're going to change the story halfway through. It will work." *I hope. If I carved them well enough.*

"They've gone now," Si-Si reported.

Mayka crept out of the pantry and hurried through the empty house. She took a hammer and chisel with her, tucking them into the pockets of Ilery's dress.

"Into the pack and basket," she told Jacklo and Si-Si. "Let's go."

Outside, carrying her friends, she joined the crowd surging from the Stone Quarter to the Festival Square. People and stone creatures were everywhere, decked out in their finery. Flesh people wore bright colors and flowery hats, and stone creatures wore ribbons around their necks and had pompoms dangling from their stone ears. Mayka lost herself in the crowd, and for a moment, she forgot why she was there. She'd never been to a festival of any kind before. She felt as if she'd plunged into sparkles. Everywhere, color. Every moment, music and laughter. The joy swept away all worries.

Almost.

All these flesh people . . . If they knew about the mark, what would they think? What would they do? *If we fail, will the mountain be far enough to be safe?*

Throughout the Festival Square, musicians played, and dancers and acrobats performed. Vendors sold food from carts, and flesh people lined up to buy it. Flesh-and-feathers birds scavenged near them, scooping up treats that people had dropped, and Mayka thought she saw Risa hidden among them.

At last she found her way to the festival stages and stood with the crowd to watch.

On one stage was a stonemason who claimed she'd created the most delicate and exquisite carvings ever imagined. As she unveiled her creations, the crowd gasped, and Mayka gasped too. In the center of the stage was a fountain in which she'd carved water out of stone. It was motionless, frozen, but every droplet, carved of translucent blue stone, was linked to another in a detailed chain. Stone fish leapt through the water — they were made of orange and milky white stone.

On a second stage was a stonemason with a collection of stone cats. They were draped around his stage, and the audience laughed as the cats refused to come when he called, exactly like flesh-and-fur cats, and he bowed after they refused, showing it was all a part of the act.

Mayka wished they'd found one of these stonemasons instead. *But then we wouldn't have known to stop Master Siorn. And he* must *be stopped.* She inched closer through the crowd to Master Siorn's stage. She caught a glimpse of Garit scurrying back and forth, and she saw the otters clustered by the stairs, hugging one another. Standing on her tiptoes, she tried to get a better view.

A vendor walked past her and shoved a bag of roasted

corn kernels under her nose. "Roast corn! Get your fresh roast corn!"

"No, thank you." She scooted away. At least her disguise was holding.

"What's happening?" Jacklo asked, his voice muffled from his basket.

"Nothing yet," Mayka said.

"I want to see! Let me fly up with Risa!"

"I don't want to risk you breaking again." He *should* be healed by now — it had been another day, but she had enough to worry about with Kisonan and the other creatures.

Muttering, he settled back down.

"What was that?" she asked him, but before he could reply, she saw Master Siorn mounting the steps up onto the platform. "Never mind. Shhh!"

He was dressed in jewels: sewn onto his robes, strung onto necklaces, and circling his head. His ridiculous hair was laced with them. Garnets, rubies, amethysts. He looked as if he'd leapt into a vat of gems. Standing in the center of his stage, the stonemason spread his arms wide.

"Hello and welcome!" he boomed. "I am Master Siorn, stonemason extraordinaire!"

Most of the audience ignored him. They continued chatting, eating, and watching dancers, acrobats, and whatever shiny event caught their eye. One lone man on a stage wasn't enough to attract their attention, even with all his sparkle.

"Today you will see miracles! Miracles that will change life as you know it. Have you ever had an ox who refused to plow? Have you ever wondered if you could trust your child's stone nanny? Have your home and your loved ones ever been at risk because of an inattentive guard?" A few people nodded along with him. "What if your stone creature were utterly devoted to your family? What if you could ensure it obeyed your every command?"

Mayka heard people muttering: "Who's that?" "Some crackpot." "Master Sorb?" "No, that's not it. What did he say his name was? Siorn?" "Hey, what are those? Eh, nothing new. Look over there."

His mishmash creatures waddled onto the stage.

"These carvings aren't new, you say?" Master Siorn said. "True! But what they do *is* new. I present to you a new mark, my own invention, inspired by legend: the obedience mark!"

That caught the crowd's attention.

Mayka felt Si-Si peek over her shoulder, half hidden by Ilery's scarf.

"Now what's happening?" Jacklo asked.

"It's beginning," Mayka said.

Chapter
Twenty-Two

Yes, it's true!" Master Siorn said. "I have perfected the long-sought-after obedience mark! It will tame all your stone friends!"

"Friends?" Jacklo muttered. "He doesn't know what that word means."

"Shush," Mayka said. "Baskets don't talk."

In a booming voice, Master Siorn introduced his mishmash creatures as they stood on the pedestals. "When I first showed you these carvings at a Stone Festival, you called them 'undesirable.' I challenge you to find them undesirable now, when they obey my every command! Garit, the fire."

Garit hurried onto the stage, to the pile of wood he'd dumped there, and he struck a piece of metal against the arm of the nearest stone creature. The flame started. Soon it was roaring.

"Stand in it," Master Siorn ordered his creatures.

The nearby crowd fell silent — his fire had caught the attention of the men and women who were closest. A few of them sat on the benches facing his stage. Others continued to mill through the square, their attention fixed on other stages or on the food vendor carts.

Mayka didn't look anywhere but at the stage.

Stone creatures wouldn't burn. It wouldn't hurt. But they'd feel the heat. One of them — the lizard with the hedgehog's body — hopped into the middle of the fire, turned around, and did a little dance.

Oh no, they're not free! she thought.

Her story hadn't worked. She hadn't carved the marks correctly, and no one had changed.

Or maybe it had worked, and the creature had chosen to go into the fire. She remembered how they'd played catch with the kitchen fire. Maybe they were just waiting for the audience to get bigger.

Either way, the audience was beginning to believe Master Siorn. All around Mayka, a crowd was forming as the dancing lizard in the middle of the fire caught their eyes. "What's going on?" "He claims he invented the mark." "Obedience mark, he said." "But that's just a legend!"

The other mishmash creatures joined the lizard in playing with the fire. They tossed embers back and forth, giggling and laughing. The one with the deer's head caught a burning stick on his antlers and swung his neck so it spun around.

"That doesn't prove anything," one woman sniffed. "Mine play in the hearth all the time. They think fire tickles. What I'd like to see is a way to keep them *out* of the fire. They track ash all over the house."

Master Siorn was done with the fire trick. He dismissed the mishmash creatures from the stage, and they hesitated — but their hesitation wasn't dramatic enough for the crowd to notice, and even Mayka wasn't sure if she'd imagined it or not.

Next, Master Siorn summoned the octopus, and it mounted the platform using four of its tentacles, then rose up on them until its face was level with the stonemason's.

"Behold, my octopus, carved in homage to the glorious and mysterious sea creatures!"

The audience began to chatter again — they'd seen the octopus last year. No one had been interested then; no one was interested now. Master Siorn and his oddities were out of vogue and had been since the days of the Stone War. The crowd began to drift, pulled toward the other stonemasons' stages.

"Ah, I sense you are not impressed yet. What would impress you? How about height? Climb!" Master Siorn ordered, and the octopus slithered off the stage and began to climb up the side of the building. "Higher!"

This caught people's attention again.

She heard snippets around her: "Why is that octopus

climbing?" "What's he trying to prove?" "Obedience mark." "But that's impossible!"

"Ah, and how about danger? What would you say when my mark proves stronger than the basic instinct to survive?" Master Siorn cupped his hands around his mouth to amplify his voice and shouted, "Jump!"

The audience gasped. "He can't!" "That's barbaric!" "That poor creature, he'll be destroyed!"

The octopus was three stories up.

If it jumped, it would shatter. Mayka clutched Jacklo's basket so hard that the handle crunched in her grip. *Don't do it. Resist.*

It didn't jump.

The audience murmured. There were few uncomfortable laughs.

Master Siorn smiled at the audience, as if this were all part of the show. "See, he responds only to *my* commands. If he can't hear me, he can't respond." He seemed unfazed by the creature's disobedience, and Mayka wondered if the octopus really couldn't hear him. If he had been closer, would he have jumped? She thought of how the creatures had hurried to prepare his lunch and wished she could have tested whether their new stories worked. She'd thought she'd carved them carefully enough, but what if she hadn't? What if she had only succeeded with Jacklo because she knew his story so well?

"But wait until you see what comes next!"

A man near Mayka muttered, "*I'm* not waiting around for this nonsense. He's endangering his own stone creatures. It's cruel, not to mention unprofessional."

"Stay," a woman said. "I want to see what he's going to do."

The otters were next.

They climbed up onto the pedestals.

Tossing them apple-size stones, Siorn instructed them to juggle, which they happily did, chucking the rocks higher and higher into the air. And then he called out to the audience, "What would you like to see them do? What would startle you? Shock you?" He pointed to one of the stone otters, the largest and strongest of them, who stood on the tallest pedestal. "Stand still, and do not move. No matter what happens: do not move."

The otter stiffened, standing straight.

"Throw your stones at him," Master Siorn instructed the other otters.

Please resist him, Mayka thought. The otters had thrown a stone at Jacklo, breaking his wing, while they had the mark. Now that they were free, they could make the audience think the mark wasn't real. *If* they were free. She watched the faces on the crowd. *Let this work!*

The crowd began to rumble: "They can't do that!" "He'll be hurt!" "He'll never stand there." "They'll never throw it." "But if they do . . . If it works . . ."

Each of the otters cradled a stone. A few tossed theirs from paw to paw, testing its weight. The large otter didn't move. He stared at the other otters.

Mayka didn't move either. Couldn't move. Could only stare at the faces of the flesh-and-blood men and women around her. The shock in their expressions was clear, but she couldn't tell if they were horrified or fascinated. Or both.

"Break him," Master Siorn ordered.

As one, the otters turned. And they threw their rocks at Master Siorn's feet. Yelping, he jumped backwards as the rocks crashed onto the stage and then harmlessly rolled off.

The crowd laughed.

Mayka felt like cheering.

From that moment, the demonstration unraveled.

"Kisonan! Kisonan, take the stage," the stonemason shouted, over the jeers and laughter of the crowd. As majestic as always, the griffin climbed onto the stage. The crowd fell silent as the legendary creature halted in front of the man who had carved him and given him life. "Kisonan, I order you to obey me: break the otter."

Kisonan studied the stonemason, then the otters. The crowd watched, listening, whispering. And then the griffin spoke.

"With all due respect, Master Siorn, I will not. If you would like to make a reasonable request, I would be delighted to fulfill it, but I will not harm any of my fellow creatures, or anyone in the audience. Nor will I cause harm or unnecessary discomfort to myself. I am a thinking, feeling being, and I would thank you to remember that, as I continue to serve you."

His voice reverberated across the square.

And Master Siorn now had one thing he had wanted: the attention of everyone in the Festival Square, including all the other stonemasons. As Kisonan finished his speech, the entire audience burst into talk and laughter.

Master Siorn's face flushed a purply red. He began to shout at his creatures. "No! You can't! You *must* obey me!"

Lunging forward, he grabbed the closest otter. He yanked the creature's arm up and examined the mark. "Someone has changed this! Who has done this? Garit?"

Garit shrank back. "When? I was with you the whole time! I couldn't have done it!"

"Someone has sneaked into my home and —"

"Get off the stage!" someone shouted. The cry was echoed by others: "Liar!" "Fool!" "Crackpot!"

"You don't understand!" Master Siorn said. "I've been tricked!"

One of the stonemasons on a nearby stage called, "Disbar him!" It was Master Zillon, Mayka recognized, the one who specialized in doors. "Take his credentials! No stonemason lies about his marks. And no stonemason asks his stone creatures to hurt one another. Your behavior is unprofessional and reprehensible."

And the other stonemasons joined in: "He's not one of us!" "You disgrace us!" "Delusional, to believe he could create an obedience mark." "We don't need a crackpot in our ranks!"

"No! I have done it!" Master Siorn cried. "Listen to me! Let me prove it! I have been set up — arrest my creatures and my apprentice, force them to tell the truth, and you'll see!"

The crowd shouted louder. "Remove him!"

And "Imagine, blaming his apprentice on top of it! Poor boy!"

Master Siorn's eyes swept over the crowd. "No! No, no, you don't understand!" And his gaze fixed on Mayka. She froze, like a rabbit spotted by a hawk. She saw his jaw drop, and then his face twisted. "Her! It was her! She did it, somehow! She —"

But he was drowned out by the crowd. Faced with taunts and shouts and boos, Master Siorn retreated from the stage. Mayka saw the otters and the griffin cheer, and she felt a smile on her own face as well.

"We did it," she whispered to Jacklo and Si-Si.

"Yay!" Jacklo said in a half shout, half whisper. He poked his beak out from under the scarf. "Where is he? I want to see!"

Tucking the scarf back around Jacklo, Mayka looked up again. The crowd was shifting around her, repositioning to watch a different stonemason on another stage, and she couldn't see Master Siorn's stage. Elbowing as she went, Mayka pushed through, trying to see what was happening with her friends.

At last, she squeezed through, bursting out in front of the

stage. Garit, Kisonan, the otters, and the others were there, cheering and hugging one another. One of the otters was dancing.

"Garit, where's Master Siorn?" Mayka asked.

"So embarrassed that he ran away!" he said, grinning. "Do you know what this means? No one — not the other stonemasons, not my family — will blame me for leaving him!"

"That's wonderful, Garit!" Mayka said.

Si-Si jumped out of the backpack onto the stage and danced in a circle around Garit. Laughing, Garit danced with her. "It *is* wonderful!" he said. "There's talk of the stonemasons evicting him from the guild for lying about the mark! They might do it too. He might be kicked out of the Stone Quarter, his chisels confiscated, for disgracing his colleagues with his behavior. He won't ever hurt another stone creature like Ava again."

One of the otters hugged Mayka. The others started dancing with Si-Si and then dancing around the octopus as he joined them on the stage. She rejoiced with them for a moment, then noticed one of the stone creatures wasn't celebrating: the griffin, Kisonan. Still as a statue, he was frowning at the empty pedestals. She crossed to him, and he spoke before she could ask him what was wrong. "We did not convince *him* that the mark failed. He knows we are responsible."

The otters stopped dancing and exchanged glances.

He was right — and Master Siorn had spotted her in the

crowd. She should have thought about what would happen *after* the demonstration. She had to get them all safely away before he returned.

"You can come with me," Mayka said to them. "Or you can go wherever you want. Explore the world. Find another city. Either way, you should leave."

"Leave Skye?" The octopus fretted, crossing and uncrossing his tentacles. Even though she'd never seen a face like the octopus's, Mayka could read the worry on it.

"She's right," Garit said. "The city council might remove his badge, but he'll blame you and try to make your lives miserable. And mine."

"You're welcome to come too," Mayka told him. "Or you could find another stonemason to apprentice yourself to. Given what happened today, I'm sure any number of stonemasons will be sympathetic and want to help you start fresh."

Kisonan warned, "It may not be so easy to escape him —"

The ground shook, as if in a slight earthquake. Mayka felt it through the stones on the street. The others felt it as well. The mishmash creatures clutched one another.

"Did anyone see where Master Siorn went?" Kisonan asked.

Another tremor.

"What *is* that?" asked an otter.

"Bad," Jacklo said. He cowered in the basket.

Another tremor, harder, and a few people cried out — the

shaking was now strong enough for flesh and blood to feel. Some scooped up their children.

Another shake.

Then another.

Steady, like the footsteps of a giant.

He couldn't have —

"Please tell me you changed the mark on the monster too," Garit whispered.

Mayka shook her head. She hadn't thought about him, only the creatures who had lined up in the workroom. He'd still been inert when she'd seen him. "You don't think he —"

Risa winged down from the roof, calling her alarm: three short chirps and one long. "Mayka! He's brought the giant! Run!" She flew over the tops of the heads of the audience.

Another stomp.

One more stomp, and the stone monster was visible above the tops of the houses. It had been coiled within the back workroom, but now it was stretched to its full size, and it was massive. The features on its face were like a bull's, but its mouth was filled with stone teeth, each as sharp as a spear. It had human-like arms that were thick with rock muscles, and its lion-like body was carved with diamond-shaped patterns that resembled scales.

It roared, and the crowd screamed.

Another roar, and people scattered. Mayka and Garit and

the others were pushed and swept along with the crowd as they tried to flee the square.

"Look, he's riding it!" Rearing onto her hind feet, Si-Si pointed. Her wings flapped, balancing her for a moment, but then she wobbled and dropped back down.

Up near the giant's neck, Master Siorn clung to the monster's shoulder. He was shouting, but Mayka couldn't hear him over the screams of the crowd.

"He is trying to prove he can control the monster," Kisonan predicted. "If he succeeds, it will negate all we have done. Watch — he will try to show how he can tame him!"

But the monster placed Master Siorn on the top of a building, and then with a roar, it waded into the Festival Square. Every step was like a thunderclap, shaking the ground.

"He doesn't look tame to me," Si-Si squawked. "He looks angry."

"Perhaps I was mistaken," Kisonan said slowly. Then he turned to them and added urgently, "I believe we should flee. *Now*."

All around them, everyone was panicking. Flesh and stone were screaming as they fled. Mayka and the others tried to run too. But there were so many people fleeing in so many different directions that speed was impossible. The monster's shadow stretched over several streets. "How is it so huge?" Mayka asked.

"Multiple stones, combined," Garit said, beside her, panting. "They're shot through with iron rods, connecting them all."

Looking back, she saw he was right — it had joints, like a puppet.

From the top of the building, Master Siorn was continuing to shout at his monstrous puppet, and it swung its massive head around, as if looking for prey. *It's after us!* Mayka thought. Kicking off her shoes, she ran faster.

The otters were weaving in and out between the feet of the fleeing people around them, and the mishmash creatures were barreling through the crowd ahead of them. Risa was flying overhead, and the octopus loped beside them. *We're too conspicuous,* she thought. Garit was visible, in his apprentice robes, and —

The monster spotted Kisonan first.

With a roar, it swiped at the griffin, but Kisonan was faster. "Climb on," Kisonan ordered Mayka and Garit. "He wants you most of all."

Mayka scrambled on. "Hurry!"

Garit climbed up behind her, and Kisonan sprang forward. He raced through the crowd, with his wings knocking aside people. The other creatures — Si-Si, the otters, the lizards, the mishmash creatures, and the octopus — scattered.

The monster stomped through a stage, knocking over the nearby stands. Wood fell and broke. Rocks tumbled into the street.

Ahead, Mayka heard trumpets blaring. "Make way for the guards!" voices shouted. "Make way!" People fanned back to allow a troop of humans to march into the square. Rushing forward, the guards began to attack the monster with two-handed hammers and axes.

Garit leaned forward. "Faster!"

Their little group raced out of the square, and the other creatures joined them. Mayka wanted to shout at them to split up and save themselves, but now it was too late. The monster had spotted all of them.

The monster kicked away the guards, and they sprawled against the buildings, knocking over fleeing people and capsizing pedestals. The monster charged forward. Each step slammed into the ground and caused the buildings to sway. Tiles fell off roofs. Chimneys toppled.

They ran, and the monster chased after them, pounding through the streets.

"Find a place to hide!" Jacklo called.

"He's too close!" Garit said. "He'll see!"

"Then we must first lose him with speed," Kisonan said, and ran faster. His wings pumped up and down. He wasn't able to fly, but the wings seemed to propel him forward. With his cat legs, he leapt onto a low roof and then to the next and the next until he was running from building to building over the rooftops. The monster lagged behind, forced to either navigate between the buildings or crash through them.

Soon they had a lead. And in a moment, whipping around a corner, they'd lost him.

Kisonan dropped to the ground with the others and scanned the street for a hiding place. "Over there!" one of the lizards cried, and Kisonan ducked into a shed filled with gardening tools and crouched down, facing the street. Everyone piled in with them.

Mayka recognized where they were — not far from the inn where Ilery was staying. If the monster followed them . . . "We have to get out of the city. Too many can get hurt here."

"Like us!" Jacklo said.

They listened as the monster stomped through the neighborhood. The guards were still chasing him, but to no avail. Every so often the monster would swat them away as if they were nothing more than irritating flies.

"Mayka's right — we have to get out," Si-Si said. "We can't just wait for him to find us."

"He knows we are nearby," Kisonan agreed. "It will not take long before he begins to pull the roofs off houses, in search of us."

"At least people don't think the obedience mark is working," Jacklo said. "That's good, isn't it?"

"Master Siorn has never been so humiliated before," said Kisonan. "We did, perhaps, too well. The worry comes, though, if the guards realize the monster *is* obeying Master Siorn."

"So what do we do?" Mayka asked. "Can we get out of the city?"

"He will see us in the open countryside," Kisonan said with a shake of his eagle head. "I believe Master Siorn wishes to destroy us. He will take drastic measures, as you can tell, to reclaim his reputation. But the worst will come when the monster *stops* hunting us, when Master Siorn's rage cools and he proves to the city, beyond a shadow of a doubt, that he can control the monster. Even if he is punished for the devastation he caused, all will know the obedience mark works."

They fell silent, listening to the monster's destruction in the city beyond. People were still screaming. Rocks were crashing onto the streets. *Calm down and think,* Mayka told herself. *Stone is calm.*

Except nothing about any of this was calm.

Maybe I don't need to be calm, she thought. *Maybe I need to be brave.*

"There's one solution," Mayka said.

All the creatures turned their heads to look at her.

She listened to the crashing and the screaming, and she felt herself flinch with every new crack and thud. "I change the monster's mark."

Chapter
Twenty-Three

That's a terrible idea!" Garit yelped. "It's a giant, rampaging monster! The obedience mark and Master Siorn's command might be the only thing keeping it from crushing the city entirely."

Mayka listened to the monster smashing through the city. *He has a point,* she thought. *Still . . .*

"It doesn't deserve to have the mark any more than any of us do."

"Yes, but I don't deserve to be stomped on," Si-Si said.

Clustering around her, the otters bobbed their heads. One of the mishmash creatures, the half hedgehog, half lizard, had curled into a ball and was rocking back and forth.

"You don't know it will choose destruction," Mayka said.

"It has only one story," Kisonan said. "That is all it *can* choose."

Crash — that could have been a building. *Crash* — or a chunk of a wall. *Crash!* She heard more screams. *He could be crushing people right now,* she thought. *I have to do something!*

"Master Siorn created it to fight and destroy," Kisonan said. "He intended to present it to the city leaders as a guard, to battle our enemies as the Great Defender of Skye. Without the obedience mark, that is all it is. That is all it knows how to do. *That* is its story: violence."

Jacklo piped up from the basket. "So give it more stories!"

"Yes," Mayka said, seizing on the idea. "I'll give it a story that isn't about destruction. Give it choices."

Garit shook his head. "You won't even be able to reach his marks — they're on his neck, near his left shoulder. And even if you do, you won't have time to carve much of anything before he swats you off."

"The boy is right," Kisonan said. "You'll be caught and broken before you finish."

"Then I'll need a story that's quick to carve but open to interpretation . . ."

It was so hard to think while the monster was careening through the city. Every rock that crashed down made her feel as brittle as a flesh-and-blood creature. She was more aware than she'd ever been of the fact that she could be broken, her friends could be shattered, and they could all be gone. *Is this how flesh people feel all the time? How do they do it, face every day knowing they could break?* She tried to take deep, even breaths, as if she needed them. The act of breathing like a flesh person calmed her a little. "Anyone have an idea?"

Mayka glanced at Garit. He was blushing so hard that his neck was red. "Um, well, when Master Siorn showed me the monster yesterday, there was a mark that I *wanted* to add, but he said no. It was simple —"

"What was it?"

He picked a stick off the ground and drew in the dirt. "That's his name, and then I just wanted to put . . ." He added a few additional lines.

"'Monster is awesome,'" she read.

Kisonan sighed. "You are such a child."

Garit squirmed. "I know. It's just . . . he's so enormous and powerful, and I wanted . . . I don't know what I was thinking. Never mind. Bad idea." He kicked at the dust, blurring the mark.

"It might be enough," Mayka said. She took the stick, knelt, and redrew the mark. She studied it. *Yes, it could work. I could use this.*

"Enough to do what?" Jacklo asked.

"Enough to make him more than what Master Siorn thinks he is," Mayka said. "We make our stories our own. It all depends on how the monster chooses to use its tale." Standing, she laid her hand on Garit's shoulder. His flesh felt soft and warm through his shirt, very different from her.

Garit still looked embarrassed, but he nodded as he scuffed his feet on the ground, next to the redrawn mark. He didn't disturb the lines.

"Only question left is how do I reach it? You said the marks are on its neck. The monster isn't going to let me get close enough to climb it, at least not willingly."

"He needs to be distracted," Kisonan said.

One of the otters scurried forward. "We can bite at his feet! It won't hurt him much, but it might help." The other otters bobbed their heads up and down.

The creature with a deer's head said, "I can poke him with my antlers."

"I can squeeze him," the octopus said.

"I can scratch," the hedgehog-lizard said.

"I can peck his eyes," Risa offered.

"We both can," Jacklo piped up.

"But your wing!" Mayka said. "You haven't even tried it yet. What if the strain of launching yourself is too much?"

"Throw me," Jacklo said. "Once I'm airborne, it will be easy."

"Absolutely not," Risa said to Jacklo. "You stay here. I don't want to have to worry about you."

"It's my choice, not yours," Jacklo said. "I am the hero of my own story. And I say I help." He met Mayka and Risa's astonished gazes unwaveringly, first one then the other.

Mayka wondered how his new story had changed him. Or had he always had this strength, and they were so busy thinking of him as silly Jacklo that they hadn't seen it?

"We'll all help," another of the mishmash creatures said, and the rest raised their voices in agreement.

The octopus unraveled his tentacles and rose up on four of them. "Let us help," he said. "He's making a mess of the city. I do *not* like mess."

The griffin surveyed Mayka. "You will not be able to climb quickly enough with your puny human hands and feet," he declared. "You will ride me, and I will take you up to the monster's marks."

"What about me?" Garit asked.

"Go to the flesh-and-blood people," Mayka said. "Tell them we're trying to stop the monster. Keep them from stopping us."

"I don't know if they'll listen to me, but I'll try."

The crashing continued — the monster was still nearby. Mayka peeked out and saw his feet. He was headed toward the Inn District. There was no more time for plans or discussion.

"Now!" Mayka cried. The creatures charged out of the alleyway. Carrying Jacklo, Mayka climbed onto Kisonan and shouted, "Go!"

The griffin ran out of the alley, and Risa flew above them. Behind her, she heard Garit running too. She didn't look back.

Only ahead.

The monster was tearing off roofs — looking for them.

When the first of the stonemason's creatures reached it, it halted and howled. Kisonan stuck to the shadows, and Mayka clung to his back. She had the hammer and chisel she'd taken from the stonemason's house.

We have to stop it, she thought. *I can do this,* she told herself. She'd helped the stonemason's other creatures — her stories had worked. This was the same. Just larger.

Closer, they ran past the guards, who yelled at them to stay back. The monster began to turn toward them. "Ready," Jacklo said. He curled tightly into a ball.

Sitting up straight on Kisonan, she hurled Jacklo as high and as hard as she could. He soared toward the monster's face, then unfurled talons first and slashed at his eyes.

The monster swatted at him, but Jacklo dodged.

Jacklo's doing it! Mayka thought. *He's flying!*

While the monster was distracted with Jacklo, Risa struck, diving for his eyes and pecking. He flailed, swinging at her, and it was Jacklo's turn to strike again. The otters and lizards swarmed over his feet.

Kisonan sprang up. Higher and higher, from rooftop to rooftop. He ran and jumped over alleys and streets, racing toward the monster, along the roofline of the city.

"Now!" Mayka called.

Kisonan leapt onto the monster, landing on his torso.

The monster cried out.

But the birds both pecked at his eyes, the otters and lizards attacked his feet, the mishmash creatures pounded at his ankles, the octopus squeezed his knee, and the monster didn't know where to strike. He flailed wildly, knocking his arms into spires and towers, as Kisonan leapt up from boulder to boulder toward the monster's shoulder.

"He's distracted," the griffin said. "Carve quickly!"

Mayka slid off his back and clung to the monster.

She saw the mark in front of her, large and clear.

Kisonan scrambled across the rough-hewn boulders that made up his torso. Whacking at his own body, the monster tried to hit the griffin. The monster stumbled, crushing the side of a building.

Mayka clung to his shoulder, trying to stay on. How could she carve when she was in danger of falling? Hugging the stone, she inched forward, crawling toward the mark.

One thing at a time, she told herself.

Reach it, then carve it.

The monster bent to swipe at an enemy on the ground, and Mayka was flipped off the rock — only holding on by one hand. A scream ripped out of her. Risa and Jacklo called to her:

"Hang on, Mayka! You can do it!"

Struggling, she pulled herself back on.

The monster swiped at his shoulder, and she fell again, this time under his armpit. She pulled out her chisel and dug it into a crack between the boulders. She used it to pull herself up.

Before her was his story. As Kisonan had said, the monster

had marks that said he'd been made to defend the city. "Defender of Skye," the first marks read. "Strong, fierce, and merciless." And following that was Master Siorn's obedience mark.

Mayka brought the hammer and chisel up to the mark. She knew what she had to carve. She pictured it in her mind.

She didn't have time for fancy swirls. Instead, she added simple lines that changed the mark into past tense so that it read "Monster used to obey Master Siorn." And then she added "And then he was free." And to that, she added the mark that Garit had drawn: "Free to be awesome."

In the middle of swinging his massive arm at Kisonan, the monster hesitated.

"That's right," Mayka called to him. "You have a new story now. *Your* story! Once upon a time, a stonemason named Master Siorn wanted to achieve greatness. He believed if he carved the largest, most wondrous creature his city had ever seen, he'd be revered. But he was wrong, because the greatness didn't belong to him. It's *yours.* You're free to be whatever you want to be! You were made to defend the city — you can still do that! You can stop this destruction and protect the city and save everyone, both flesh and stone, if you choose. You can be the hero of Skye, strong and fierce! It's up to you to take control of your story and *be awesome!*"

He turned and began to stomp back through the city.

She saw Kisonan running beside them, on the rooftops. "Jump when I say to jump!" he called.

I can't! I'll fall! I'll break!

"Trust me, as I trusted you!"

She readied herself.

"Now!" he cried. "Aim for the purple!"

She jumped off the monster toward a purple awning — and landed, cradled by the tough fabric. Kisonan leapt down to her, and she scrambled onto his back. She held on as he ran to the next building and up to the peak of its roof, where they could see.

Together, they watched the monster lumber toward the Festival Square. Buildings shook in its wake. Roof tiles tumbled to the street and shattered.

"Did you succeed?" Kisonan asked.

"I think so."

"What will he do?"

"I don't know." She hoped she'd made the right choice. She'd done her best with the story, but now it was up to the monster. Below, she saw a great swarm of flesh-and-blood people had gathered, both guards and ordinary men, women, and children. They were shouting and pointing, both at the stonemason's creatures and at the monster. Garit was with them.

Standing for a better view, Mayka watched as the monster tromped toward the Stone Quarter. Master Siorn was a tiny figure on top of the building.

The monster approached him.

Stopped.

Picked Master Siorn up in his rock hands.

And then walked out of the city.

As the monster passed, Mayka heard the stonemason screaming, "Stop! Put me down! Obey me!" The people of Skye heard him too, and they watched as the monster did not obey.

Chapter
Twenty-Four

Je did not return.

Not the monster, and not the stonemason.

Mayka waited on top of the roof for a long time, watching the horizon, while people swarmed below, tending to those who had been hurt by fallen stone, clearing the debris from the street, and comforting one another. Several blocks had been damaged by the monster, in a swath that led from the Festival Square to the Inn District.

The two birds perched beside her, and Kisonan stayed as well, holding himself still and watching the horizon with them. When the first few stars began to appear, Kisonan spoke. "I do not think he is coming back. Strong, fierce, and merciless, the monster defended Skye."

Far below, in the square, the owl was wailing about curfew, but Mayka ignored him. Let them come up here, if they wanted, and drag her down. She wasn't ready to leave yet.

They waited through the night, watching the stars march across the sky.

Only when sun rose again and the monster did not return did Mayka and Kisonan come down from the arch — it wasn't an easy climb, since they hadn't gotten up there in a normal way. But she used her chisel and hammer to make handholds for herself, and Kisonan had his claws. The two birds, of course, flew.

The Stone Quarter was a disaster. Master Siorn had marched his monster *through* the wall to the Festival Square. Mayka saw stone creatures out cleaning with their stonemasons, going through the rubble looking for what was salvageable.

At Master Siorn's, the house itself was standing, but the back was torn open — the monster must have stomped out through the back wall of the workroom.

She hurried toward the door, and the otters came out to greet her. "You did it!"

"We all did it," she said, examining them — all of them seemed whole, though one had a chip in its tail. "He's gone, and I don't think he's coming back. The monster carried him off. Is everyone okay? Is Garit here?"

"Inside," they said, and then they clambered over Kisonan, greeting him.

She found Garit in the workroom.

The wall had been shredded, and the roof was ripped off. Sunlight poured in, and stone dust twinkled in the air. Jacklo and Risa flew in from above.

Garit was still dressed in his apprentice gear, but he had a bandage around one arm. He was cleaning up rubble around the worktables.

"It worked," Mayka said.

He smiled, a broad happy smile, as if his home hadn't just been destroyed. "It really did. And no one blames me for what he did, or what he tried to do."

Mayka smiled back.

"Everyone's saying the mark was a disaster."

"Good," Mayka said.

"Even better, they know that stone creatures were the ones who stopped the monster," he said. "Lots of people saw you all attack him. You're heroes. There's a bunch of different stories already about what happened. No one knows you changed the mark."

"Good. Very good. Let them tell whatever stories they want. So long as the stories have a happy ending." Out of the corner of her eye, she saw the other creatures filter into the workroom: the otters, the mishmash creatures, Kisonan. "We're going back home. I just wanted to make sure all of you were okay first."

"We're fine," Garit said, "but Si-Si . . ." He knelt next to the little dragon and then looked up at Mayka. "Will you stay long enough to help me finish her? You're good with marks. I could use your help."

Mayka opened her mouth to say that she was needed at home, but then she closed it. *He thinks I'm good! I think . . . maybe he's right.* She could take the time for this. She had already found the perfect stonemason for her family. Mayka glanced at Risa and Jacklo.

"Of course you have to help her," Jacklo said.

Risa nodded. "Of course."

Si-Si beamed at all of them. "Really truly?"

"Really truly," Mayka told her.

Garit taught her as they worked, explaining techniques she'd seen Father do so naturally, breaking them down into steps. She practiced on shards of stone, and then she and Garit worked on Si-Si, reshaping the little dragon so that her wings would hold her. While they carved, Mayka told him about the new story she'd given the monster, and then, when he asked, she told him other stories, about Father as she knew him and her friends on the mountain.

As they worked and talked, flesh-and-blood people began to arrive. First were guards, who came to thank them. Others — men, women, and children of all ages — came to gawk at them, the stone creatures who had attacked the monster.

At dawn the next day, Ilery came with her parents. The mishmash creatures fed them breakfast while Ilery visited with Mayka. Garit continued to work on Si-Si while the two girls talked.

"The mural is gone," Ilery told her. "I'm sorry."

Mayka considered it for a few minutes. "It's okay. That's not the way I remember Father anyway." She thought of the image of the two graves. He may have carved her to replace his daughter who died, but did that make Mayka any less of a daughter to him?

No, she thought. *I was his daughter too. He loved me.*

She'd never doubted that, and she wasn't going to start now. She was sure he'd loved his first daughter, and he'd loved her too. She was just as real to him. "To me, to all of us, he was Father, not the famous Master Kyn. He made us, and he loved us." Saying it out loud made her feel better. He may have been a hero to Skye, but she had her own stories about him, and she liked those better anyway. He was happier in her stories.

"What will you do now?" Ilery asked. "Will you stay, or do you still plan to return home? I've heard the council is going to end the curfew, and there's even talk of not rebuilding the wall around the Stone Quarter — the people liked that stone creatures stopped the monster, and all the stonemasons have been denouncing what Master Siorn did. Things are going to get better for stone creatures here."

"I belong at home," Mayka said. "We're going to leave as soon as Si-Si flies. But the offer still stands for you to visit me."

"I will someday," Ilery said, "when I can."

"Whenever you want to," Mayka said. "You're always welcome."

After they finished carving Si-Si's body, Mayka lay on the floor with papers in front of her. She drew, sketching out mark after mark, telling of Si-Si's wish for the sky, her wish to be free of the earth, her wish to be one with the wind, like the dragons of legend whose story she bore.

Peering over her shoulder, Garit frowned. "But that's not like any of the flight marks I've ever seen. It's all about wind and the sky. It doesn't even match what's on the birds." He pulled out his notes. "See, I've studied all the attempts at flight marks by dozens of stonemasons over decades." He then brandished a fresh piece of paper, with new marks on it. "And here's what I think we should do, based on what they've already tried."

Mayka looked over the marks, both Garit's and the other older stonemasons'. All of them, without exception, were about the mechanics of flight: lift, thrust, balance. Garit's was more advanced, but it was still all about the technical details of how to fly. It didn't touch the heart of what it meant to soar, free on the wind, with the sun above and the world with all its worries and regrets shrunk small below. "Mine will work. Si-Si, what do you think?" Mayka asked.

"Mayka's marks tell my story," Si-Si said. "Carve those."

And so they did, carefully and painstakingly. Garit did the majority of the work, since he had both more experience and more training, but Mayka was there every step of the way, guiding the lines and carefully watching to be certain the story was right.

At last, when it was finished, they stepped back and studied Si-Si.

She was the same, but sleeker, with bubbles of air within her that reflected the light shining through her stone. She spread her wings. "Are you certain this will work?"

"It doesn't matter what I think," Mayka said. "You have the story now. You just have to make it yours."

"We'll fly with you," Risa said. "Follow us." She flapped her wings and took off in an upward spiral. Sunlight glittered above her, and soon she was a dot against the sky.

Jacklo stayed with Si-Si. "You spread your wings and then push down, catch the wind beneath them. And then — look to the clouds!"

Si-Si began to flap. She rose off the workbench.

"You're doing it!" Garit cried.

The little dragon smiled. One wing flapped harder than the other, and she veered to the side and crashed into a boulder.

Garit started to go to her, but Mayka put a hand on his arm to stop him.

Si-Si righted herself. With Jacklo and Risa encouraging her, she flapped again, and this time rose higher. She spiraled up with the birds toward the hole in the roof. Wobbling in the wind, she flew unsteadily toward the sky.

She looked awkward and ungainly, as if she was about to crash at any moment.

But she flew.

As they watched, she flew higher and higher, free of the earth and one with the sky.

Chapter
Twenty-Five

ayka left the city at dawn, with Jacklo and Risa riding on her shoulders. Her friends Garit and Kisonan, as well as Si-Si, walked with them as far as the gate.

"You can come with us," Mayka told Si-Si.

Si-Si spread her wings. "I've so much to see first. There's a whole valley to explore! But thank you for making me into who I am."

"You did that yourself," Mayka said. "All we did was make your outsides match your insides. Your heart could already fly." She knelt and hugged the little dragon, then she turned to Garit and Kisonan. "And the offer's open to you too. Anytime you want to climb a mountain."

"Thank you," Kisonan said gravely. "Be well, and may your story continue as long as you wish it to."

"Yours too." She asked Garit, "Will you be all right?"

"I'm going to try for my stonemason badge," Garit said.

"After carving Si-Si . . . Well, I think I can do it. And if I succeed, then I'll be able to help my family for certain."

"You'll do it. I know you will." She hugged both him and Kisonan.

Then Mayka, with Jacklo and Risa, walked out the gate, as the giant stone turtle smiled down at them. Every time Mayka looked behind her, her friends were still there, watching and waving. And every time, she waved back too.

The city faded into the distance as they walked on. She guessed the fields to the east had been trampled, but in this direction, the countryside bore no damage from the monster — in fact, it looked exactly the same as it had when she'd come to the city. She half expected it all to be different, since she felt so different from when she'd arrived. She kept to the road, jogging as she went, and didn't try to talk to anyone.

A few travelers called out to her. She greeted them with a wave, but didn't pause.

No one tried to stop her. She ran with purpose. She wasn't lost.

When night came, she kept going, slowing to a walk so she wouldn't fall. Jacklo and Risa sometimes flew and sometimes rode. Night blanched into day and then faded to night again.

They passed the field where they'd met Si-Si. They passed the farmhouse with the horrible farmers — she gave it a wide berth.

Ahead was their mountain.

As she drew closer, she felt as if something inside her was singing. Jacklo and Risa flew off her shoulders and into the trees. They darted in between the birches and pines, and Mayka smiled. She ran faster.

She scrambled beneath the trees, waded through the streams, tromped over the underbrush. At last, she found the cliff and climbed the stone steps.

Ahead of her, the birds cried, "We're home! We're home! We're home!"

And as she ran up the mountain and burst out of the forest, she saw their cottage. Her family was all there, rushing toward her: Dersy and Harlisona, Kalgrey the cat, Nianna the owl, Etho the lizard, and Badger. Even the fish were poking their heads up in their lake.

The chickens were reacting to the excitement, pecking and chattering in their pen, and the goats were butting against the fence. Laughing, Mayka dropped to her knees and hugged as many of her friends as she could at one time.

"You came back!" Dersy cried. "Oh, you're back! You're here!"

"But where is the stonemason?" Kalgrey asked. She looked to the woods.

"She's here," Mayka said. "She's me. Or I will be, once I've practiced enough. Come on, I have much to tell you, and the sun is setting."

Together, they climbed onto the roof of the house, and

Mayka, with Jacklo and Risa, told them all their story, how they'd gone into the valley and come back again. She told them about Si-Si and Garit and Ilery and Kisonan and Master Siorn and the monster and the great city of Skye, once home to their father, the man who had carved them all and begun their stories.

And the stars traveled across the sky.

When the sun rose, Mayka climbed down from the roof of the cottage and went inside. She stood in front of Father's tools. They gleamed, polished but not used, as they had for all the years since he'd died. She reached a hand toward one and then stopped.

What would he think? Would he be proud?

He'd never imagined she could carve, never mentioned it as a possibility, so she'd never thought it was possible. But in the city of Skye, she'd done it. She'd even helped Si-Si fly.

Mayka took a chisel off the wall and a small hammer. They fit nicely in the palms of her hands, as if they'd been waiting for her. She went outside.

The mountain was full of rocks she could practice on.

And so she did. She carved and cut and chiseled. Just shapes at first: a cube, a cylinder, and then she began on more complicated carvings.

When she completed a flower, she knew she was ready.

She began on herself first: carving her own story into her stone. She chose a spot she could easily reach: her legs. On the legs that had helped carry her away from home, she wrote the marks that told of her journey. *I am Mayka, who left home to save her old friends, and returned home after saving her new friends. I am a storyteller.*

It took her three days to figure out and carve all the marks she wanted, and she spent those days by Turtle, staying with him the entire time. And then when she'd finished on herself, she cleared the moss from his back and carved him, deepening the marks that had faded and adding more, about how he had stopped and then reawakened.

The others watched. They were there when Turtle took his first step forward. They were there when he saw the yellow flowers she'd planted around him.

"Welcome back," she said.

In his slow, soft voice, he said, "It is nice to see you again. I had thought I wouldn't wake."

"I woke you," she said. "And I'll keep you awake." On the overlook, with the view of the valley, she told him the story of her journey, and he listened to every word.

When she finished, he said, "You are your father's daughter. He would have been proud of you. He already was proud of you."

Mayka hesitated. She wasn't sure she wanted to ask her next question, because she wasn't sure she'd like the answer. But she had to ask. "Did Father carve me to replace the daughter he lost?"

"Yes," Turtle said. "But he loved you for you." He swung his head slowly to look out across the valley. "He loved us all for who we were, and we loved him. Your city badger was correct — the stone creatures who fought beside him did so of their own free will, out of love and respect . . . the same reasons Jacklo and Risa accompanied you to the valley, the same reasons the stone creatures fought beside you against the monster in your tale."

Mayka felt as if something had been healed inside her, a piece of her that she hadn't even known was cracked. "I'm glad you're awake, Turtle."

Echoing her, her family cheered. "Carve us!" Dersy cried. "Fix all of us!"

And she began the process of recarving her family, deepening their marks and smoothing them. She didn't add new marks to any of them unless they requested it. Both Jacklo and Risa wanted a new mark, to represent their journey, but the others wanted to stay as they were.

During this time, Turtle began his walk back from the cliff to their home.

When she had recarved her friends, she hung the tools in the cottage and spent time with her family, as she'd always done. And then, a few months later, she picked up the tools and began to carve again: new creatures with new stories about journeys and adventures. Rabbits, squirrels, birds, minks, foxes, cats, badgers . . . She released them into the world when she was done.

As the years passed, some of her creations returned. Some

stayed. Some came only to be recarved. Some wanted new stories added to them, to reflect all they'd experienced out in the world. They told tales of the valley and of distant lands beyond the mountains, with plains and savannahs and deserts and oceans.

Other stone creatures began to come, making the pilgrimage up the mountain. They wanted to meet the Carver on the Mountain. Jacklo and Risa kept daily watch at the cliff, to guide those visitors up the steps and then the rest of the way to the cottage.

Mayka learned there were stories about her, down in the valley, each less accurate than the last, but all of them talking about a brilliant carver who breathed life into stone, carrying on her father's legacy. She liked that story.

One day, when she was carving fur into the back of a stone squirrel, Jacklo came flying toward the cottage. "Mayka! Mayka, she's here! She came! Come see!"

Mayka apologized to the squirrel for the interruption, then put down her tools and followed Jacklo to the cliff. She walked carefully through the streams and peered down over the rocks.

A woman was at the bottom of the cliff. She looked to be twenty or thirty years old — it was difficult to judge human age, especially at this distance — and she carried a baby in a scarf tied to her hip. She also had a scarf tied around her hair.

"Mayka?" the woman called. "It's me, Ilery. Remember me?"

"Of course I do! Jacklo and Risa, show her the steps."

Guided by the birds, Ilery climbed the cliff. When she reached the top, she hugged Mayka, laughing. "You're really here! I heard the tales, and I thought it was you — they call you the Secret of the Mountain and the Maker of Miracles. And sometimes just the Stone Girl."

"I'm glad you came," Mayka said.

"I look old to you, don't I?" Ilery said. She gestured to the baby at her hip. "This is my daughter, Flika. We've been looking for a new home."

"Then you found one," Mayka said, and she led her old friend to the cottage of shining marble with the garden in front and fishpond beside it.

"Oh, Mayka, it's exactly as I pictured it!" Ilery said. "It's perfect." The rabbits and other animals hopped around her, curious. No flesh-and-blood person had ever visited them before. The animals fetched her food, and the fish helped provide the water. Mayka showed her to Father's room with his unused bed.

Over the next several days, Mayka carved a cradle for the baby. Its base was stone, but they used blankets for the mattress. There was goats' milk to feed the baby and Ilery, and food from the garden, plentiful, with honey from the wild bees to sweeten it.

"You can stay as long as you want," Mayka told her.

"I'd like that," Ilery said.

Over time, Mayka learned that Ilery had left an unhappy

home. She'd wanted to start a new life for herself and her baby, and she thought the mountain would be a good place to come and figure out what she wanted her story to be.

Three years after Ilery came to live with her on the mountain, another friend came: Garit. And with him, another surprise. Si-Si.

Mayka saw that Garit had aged too. She introduced him to Ilery and Flika, now a sturdy toddler, and he greeted them kindly.

Si-Si introduced herself to Mayka's friends, "I am Siannasi Yondolada Quilasa, but you can just call me Si-Si."

"Hi, Si-Si!" Jacklo said. "Want to fly with us?" The other birds that Mayka had carved—over a dozen in all—crowded around her, chirping and tweeting and chattering.

"Oh! Yes!" Si-Si cried. "You can all fly?"

"Of course," Risa said. "Come fly!" And Si-Si took to the air in the middle of the flock. Mayka, Garit, Ilery, and Flika watched them as they circled above the cottage and then flew toward the peak.

"Tell me of your adventures," Mayka said to Garit.

He smiled. "I'm Master Garit now." He showed her the patch sewn into his leather garments. "It's not as permanent as stone, but it means almost the same thing. It says I became a stonemason in truth. I have a shop in the Stone Quarter, and

I've performed in several festivals. People . . . well, they're nicer to stonemasons and stone creatures now. There's no wall around the Stone Quarter, and there's no more curfew for stone. We can all come and go whenever we please. My family visits me all the time — with the money I send them, they can afford to now. And Si-Si comes to see me too, in between her adventures. Things are good."

"What brings you here?" Mayka asked.

"I heard a story about a Master Carver living in the mountains," he said. "I came to find her and learn from her. It's said she can carve birds that can fly and fish that can swim."

And so he stayed, for many months, and they carved together and learned from each other. And eventually, Ilery and Garit told Mayka they wanted to be married. Mayka went back to the valley and the city of Skye to see them wed, and she visited with Kisonan and a new stone creature named Ava in honor of Garit's broken friend, in the rebuilt stonemason's house.

Then she returned to her mountain.

In the years that followed, Ilery and Garit came to visit her many times, and when Ilery's child was old enough, she stayed to be Mayka's apprentice.

And so time passed, and their stories went on.

Acknowledgments

Years ago, my husband bought me a small stone rabbit for our flower garden. Every spring, I used to dig it out from the dead leaves and sticks and other debris, but then one year, I couldn't find it. I joked that it had come to life and hopped away . . . and then I started wondering where it would have hopped to. And so Mayka, the stone girl, with her stone animal friends, was born. I like to think she's befriended my little rabbit and taken him in.

Thank you to that little lost rabbit. And a special thank-you to all the non-stone people who brought Mayka and her friends to life: my amazing agent, Andrea Somberg; my brilliant and wonderful editor, Anne Hoppe; and the incredible team at Clarion Books and Houghton Mifflin Harcourt: Amanda Acevedo, Lisa DiSarro, Candace Finn, Sharismar Rodriguez, Jackie Sassa, Tara Shanahan, Tara Sonin, Rachael

Stein, Dinah Stevenson, and the many awesome others who took up chisels and hammers and created a path for Mayka to walk into the world.

Special thanks as well to my family — your stories are carved on my heart and soul.